NEW YORK REVIEW BOOKS
CLASSICS

WISH HER SAFE AT HOME

STEPHEN BENATAR was born in London in 1937. He has taught English at the University of Bordeaux, lived in Southern California, been a schoolteacher, an umbrella salesman, a hotel porter, and an employee of the Forestry Commission. He began writing as a child, but did not publish his first book, *The Man on the Bridge,* until he was forty-four. Subsequent works include *Wish Her Safe at Home, When I Was Otherwise, Recovery, Letters for a Spy,* and *Two on a Tiger and Stars,* a book for young readers. Benatar has four grown children and currently lives in West Hampstead, London, with his partner, John.

JOHN CAREY is Arts Emeritus Merton Professor of English at Oxford University. He has appeared as a host and commentator on numerous television and radio programs in England and is the former chief book reviewer for *The Sunday Times.* Among his books are *The Intellectuals and the Masses, What Good Are the Arts?, Pure Pleasure: A Guide to the Twenieth Century's Most Enjoyable Books,* and a biography of William Golding. He has chaired the Booker Prize committee twice and in 2005 was the chair of the first international Booker Prize committee.

WISH HER SAFE AT HOME

STEPHEN BENATAR

Introduction by
JOHN CAREY

NEW YORK REVIEW BOOKS

New York

THIS IS A NEW YORK REVIEW BOOK
PUBLISHED BY THE NEW YORK REVIEW OF BOOKS
435 Hudson Street, New York, NY 10014
www.nyrb.com

Copyright © 1982 by Stephen Benatar
Introduction copyright © 2007 by John Carey
All rights reserved.

Frontispiece: Donato Barcaglia of Milan, *Street Orderly Boy*, Paddington
Street Gardens, Marlyebone, London; photograph by John Murphy

Library of Congress Cataloging-in-Publication Data

Benatar, Stephen.
 Wish her safe at home / by Stephen Benatar ; introduction by John Carey.
    p. cm.
 Originally published: New York : St. Martin's/Marek, 1982.
 ISBN 978-1-59017-335-0 (alk. paper)
 1. Single women—Fiction. 2. Mental illness—Fiction. 3. Bristol (England)—
Fiction. I. Title.
 PR6052.E449W5 2010
 823'.914—dc22

                              2009036316

ISBN 978-1-59017-335-0

Printed in the UK by CPI Bookmarque, Croydon
10 9 8 7 6 5 4 3 2

INTRODUCTION

I FIRST read *Wish Her Safe at Home* when I was chairing the judges of the 1982 Booker Prize. The rules were that each publisher in the UK could submit two novels—the assumption being that they would choose the best two on their list. That meant that about one hundred novels—the top titles of the year—were submitted. The judges had to read these in about four months, so it was wise to keep notes on each one to prevent them all merging into a mental fog. With me the notes often amounted to no more than a few lines. But the other day I looked up what I had recorded about *Wish Her Safe at Home*, and found that it occupied a whole enthusiastic page of my miniscule handwriting. I listed about forty page references, and reminders of what seemed (and still seem) to me the most brilliant passages. At the top of the page I wrote a general summary:

"Impressive study of woman going quietly and genteelly crazy. Skill of the presentation is that all is seen through her mind, so when she comes into contact with the outside world you understand her and feel awkward about her craziness."

"Feel awkward about" is the nub of it, and it appeared to me to sum up the reaction of my fellow judges when I started to enthuse about the book at our first meeting. Anyone who has done book-prize judging will have got used to the vast differences in personal taste that expose themselves once you get down to the job of selection. The assumption that five people of pretty similar cultural background will feel more or less the same about a book they've all read carefully is exploded in the first five minutes of discussion. And it was exploded on this occasion, but with a difference. My fellow judges were all highly intelligent people, whose opinions I respected. But their response to my advocacy of Benatar's novel was something between embarrassment and physical discomfort, almost as if I'd made an indecent suggestion. I don't recall precisely what they said, but I am clear that it didn't amount to a reasoned and systematic critique of the novel. It was more like a semi-articulated wish to drop a disturbing or distressing subject.

So, as it was four against one, we dropped it. But in retrospect their unwillingness to countenance further discussion seems to me a tribute to the book's power. It had got under their skins, and no wonder. For it is one of the most disturbing books I have ever read, and, though it may seem a strange compliment to pay to a work that I consider a masterpiece, I can think of quite a number of people whom I would counsel against reading it. It disturbs, to put it bluntly, because Rachel, the mad narrator, is very like us. Admittedly, she takes things to extremes. Traits that we all recognize in ourselves are, in her case, blown up into intense inner (and sometimes public) dramas. Nevertheless, they are the same traits. We all, all the time, carry on an interior monologue which pressgangs the people we meet, even chance acquaintances and passersby, into our private fictions and fantasies, and allocates them roles in our plot. This is because people are opaque, but social life forces us to interpret their motives and meanings. Any conversation exposes us to imagined, or intended, slights, rebuffs, invitations and unspoken messages. We have to read others as they have to read us, and where there is reading there is bound to be misreading, and doubt about which is which. It is out of this network of complexities that Benatar creates Rachel. She is a mistress of misunderstanding. Her first encounter with the amiable assistant in the chemist's shop, for example, mimics with painful acuteness the universal process of tension, hope, invitation and apprehension that structures human interaction. It shows us ourselves in a mad mirror. It reminds us how thin the boundaries are between the mad and the imaginative, the mad and the sensitive, the mad and the acute.

That Rachel is a version of our secret selves helps to explain one of the most curious things about the book—the fact that we are, from the start, on her side. We fear for her. Our hackles rise when others approach her. We harbour black suspicions about anyone who seems out to deceive her. Benatar encourages this paranoia in us by not letting us know about other people's motives. How trustworthy is Mr. Wymark? He is a lawyer, which ought to put him beyond reproach, but we feel uncomfortable about his being so friendly with Roger and Celia, the beneficiaries of Rachel's generosity. And how trustworthy are they? Do they target Rachel right from the start? Is Roger perfectly aware, when he strips off to do the gardening, that he will inflame poor Rachel's desires? Does he tell Celia, when he gets home, that there's a crazy old bat ripe for exploitation, and that if they play things right she'll be eating out of their hand? Is their invitation to Rachel to be Thomas's godmother just a cynical ploy? Or perhaps only Roger is the devious one and Celia, at any rate at first, hangs back or feels awkward and ashamed about what her husband is doing? It's possible to read her tongue-tied, embarrassed behaviour like that, just as it is almost impossible to read Roger's smarmy denials of any age-gap between Rachel and himself as honest and aboveboard. When Celia says "Just so long as you don't believe we're insincere, we really couldn't bear that, could we, darling?" the atmosphere crackles with suspicion. It sounds like a callous injoke. Or are all these fears just our imagination? Are we, like Rachel, seeing things askew when we invent base and unscrupulous motives for two perfectly decent, friendly young people?

Her memory of Tony Simpson, the boy who almost made love to her, arouses our doubts and anxieties in a similar way. We know enough about the twenty-year-old Rachel, by this time, to consider her socially maladjusted to quite a serious extent, and this makes the boy's attentions seem ugly and false. Is he, we wonder, doing it for a bet? Did he intend to boast afterwards, among his chuckling cronies, about having sex with a freak? Doesn't it give the game away when he begs her not to tell of his failure if she should ever meet "any of the others" and they should "allude to this in any way"? But, after all, this might just be the discomfiture of a young man who feels himself disgraced and doesn't want his friends to know. Benatar doesn't allow us anything definite to hang our suspicions on, yet he arouses them. As the scene develops, the relationship shifts. The boy feels ashamed and diminished because of his premature ejaculation, but Rachel's reaction is intelligent and loving. She strives to restore his damaged self-respect, and her generosity, it seems, evokes a generous response in him. His assessment of her appears to change: she has ceased to be a joke for him and has become an object of love. Of course, this story we make up about the boy and his motives may all be false. For that matter, Rachel's account of the episode, which is all we have to go on, may be far from the truth, for she is scarcely the most reliable of narrators. Benatar has lured us into fiction-making, and so, again, brought home our kinship to Rachel who, like Benatar, is a fiction-maker above all.

Because we feel protective on Rachel's account, we worry when she does not. The letter from the bank telling her she is £15 overdrawn is a chill blast for us, a premonition, we fear, of ruin and want. But Rachel blithely sweeps it aside. The portrait of Horatio Gavin, which she builds her new life around, may, we are uncomfortably aware, not be a portrait of Gavin at all. The dealer who sells it to her evidently has no idea who the sitter was; to him, he is only "the unknown cavalier"; but Rachel ("Unknown, indeed!") assumes he is simply ignorant. What haunts us is the thought that she may find out her mistake, if it is a mistake. We are anxious that her illusions should be preserved. We do not want to see her reduced to despair. So we are constantly on tenterhooks in case her ability to reinterpret events to suit her fantasies should falter or collapse. In the same way, we're edgy with apprehension when she's among other people, in case her madness should become apparent. The church service—one of the cleverest scenes in this matchlessly clever book—is a torment to us because, thanks to the cunning of the narrative method, we can't be sure how much, if anything, Rachel says out loud, and how much is just interior monologue. "'Some hope!' I said—I thought quite wittily—staring around me in defiance." That certainly sounds as if she speaks, and we shiver with embarrassment at the possibility.

Her character is complex but entirely convincing. At its core lies fear of suffering, not merely her own but that of others. Because she is highly sensitive, other people's pain hurts her. The fate of little Alfredo Rampi is a horror she hardly dares to let her mind approach. Among the griefs over others' suffering lodged deep in her memory is the death of the gentle young man in Paradise Street who had a club foot and kept a rabbit in the back yard, and was knocked down and killed when she was ten. The embarrassing scene on the train when she holds forth about a hanging, drawing and quartering to a hard-of-hearing fellow passenger is an index not of social maladjustment but of pathological hypersensitivity—"I've just read the most frightful description . . . and I just can't stop reliving it." Because she is so defenceless against the world's cruelty, she can only withdraw. She builds an imaginative life that will shut out the real, and she has done this since childhood. In those early days she hung in her bedroom seven pictures torn from magazines, and used to inhabit them "almost literally," living in seven different countries, with seven different professions, and fictional families and friends culled from her favourite books. This decision to retreat and spend her life among fictions that have become embedded deep inside herself, explains why, though she cares about others' pain, she is so resolutely and desperately self-absorbed: "When it came down to it there was no one I really cared about. Nothing that happened to others could genuinely affect me." This truth which she bravely forces herself to confront is paradoxically evidence not of callousness but of sensitivity.

Her instincts and desires are good and entirely commonplace

—you could almost say universal. She wants to be loved, she wants to be admired, she wants to be a success, she wants to give others pleasure, she wants to stay young. Unfortunately she learns quite early in life that she is unlikely to fulfil any of these ambitions: "I lacked both character and know-how and had always been unusually timid." Given these drawbacks, there are really only two alternatives open to her. She could opt for despondency and depression—"the glooms," as she calls it—and she knows how dreadful that can be. She remembers the desolation she felt at menopause. She recalls feeling "sick with deprivation and jealousy" at the thought of Roger and Celia making love. These black moments must, she realizes, be avoided at all costs. So she chooses the other alternative, which is to pretend that her ambitions have been fulfilled—that is to say, to go mad. She can afford the luxury of madness only because of her great-aunt's bequest. Without that, she would have had to stay in her grim flat with Sylvia, would have had to carry on in commonplace misery. Instead she is able to rewrite her childhood as joyous and loving, mingle with stars, be a star herself and become, eventually, a "bride of Christ." The religious ecstasy she ascends to is an entirely plausible extension and fulfillment of her imaginative life. Her allusion to King David at her leaving party (so side-splitting to her raucous and stupid colleagues) shows that she has been brought up to know about the Bible, so where else should her imagination go for its ultimate flight? Further, the phenomenal powers of self-deception she has trained herself to exercise, that enable her to see everything in a false light, make her—as some would say—a natural candidate for religious belief. Faith can move mountains . . . or, in Rachel's case, varicose veins.

The veracity of her psychology is worth emphasizing, because a mere summary of the book might give the impression that it is fantastic or comic. Though it is composed almost entirely of Rachel's fantasy, and most of its episodes are ludicrous, it is terribly and seriously real. It is also, I believe, wholly original. Theorists hold that there are only a dozen or so fictional plots, all of them present in classics of early literature, which later works re-jig. But Benatar's work does not correspond to any of the prototypes, so far as I can see, or only in ways that are so remote as to emphasize its singularity. You might say that a story about someone who is inherently good, but also mad, and who suffers chronic delusions about herself, which her adventures expose, often with ludicrous results—you might say that this resembles the plot of Cervantes's *Don Quixote*, which is certainly one of world literature's master plots. But the differences are greater than the similarities. Rachel is alone—she doesn't have a comic servant or protector as Don Quixote has, and more importantly we see everything from inside her head, whereas Cervantes's mad knight is viewed externally. It matters too, of course, that Rachel is a woman, and Benatar, by some extraordinary feat of sexual ambivalence, has entered a female consciousness in a way that very few male authors have been able to do (or so it seems to me—women readers must be the ultimate judges). At all events, these disparities make the *Don Quixote* comparison look way off target. Yet no other prototypes suggest themselves.

So my fellow Booker-judges seem to me, looking back, to have been even more wrong than they appeared at the time, and my offence, in cravenly giving way to them, instead of sticking to my guns, looks the more woeful. I hope this Introduction will be some kind of expiation.

—JOHN CAREY
Merton College, Oxford
Summer 2007

As before, this book is lovingly dedicated to my family—
with, now, a special thank you to Prue, for suggesting minor
but useful alterations for the present edition.
(Also, a thank you to your cohorts, Katie and Pascale).

It is dedicated, too, to Charlotte Barrow.
I'll always be grateful that—back in 1982—
you rescued my manuscript from the slush pile.

And, lastly, to my partner John. Thanks, doll.

WISH HER SAFE AT HOME

I

MY GREAT-AUNT in middle age became practically a recluse and when she died I remembered very little of her, because the last time I'd visited that stuffy basement flat in St. John's Wood had been thirty-seven years earlier, in 1944, when I was only ten. So perhaps my most vivid recollection was of hearing her tell us, my mother and me, on at least half a dozen occasions, like a favourite fairy tale, the full unchanging story of a play called *Bitter Sweet*. Looking back I couldn't rationally believe it was the only show which she had ever enjoyed but she nearly made it sound like that: still spoke of it—some fifteen years after she had seen it—as though she had been present just the previous night. And then unfailingly she entertained us with the same two songs. She would stand up, this rather dumpy woman, and either with hands touching her bosom or else with arms thrown wide, her eyes intense and misted, her full voice slightly husky, would render these ballads so throbbingly that my mother and I had to gaze into our laps and I would drive my nails into my palms—surely providing, for both of us, a rare moment of togetherness. And almost forty years later I could still hear, very clearly, my Aunt Alicia as she sang, "Although when shadows fall I think if only..." There'd be a brief and sacramental hush:

> ...somebody splendid really needed me,
> Someone affectionate and dear,
> Cares would be ended if I knew that he
> Wanted to have me near...

Unremarkably those few lines stayed with me without my making any effort and one afternoon, during break, I surprised all the other girls in the playground by suddenly bursting forth. The most popular songs of the period were "Swinging on a Star" and "Don't Fence Me In" and morale-boosting, lump-in-the-throat things like "The White Cliffs of Dover," but this one became an instant hit, a curiosity, and I was frequently asked for it: "Rachel's party piece." It seemed to bring me both acceptance and renown and I used to do some wicked take-offs of the old lady (fifty-seven, when I last saw her), my exaggerations growing ever more exaggerated. Often, of course, I'd feel guilty; vowed I would put an end to it. Back in the light of day, though, I'd tell myself it didn't do my great-aunt any harm and it certainly did *me* a fair amount of good, of a kind. I could uneasily reconcile it with the knowledge I had even then: that I very much hoped, one day, to find my place in heaven.

Each time my mother and I came away from Neville Court my mother would say something like, "Poor Alicia. One can only humour her."

"Is she mad?" I once asked.

"Good heavens, no. Or at least..."

I waited.

"Well, if she is," she went on, "she's perfectly happy. There are many who'd even envy her that type of madness."

To myself Aunt Alicia didn't seem a template for perfect happiness: stout, downy-cheeked, heavily dusted with powder; wearing dresses which, as my mother said, must have hung in her wardrobe forever and had probably been unsuitable even when new; a woman, as it appeared to me later, who was always searching for something unattainable in the dark corners of that lush and overheated room, possibly for somebody splendid, affectionate and dear. No, when I was ten years old I didn't regard her as being in any way enviable. Nor, indeed, when I was twenty years old. Or thirty... or whatever.

And then my mother said:

"Actually your father did once mention a strain of insanity in his family." Pause. "So all *naughty* little girls had better watch out, hadn't they?"

She laughed, so I knew this last bit was a joke. In any case I wasn't particularly naughty. By and large I was a quiet child who didn't seek attention. I'd have been appalled—and terrified—to think of what was shortly going to emanate in the school playground.

Aunt Alicia was looked after by a large and blustering Irishwoman called Bridget, who may once have saved my life by crying out as I was about to turn the kitchen light on with wet and soapy hands; and when my great-aunt moved away from St. John's Wood without informing anyone of where she was going, or of why she was going, Bridget went with her. Even the porter hadn't been left a forwarding address; nor could he bring to mind the name of the removal firm. We received no Christmas or birthday cards and gradually I forgot all about Neville Court and the weird, reclusive life being led there. Both that snatch of song and the impersonations—if that's what they could ever have been called—became things of the past.

And even when my mother died I heard nothing. I vaguely supposed Alicia too was dead.

But she wasn't. At that time she'd have had about a dozen more years to go.

Later I learned that she and Bridget had repaired to Bristol; and that there, when Bridget had committed suicide at the age of eighty-four, Aunt Alicia, ten years her senior, had gone on living in the same house with Bridget's body: a state of affairs which had come to light only after two weeks—two weeks of sleet and snow and freezing temperatures. Bridget had then been removed to the mortuary at St. Lawrence's, and Alicia to a geriatric ward in the same hospital.

"Tragic," said Mrs. Pimm, the almoner, when I finally took it into my head to make enquiries. "Tragic," she said, her round face shining with health, and now, all this time later, even with enjoyment, with a storyteller's relish. "The old lady only lasted for a month or two. And to end up like that: too awful to be thought about, much less spoken of! And when you consider her background! Well, it was obviously well-to-do, middle-class, solidly Victorian. A nanny. Little bottom lovingly powdered with talc... A pretty child I'd think; and probably made much of..."

Mrs. Pimm pursed her lips and shook her head and there was silence: an unconvincing moment of requiem. Her small office, white and functional for the most part, contained a framed photo of her family on the desk; and two large watercolours on the wall, both depicting gardens. "Like the woman with the cats," she said.

"Cats?"

"Oh, yes, didn't you read about that? Nine of them. Pets. But when she died—and she, too, was a ripe old age—poor things, they couldn't get any food, so they started eating *her*... and, afterwards, one another. Well, that's nature, I suppose, but as the youngest of my kiddies said to me, "Mum, what if they didn't *wait*?" Well, I soon shut her up, of course, but just the same I couldn't stop imagining."

I shuddered.

"And I often think of *her* little bottom being dusted as well, her rosy little lips being kissed by scores of doting relatives—the flesh, you see, had all been torn away around the mouth." She closed her eyes and gave a series of solemn nods.

"Horrible."

"I'm sure she never thought she'd come to that."

Her laugh in some way wasn't callous. It was aimed against the irony of life itself, rather than at the poor woman with her nine sharp-clawed cats.

"Linda Darnell—such a beautiful actress—dying in a fire," she said. "C B Cochran slowly scalding to death in his bath. Up till then, you know, nearly anybody would have envied them... the glamorous, successful lives they'd both enjoyed."

She clearly had a catalogue of such disasters. And yes, too, there *was* almost a relish: a compensatory garment to wrap about herself to make up for the lack of beauty or glamour or success she felt existed in her own life.

The office had grown increasingly claustrophobic: walls closing in on you, ceiling moving down. You couldn't like her. She told me of a man who had jumped from a window in New York. Oh, yes, he had certainly meant to kill himself and he'd succeeded. Poor fellow. He had also killed the gentleman he'd fallen on top of. "He must have thought that nothing could get any worse. But he should have listened to William Shakespeare, shouldn't he? Things can *always* get worse."

No, you couldn't like her.

And yet I sat there, and yet I listened. Why? Eventually I drew her back to the subject of my great-aunt.

"Naturally," she said, "you realize she was gaga? The mystery is...how she and that Irish woman ever managed to survive; survive for thirty-seven days, never mind thirty-seven years! Sometimes, according to the neighbours, they could be sweet as pie; but sometimes you would hear them scream and it was just like they were doing each other in! Like Bedlam, said the neighbours—well, only thank heaven for such good thick solid walls! There were endless complaints to the council."

I asked what had become of these complaints but Mrs. Pimm may not have heard me.

She said: "You'd expect to have a bit of peace, wouldn't you, when you've nearly completed your voyage? The start of a golden age. The rays of the evening sun reflected on the water. And the filth," she added, "the squalor. The mountain of rubbish in one of those nice big airy rooms..."

But I had already heard about that; *and* witnessed the effects of it.

She saw me out—insisted on escorting me to the main door.

"Still, there you are," she repeated. "I suppose none of us can say what lies around the corner."

I think that, somehow, she intended this to be reassuring. While she went back to her coloured photograph of a similarly apple-cheeked husband and three gormlessly grinning daughters, went back to her summer gardens filled with roses, I reflectively made my way to the bus stop and remembered Bridget letting me run my finger round the mixing bowl as she transferred the cake tin to the oven. I remembered her telling me of the pictures she'd seen on her days off, and about her two strapping nephews in Donegal who were both waiting to marry me.

Naturally, I remembered my great-aunt, as well. Heard again her account of swirling ball dresses—all of them in different shades of pastel—and of Lady Shayne, the erstwhile Sarah Millick, flouter of convention and runner-off to happiness (and tragedy, too, yet would she then have sacrificed the one in order to avoid the other?), now white-haired and seventy but retaining her youthful figure and dressed in an exquisite gown.

During the final moments of the play, due to the self-absorption of all those who had earlier been surrounding her, she is left alone on stage.

Slowly, she moves across it to the centre. At first she stands quite still. Then she begins to laugh. A strange, cracked, contemptuous laugh. Suddenly she flings wide both her arms—

> "Though my world has gone awry,
> Though the end is drawing nigh,
> I shall love you till I die,
> Goodbye!"

And I thought of this as I waited patiently for the bus to move off: the one matchless evening in my Aunt Alicia's long but disappointing life: an evening of empathy, transcendence, exhilaration; and almost surely—at forty-two or forty-three—of hopes of a romance.

2

"OH, SYLVIA! I don't believe this! Listen!"

It was a Saturday and we were sitting over a late breakfast, she with that morning's paper, myself with the previous day's. I had been reading some of the Personal Ads: "Love is a red silk parachute. Take care. Swarms of kisses."

"Divorced? Separated? Single? Meet new faces at private parties."

I had been uncharitably assessing the happy couple shown issuing this invitation—especially the man—when my eyes, seemingly one step ahead of my mind, slipped across to something familiar in the next column. I gave a gasp. I had caught sight of my own name.

"No!"

And it was as if I'd been imprisoned in a glass booth, with a heavy fog swirling about it.

"Oh, Sylvia! I don't believe this! Listen!"

My flatmate, having lowered her own paper, noisily, was now staring with a frown, her eyes screwed up against the acrid smoke from her Marlboro. "Well, come on then! Give!"

I read it out carefully. "Would the person born as Rachel Waring, last known to be living in Marylebone in 1944, please contact Messrs Thames & Avery (reference Wymark), Bristol 5767, whereupon she will learn something to her advantage."

There was a pause.

"Christ!" said Sylvia. The humming continued in my ears—how I felt distanced from reality! "Lovie, don't just sit there!

Bloody well get on the blower!" She started to cough—almost automatically—yet for once my stomach didn't tighten.

"It must be Aunt Alicia," I said.

"You've never mentioned any Aunt Alicia."

"I didn't realize she was still alive."

Sylvia spluttered with laughter and the laughter turned into another of her coughs. "Let's damned well hope she isn't!"

I looked at the paper again. "Whatever made her go to Bristol?"

"Oh, who cares? Jump to it, Raitch! Make a dive for those solicitors!"

But it soon transpired that Messrs Thames & Avery didn't practise law upon a Saturday.

During Monday lunchtime Sylvia rang me at the office. "Well?" she demanded. I could picture her flicking the ash off her jumper as she spoke; you can often come close to hating someone for the most shamingly trivial of reasons.

I confirmed that it had indeed been Aunt Alicia.

"And *was* she filthy rich?"

"No. It seems she left a pile of debts."

Yet the debts weren't really so large and a sale of some of the furniture, Mr. Wymark had suggested, would more than cover them. Although he wasn't an expert, he had said, he believed there might be a few good pieces beneath the cobwebs and the dust.

"And was *this* the something to your advantage?" exclaimed Sylvia. Yet, notwithstanding her disgust, I thought I detected a faint note of relief. "So you're telling me you *haven't* come into millions?"

"Not quite."

"Well, damn and blast! Bang goes that whopping great present I was hoping for!"

So I might have been mistaken.

Then common sense reasserted itself. "But there must have been something?"

"Yes, something," I conceded.

"Well, out with it, for Pete's sake!"

"Her house."

"Her house? Her *house*! Rachel Waring—my, my—aren't *you* the wicked tease!" She gave a whistle, then a laugh. "Did they say it's in a decent area?"

"In a decent area; but far from in a decent state. Well, two old women on their own—and I gather they were senile. You can imagine."

"Christ. That does sound like a cosy setup. But never mind. When are you going to see it?"

She added, almost immediately, "Next weekend? And that'll give me a valid excuse to miss that do of Sonia's."

But I had planned against this moment; and in spite of feeling apprehensive, had planned against it with some satisfaction.

"Well, actually I was thinking of going tomorrow. Taking the day off."

Several seconds elapsed.

"Are you still there, Sylvia?"

"Yes, just as you like, my dear. It's your house, of course." Her tone suggested funeral.

"Saturday, you see, wouldn't be quite so convenient for Mr. Wymark."

Oh, weak, weak!

And Mr. Danby wasn't much happier about it than Sylvia. Well, Miss Waring, my congratulations! This could hardly have happened to anyone more deserving. I couldn't be better pleased.

But why such a rush? I assume that—with any luck—your house won't have fallen down by Saturday?

In all the eleven years I'd worked in Mail Order, in all the seven that I had been his second-in-command, I hadn't once asked for more time off than it took to have a tooth filled or a symptom diagnosed.

All right then, Mr. Danby, so this is where you'll have to learn. Learn about every dog having its day and every worm its turning point.

Therefore I went in as usual on Tuesday, Wednesday and Thursday. On Friday I telephoned to say I was unwell.

Then ordered my taxi for the station.

Not much difference, you might say, between a Friday and the Saturday. But you'd be wrong.

In the first place it expressed a newfound sense of independence; I was a person of property. It also meant I could travel alone. It meant I could read a novel during the journey; go to any type of restaurant I fancied; have a silly little sense of adventure.

It meant I could be me.

And the hitherto dull, diffident, middle-aged woman who said to the taxi driver, "Paddington, please," felt in some respects more like a girl of seventeen setting out for exotic climes. At seventeen I might have gone to Paris. This would have been in a party of five other girls and could have been momentous: leading to the kind of opportunity that only comes from getting to know the right sort of people. The girl whose parents had placed the ad was certainly one of the right sort of people. During the hour or so I spent with her at Richoux she was self-assured and kind and charming. It was impossible not to imagine all her friends being very much the same.

Yet I had never been away from home—not without my mother—except once when she was ill and our upstairs neighbours had volunteered to look after me. Irrationally (and I knew it was irrational) anywhere more than fifty miles from London seemed to me un-normal, lacking in amenities, almost hostile; and at the very last moment I did what I had sworn this time I wouldn't do—I lost my nerve. I felt so grateful to my mother as she came away from the telephone, and yet, at the same time, already disappointed and even resentful: grateful she didn't look displeased, resentful for practically the same reason. That afternoon she took me to see *The Lavender Hill Mob* at the New Gallery in Regent Street. But at seventeen I might have gone to Paris... and I was convinced it would have changed my life.

"It's obviously a moneyed sort of family." (I had said this, sullenly, next morning over breakfast.) "I'm surprised you didn't try to make me go. I know how much you idolize the rich."

My mother had come round the table and slapped my face. But she hadn't suggested I should ring again to ask if I could change my mind. I waited for her to do so, in timorous suspense.

I hadn't suggested it, either.

Thirty years later, however, embarking on my first real escapade I was seventeen once more; and I was setting off for Paris.

3

THE EXTERIOR of the house was beautiful. Terraced, tall, eighteenth-century, elegant. Oh, the stonework needed cleaning and the window frames required attention—as did the front door and half a dozen other things. But it was beautiful. I don't know why; I just hadn't been expecting this.

"Who was Horatio Gavin?" (Philanthropist and politician—had lived here, apparently, from 1781 until his death in 1793.) "Perhaps I should have heard of him?"

Mr. Wymark's eyes followed mine to the plaque between the ground-floor windows. He was a young man: small-boned and, underneath the well-cut overcoat, neatly dark-suited.

"Oh," he said vaguely, "he did a lot for the poor. Tried to introduce reforms. That kind of thing."

"Nice."

"Yes. But if I remember rightly he didn't meet with much success. Ahead of his time, most likely."

I warmed to him still further, this former resident. From a distance there is always something a little touching about failure.

We went inside and for some reason—with my high heels clattering on bare boards—began our exploration at the top. Not counting the basement there were two large rooms to each of the three floors. I wondered at first how Aunt Alicia had negotiated the steep stairs; and Bridget, too, of course. The answer was they hadn't—in any case not during their latter years. They had mainly been confined to the ground floor.

The topmost rooms had an air of Dickens. You almost expected to see Miss Havisham sitting solitary in the twilight, always the spinster in her wedding dress, swathed in cobwebs and depression.

It was like a museum with no curator to disturb the dust. The larger exhibits up here comprised several chests of drawers, a mahogany wardrobe, two single divans, a harpsichord and a loom.

"As I say," remarked Mr. Wymark, "there are evidently a few good pieces."

I nodded. I didn't remember the harpsichord but the loom was something I had seen. And perhaps my great-aunt had been standing close to it on one occasion as the tea was brought in. "Bridget, why must you cut such horribly *thick* slices?"

"Ah, do you good, you know it will."

"Such doorsteps; no refinement. So utterly *Irish!*"

"Excuse me for asking"—this wasn't Bridget—"but are you in a position to spend money on all of this? It would probably cost you thousands, yet you'd quickly make it back. And by the way I know a handyman I'd be happy to recommend. Also, as it happens, when you *do* place the house on the market I know someone who—"

"But I've no intention of placing it on the market."

He was clearly surprised. I was as well, probably more so. I seldom made snap decisions.

"Oh, I'm sorry," he said. "I was under the impression ..."

And understandably. Before I'd seen the house it hadn't occurred to me that I might want to keep it. My roots were in London; my friends too, such as they were, my work and my interests. The familiar might be tedious and unsatisfying. But it was comfortable; it was secure.

"You mean then," said Mr. Wymark, "you see it as a letting proposition?"

"Good heavens, no. I mean that I intend to live here. Yes, really! There's something about its atmosphere that's ..." I fumbled for the right word. "Well, that's practically *seductive*! Don't say you haven't felt it?"

But he only answered dryly: "I'm afraid you haven't seen the ground floor yet. Not properly."

I ignored this.

"It's odd: I've never regarded myself as being susceptible to atmosphere. But I think my great-aunt must have been more welcoming than I remember."

He said nothing.

"Or perhaps it's an impression that was left here earlier. Prior to 1944?"

For in truth "welcoming" wasn't an adjective I should have associated with Alicia. Those that sprang to mind were more like "long-suffering" or "melancholy"—except of course when she'd grown animated by thoughts of *Bitter Sweet*. Bridget had been the welcoming one.

But at least nothing that Mrs. Pimm was later to tell me of screaming and cursing could radically alter my remembrance of powdered softness; of wistful gazing into dark corners; the fact that in the kitchen my life might once have been saved, the cake mixture had tasted good, there were stories of films to enthral me and of strapping young men impatient to marry me.

No, it was merciful: the old ladies' feudings weren't going to leave any greater imprint on myself than they appeared to have left on the house. It was a shame it couldn't invariably be like that; that last impressions were so often the ones which endured. How many of us would want to be remembered for what we finally became?

It occurred to me suddenly that Bridget—on arriving in Bristol—would have been forty-seven: my own age at present. A sobering reflection.

Plainly the pair had lived, slept and washed—*and* cooked—in one of the rooms on the ground floor. There was a grease-encrusted Primus between two camp beds; there was a ewer in a basin (the basin ringed with scum); there were long velvet curtains, originally wine-coloured, hanging at the windows. The nets were grey—almost *dark* grey—so rotten that at the merest touch they might disintegrate.

I noticed that the Primus stove was called "The Good Companion."

And this was where the vegetation was, too: all those overgrown pot plants—or their successors—which had been such a feature of St. John's Wood. Nearly a dozen. One of them, incredibly, showed signs of life.

In contrast the other room was bare. Here, I was pointedly informed, had the refuse of many years amassed into something to rival the town tip; in the centre it had even touched the ceiling. And although the council had fumigated, although the rodent inspector had laid his poisons, still the air was fetid, the walls damp, discoloured—the paper hanging in places like the peeling skin of mushrooms.

The solicitor smiled at me, affably. "Does any of this shed a different light?"

"Not at all."

In the narrow back garden, little more than a wasteland with concrete by the door, there was a very nasty WC (they couldn't have used *that*, surely?) and a couple of coal bunkers.

Mr. Wymark was observing my reaction. It struck me quite abruptly that I didn't like him—not only that I didn't like *him* but that these days I didn't appear to like anybody very much. Everywhere, it seemed, I sensed ulterior motives.

I gave myself a little shake. When I was an old lady I should clearly have the most terrible persecution complex. I'd lock every door, window, drawer and cupboard, see double meanings in everything that people said, wonder why so-called friends didn't write—or else wonder why they did; watch eagle-eyed the customer in front of me at the checkout to make sure she didn't put *my* goods into *her* shopping bag; check and recheck my slip from the cash register—had the girl gone haywire or was there something about me which she didn't like?

No. No. *No*!

I smiled.

I looked at him afresh.

He was a dark-haired, smoothly shaven, self-possessed young man who plainly meant the whole world nothing but good. I said, "Well, thank you for showing me all this, Mr. Wymark. You've been most kind. Now come and let me buy you a cup of coffee and a Chelsea bun." In my own ears I sounded just like anybody's favourite aunt.

But he glanced at his watch, abstractedly mentioned another appointment and said that if I didn't mind he would see me later at his office. Or could he drop me off somewhere?

He waited while I gave water to that one surviving plant and spoke to it encouragingly. He seemed reinvigorated; it was as if I'd watered *him* at the same time, spoken to him in the same soft and persuasive style. "I can see you've got green fingers," he said.

"My mother would never have agreed with you!"

"Anyway, I can certainly put you in touch with somebody who has: a fellow who'll be able to work such wonders on your garden! A friend of mine...an undergraduate. Name of Allsop."

I thanked him and again told him he was kind. "And you seem to be wonderfully well-connected!"

"I've lived in Bristol all my life."

"Have you indeed? So did you ever meet my great-aunt?" I had meant to ask him earlier. "And if so what did you think of her?"

"Are you referring to when she made her will?"

"Yes."

"I'd have you know, Miss Waring, that at that time I wasn't even *born*."

"Oh dear! Was it so very long ago? You make me feel quite ancient."

I added quickly:

"But it's not as if I'd gone completely mad. She might have had more recent dealings with your firm?"

"Of course she might. But in fact she didn't."

Then, with a feeling akin to sadness, I watched him drive away: this dark-haired, smoothly shaven, self-possessed young man who so plainly, it appeared, meant the whole world nothing but good.

Yet he didn't return my wave and I thought that for some reason he clearly hadn't taken to me.

4

"I THINK I should like to have been somebody's favourite aunt," I said. "I think it might have been fun." This, to the woman whose table at the teashop I had asked to share.

She smiled, hesitated, finally remarked: "Well, perhaps it's not too late."

"No brother, no sister, no husband—somehow I get the feeling it might be!"

"Oh dear."

"Did you ever see *Dear Brutus*?"

"*Dear Brutus*? Yes! A lovely play."

"Wouldn't it be fine if we all had second chances?"

She nodded, now looking more relaxed. "Oh, I'd have gone to university and got myself an education!" I reflected that she probably needed one. "But otherwise I don't think I'd have wished things very different." She gave a meaningless laugh and started gathering up her novel and her magazine. Poor woman. What a lack of imagination. (And what a dull, appalling hat.) Yet I realized that I envied her.

"What about you?" She said it as if she felt she had to. She was pulling on one of her gloves.

I had a moment's sudden unease upon the question of my own hat.

"Me?" I had always considered it pointless engaging in a serious conversation unless you were prepared to give it your all. "Well, I suppose, chiefly, I wouldn't have been so stupidly kind to my poor mother."

20

Yet it seemed I had embarrassed her. "Oh, but I'm sure your mother appreciated it! Indeed I'm certain she did. Ah, but there's my bus! So sorry to rush off like this..." She smiled back at me from the doorway and dashed into the street.

I hadn't noticed any bus.

"No." I shook my head. "She took it solely as her due. But that's the old, old story. Nothing new under the sun, as they'll always tell you."

Yet this was a happy day. Not one for letting in the glooms. I picked up my bill, totted up the figures.

And, after all, it was hardly as though I'd ever won a beauty contest, was it? Therefore no real reason to suppose that—if I hadn't been stuck at home—I'd have been whisked off by some gentleman like Mr. Darcy or Rhett Butler or Jervis Pendleton. No real reason at all.

Or was there? I pulled on my own gloves with gay decisiveness. Yes, it seemed so important to be gay. In London I was seldom gay; at work, practically never. I sat at my table and pondered and grew increasingly elated. It was as if I'd received a revelation. Here in a tearoom along with the fruit scones and the jam doughnuts. I wasn't even sure what had led up to it. Previously, of course, I had often discovered the secret of happiness: courage on one occasion, acceptance on another, gratitude on a third. But this time there was a rightness to it—a certainty, simplicity— which in the past mightn't have seemed *quite* so all-embracing. Gaiety, I told myself. Vivacity. Positive thinking. I could have cheered. Still sitting at my table in the empty café I knew that concerning the house I had made the right decision. Bristol, merely a name to me before, was going to treat me well, provide me with a new start. London in my imagination had now become grey; maybe always had been? Bristol was in flaming Technicolor.

They were as different to each other as Kansas from the Land of Oz.

5

My mother was such a silly person. I explained this to the woman from the teashop as we strolled around the park; not that I felt I needed to. My mother was always so concerned, I said, with what she considered correct behaviour.

"And there's something in particular which can *still* make my stomach clench."

"Oh, my!"

"Yes! When I was a child she told me I should always decline a gift of money. And I don't mean just from strangers but from relatives. And I can remember saying repeatedly, 'No—no, thank you—I simply can't accept it,' but then, after a fair amount of coaxing, 'Oh well, that's extremely kind of you,' and later to my mother, 'Yes, I tried. I really did try.'"

The woman with the hat made sympathetic noises.

I went on.

"On one occasion an elderly cousin of my father's offered me something and got the customary response. So he simply gave a shrug and replaced the pound note in his wallet. 'Very well, in that case, if you really don't want it . . .' My disappointment must have showed. He pulled the wallet out again. 'It isn't that I don't want it,' I mumbled, with a burning face, 'it's just that . . .' 'Just that what?' he asked.

"'I was trying to be polite.'

"'Rachel, don't try to be polite. Just try to be natural. Be a child.'

"And another time (the two things are connected) my mother

was in hospital one Easter and I was staying with the elderly couple who lived upstairs. Well, on the Sunday morning there wasn't any egg beside my plate—of course, I hadn't been expecting one—but what there was, was a packet of Ross's Edinburgh Rock. When I took my seat I saw it and felt jubilant; you didn't get so many sweets in those days. Yet I didn't say anything because, again, I had been told never to assume that something was yours until you'd actually been given it. But after a while Mrs. Michaels, who was a funny little woman, spindly-legged, slightly hunchbacked, jumped up from the table with a small cry of distress and exclaimed to her husband as she went, 'It was meant as a surprise. So why isn't she pleased?'

"Well, I sat there in shocked silence for a minute, gazing dully at the gift, and then I said quietly, 'But I am. Very.' Yet by then Mr. Michaels had gone after his wife and there was nobody left to hear.

"There was nobody either—but this I was glad of—to see the silent tears which trickled down my cheeks.

"And I didn't know what to do with the rock. I carried all the dirty dishes to the sink and washed them and put away the cereal packet and the butter dish and the marmalade but in the end I just left that packet on the table. I couldn't think what to say."

I shrugged.

"Well, it simply disappeared and wasn't spoken of again. I stayed with the Michaels for a further three days. It seemed a terribly long visit."

"How deeply unfortunate!" said the woman.

"So, yes, my mother was a very silly person. Snobbish and small-minded and manipulative—and altogether altered from the time my father was alive. With him around, who knows, she might have gone on being the mother of my earliest recollections. With him around I can't begin to tell you how different my own life would have been!"

"No, I feel sure of it."

But I raised my hand with a commendably stoical gesture. "Oh, well. *C'est la vie!*"

A duck—rude thing—displayed its bottom. Perhaps the lady from the teashop would have gained in interest if she had done the same. "Oh, there's your bus!" I cried. "Be careful with your basket!" I watched her running to the park gates and dropping her library book, the *Woman's Weekly* and a ball of lime-green wool. Her hat slipped down over her eyes. It suited her. It made her look more stylish.

6

SYLVIA was angry (*extra* angry) when I phoned to say I'd be spending the night in Bristol. "When the bloody hell did you decide that?"

"Oh...about an hour ago."

So it was as well I'd had the forethought *not* to bring my toothbrush. My hand had hovered over it that morning ("Just in case," I'd told myself, for it had then been nothing but the barest possibility) yet native cunning had prevailed. I had slipped a nightdress into my handbag, and a fresh pair of stockings and knickers, and left it at that.

In the taxi though—since I was now a teenager again and on my way to Paris—the barest possibility had progressed from rank outsider to odds-on favourite. At Paddington I had asked for a weekend return.

And, roughly eight-and-a-half hours later, I was hoping that Sylvia would soon be pacified by the cheerfulness of my manner. "Is it still drizzling up in town? Here, right from the word go, it's been lovely! Quite lovely! Right from the moment I got off the train!"

"Oh, my day is now complete," she said. "Thank you so much." She hung up.

Well, I needn't feel guilty, I told myself. She was only being Sylvia. I got my toothbrush and my tube of toothpaste at a local chemist's. "Not too bad a winter so far," said the grey-haired man behind the counter. We were now in the last days of March.

"Oh, what a pessimist!" I exclaimed. "The winter's over."

He laughed. "Yes, you're right."

I questioned him about the town. "As a matter of fact I shall shortly be coming to live here."

"You won't regret it. It's a nice place."

I was glad to be discussing my plans. For one thing, it made them more official. Having just spoken to Sylvia—but naturally not having apprised her yet of my decision—I knew that back in London I might falter. I needed to have people to whom I had committed myself.

"Then we'll be seeing you perhaps?" remarked the chemist.

"Certainly."

"Hope so, anyway."

As I walked along the street in the pale evening sunshine I pondered those last three words. *Hope so, anyway.* It seemed a strange thing to have said, a little unnecessary even, unless he'd truly meant it.

I smiled. There was no doubt about it. This was a most delightful town.

Then I quickened my pace and felt blissfully aware that spring *had* come. A charming red frock caught my eye in the window of a dress shop. I stood gazing at it for well over a minute, conscious both of my own reflection and that of the world behind me.

Disappointingly, the shop was closed.

Never mind. For dinner I chose some of the most expensive things on the menu. Now do be careful—I tried to sound a warning—yet it was a four-star hotel and I had a real feeling of being on holiday. Afterwards I again wandered round the city centre, cautious to keep only to its main thoroughfares, and came across a small arts cinema where they were showing *A Streetcar Named Desire*, one of my favourite pictures. All my life I had searched for pointers. Today I felt that everything was telling me how right I'd been: simply to trust my instincts.

As usual (this was my third time of seeing it) I loved that bit where Blanche sings in her bath,

Oh, it's only a paper moon,

> Floating over a paper sea,
> But it wouldn't be make-believe,
> If you believed in me...

and I was very much moved once more by her pathetically brave declaration: "I have always depended upon the kindness of strangers." Many years ago I had been told I looked like Vivien Leigh. This was the only meaningful compliment anyone had ever paid me and I had tried to savour it sparingly. Over the years, though, it had gradually turned sour. But that night in Bristol I again derived from it a gentle satisfaction.

The following morning I went and bought the dress.

It fitted perfectly. A further confirmation.

"I saw this frock last night. Half of me was petrified it wouldn't be here this morning. The other half knew perfectly well it would —that it would wait for me, if necessary, for ever."

The assistant was fortyish and svelte. "Yes, madam, it's very lovely, isn't it?"

"I don't imagine anyone could call it dull?" I turned admiringly before the mirror.

"Good gracious, no!"

I told her I couldn't bear to change back into my skirt and jumper, happy though I'd always been with them, and she very sweetly stowed these into one of her smart carrier bags and added my receipt and the card of the establishment—"What," I said, "no tissue?"—we had quite a little laugh. Fortunately my elegant black shoes were exactly right for the dress. As were my hat and coat and handbag. I felt like a model.

It was another mild morning and even with my coat buttons undone I didn't feel at all cold. I went back to the chemist's to buy a bar of soap but my friend of the previous evening wasn't there: merely a podgy adolescent who had mild acne and a shiny nose and wore a too-tight overall.

A slightly jarring note. But there was bound to be a reason for it. I didn't let it throw me.

7

IN THE train I sat opposite a man who had a biography of William Wallace lying unopened on the table. I felt so sorry for poor William Wallace; but for some while I attempted not to think of him, tried solely to think about my own book. I couldn't. At last (though not wanting to reveal either my straining curiosity—the title had been upside-down and difficult—or to give away a possibly surprise ending) I said to the gentleman—who was old enough to make me feel I wasn't being in the least bit forward—"Do you mind if I talk to you for a moment? I've just read the most frightful description of a hanging, drawing and quartering and I'm afraid I can't stop reliving it."

I had to repeat my request but he didn't appear at all put out. He'd only been looking through the window.

"Really," I said, "we have no right—ever—any of us—to complain or get depressed, do we? Not about a thing."

"What's that? I'm sorry. I didn't quite catch the last part?" He had leant forward.

I again repeated what I'd said. "Not about bills or the things that people say to us or even illness. Not even cancer when you come to think of it."

"That's probably true, my dear, but—"

"Just *imagine*: waking up in the morning, possibly from some rather pleasant dream, and suddenly remembering..."

"I'm sorry?" He had now cupped his hand to his ear and I raised my voice yet further.

"Not that I honestly suppose you'd have managed to get much sleep."

"I wasn't dozing," he said gently. "At least, I don't believe I was."

Poor man. It happened to the majority of us; might even happen one day to myself. All the more reason then to be patient and not yield to any base temptation to exclude. I raised my voice still more.

"I mean, imagine. Having your... thing cut off! Stuffed inside your mouth! And then they start the disembowelling..."

He stared at me, wordlessly, and I knew that I'd made contact: his eyes were showing something of the horror.

"Your stomach cut open, your entrails pulled out..."

I suddenly realized just how loudly I was speaking and registered the relative, indeed unnatural, quietness of the whole carriage. I glanced about me. Along the full length of the compartment, heads were craning round, people were looking over the tops of their seats. I heard giggles.

I coloured and smiled apologetically at the old man. I picked up *Pride and Prejudice* again. I felt such an idiot.

8

"Sunday, bloody Sunday!" declared Sylvia. "Bloody awful fucking Sunday!"

I hated it when she talked like that.

"But why? Why are you taking it this way? You'll very easily find someone else to share the flat with."

"I must say it's so lovely to be missed!"

"Naturally I'll miss you."

"Oh, pull the other one! I don't suppose you've ever missed anybody in your entire life—not if you want to hear the truth!"

We were meant to be digesting our lunch. I had thought that while we were sitting over coffee and struggling with the crossword it might be a relaxed and opportune moment in which to reveal my intentions.

But my Sunday lunch—as I found so often happened with any meal eaten at home—was turning to a lump.

"That isn't true," I said, both angry and ashamed. I tried to think of all the people I had ever missed but unsurprisingly the atmosphere wasn't conducive to compiling lists. For the time being I could think of only three people: my father and Tony Simpson and Paul (whose second name I'd never known), the young picture framer with the rabbit. "And of course I'll miss you, Sylvia. But you speak as though—oh, how can I put it?—as though we were *married*," I said.

And for the first time I suddenly wondered whether just possibly... But, no, the thought was too incredible; too remote from anything in my own experience. Lots of women had slightly mannish ways, didn't they? Even the fact of my having formulated the question was startling and ridiculous. I rapidly dismissed it.

"And if it were a goddamned marriage," she was saying, "I know just what kind of marriage it would be! The kind that breaks down the moment the bloody man becomes successful. Which is precisely, if you want to know, what happened to my own mother."

And then—most awfully—she began to cry.

I was amazed. I was the one who cried, did so quite often, cried with the quiet grey desperation of it all. Not Sylvia. Sylvia didn't cry. I felt not merely amazed, I felt inadequate. Here she sat and blubbered unrestrainedly and all for what? Surely it had to be about more than just our current situation? I had so very little idea; and that seemed terrible.

During those ten or fifteen minutes I came my closest to giving in. Yet she wasn't my responsibility—no one was—and I found an inner core of strength, of self-preservation. This both surprised and saved me.

Perhaps it shouldn't have surprised me.

Later that afternoon we had some further conversation. "You know you'll never get another job?"

"Well, there's always the dole," I answered brightly. "And I *have* got a bit of money set aside. For ages now I've been quite careful."

"Not to mention mean."

There was a silence. I thought of how just the previous morning I'd overtipped the chambermaid and of how, on the evening before *that*, I'd even more absurdly overtipped the waiter. He had actually been rather cute.

Cute. A new word to enter my vocabulary. A Bristol word. Even in these present circumstances I could feel strangely pleased with it.

"Do you really think I'm mean?"

"No. You can't be. That house will cost a fortune."

It wasn't quite an answer. I now remembered the leather writing-case I had given her at Christmas, the cardigan on her last birthday. But I didn't want to risk more tears. I only said—perhaps a shade coolly—"Well, anyway, whatever I do spend on it will doubtless be an investment."

"Something to bequeath to your children?"

I didn't answer. There really seemed no point.

"Do you truly intend, then, to start sponging off the state?"

Again I wouldn't let myself be drawn.

"Oh, bloody hell!" she exclaimed, after a pause. "I always said that you were feeble."

"Yes, you did," I agreed, more equably.

"Without your job what have you left? What shred of dignity?"

Without Mr. Danby, you mean, and the clocking-in each morning and the clocking-out each evening (they sort of almost trusted you at lunchtime) and the boring day-to-day routine and the banal repetitive conversations and the yawns and the silly jokes and the waiting about in wet weather for a bus that, even supposing it stopped, you knew you'd have to fight to get on? Not to speak of that Monday-morning feeling which inevitably marred much of Sunday afternoon? (With the exception—fairly unsurprisingly—of this one; it was hardly the shadow of tomorrow that was beclouding things at present.) And the alarm clock set for 6:30 on five days out of seven? Yes, indeed. Without all that, what *had* you left?

"I've got a house that maybe God always meant me to have."

Sylvia stood up, heavily. "Well, if you're going to get all pompous about it I think it must be time I went to make the supper."

"I'm sorry. I didn't mean to sound pompous."

"You know, I can just see you one of these days turning into a religious maniac," she told me at the door.

"I don't know why."

"Oh, a lot of old maids get taken that way. Nothing better to do with all that time on their hands." Her cigarette momentarily got the better of her. "Or perhaps you'll go in for looking after cats."

"I doubt it," I said. "I don't especially like cats—or what I mean is, I don't get soppy over them. And *must* you smoke if you're about to go and do the food?" I had been fully intending to see to it myself; I had forgotten it was her turn.

"The house will stink of pee," she said. "You'll become an old eccentric like your aunt." She chortled, then spluttered. "You too can have your own private scrap heap. Something to sit on at the close of day."

Poor pitiful Sylvia. She was simply trying to wound. Bizarrely I again found it rather moving, this late realization of her sad unspoken dependence upon me; even if I most definitely didn't want it.

And yet there *was* one way in which she had managed to hurt me. I knew I wasn't mean—at least I hoped I wasn't—but I did have to admit that in the whole of my adult life there was only one person whom I'd ever truly missed. And even that had been over twenty-five years earlier.

That Sunday night I lay awake for ages. It seemed an unfair truth to have to confront during those bleak and exaggerative small hours: that when it really came down to it there was no one I honestly cared about. That nothing which happened to others could genuinely affect me.

In real life I had never seen an instance of unspeakable agony. Newspapers, even the news on TV, created simply a transient impression. Apart from the times when I cried for myself it was only novels and films that could actually move me to tears. I was a freak, without compassion.

So I said a prayer: a prayer for someone whom I could care about, care about abidingly; someone for whom I would give up anything—life, looks, liberty, possessions—and on whose account, if necessary, I would wage war just as passionately as I would ever wage it on my own. *More* passionately. It was a prayer which harried me all night.

But towards the morning I regained some sort of peace. Some sort of dull perspective. I could even laugh.

"I'm afraid, God, I was probably a bit demanding! Oh dear! Perhaps you're going to see me now as something of a handful?"

Or wasn't that respectful? I was glad at any rate to have kept my sense of humour—glad at any rate that even in London, and after the kind of night which I had just experienced, I could retain a vestige of my gaiety.

9

"AND," I HAD said, "I *have* got a bit of money set aside." In fact it was just over £20,000: mainly what my mother had left me.

I hadn't liked my mother—as the woman from the café could doubtlessly have told you. On one occasion I'd dreamt vividly that my father had returned in the dead of night, shiningly resurrected, no scars or stitches from the mine. He'd left a kiss on my forehead, an apple and a book beside my pillow and when I'd stirred and sleepily opened my eyes had winked at me outrageously, jerked his head and drawn a hand across his throat... after which he'd slowly disappeared into the wall, still blowing me kisses. I had at once pushed back the bedclothes and tiptoed into my mother's room—and there sure enough had found her staring at the ceiling all glassy-eyed and with her throat cut. It wasn't a nightmare. I went back to my own room and gave my hair a hundred brush strokes then got back into bed and ate the apple. "Thank you, Daddy. I do love you." Whereupon I picked up the book he'd left me—I was always an avid reader—and started on another dream.

But that was the one I remembered in the morning: patchily at first but coming back to me with ever-greater clarity as I lay quietly endeavouring to recall it. And before I got dressed I wrote it down in my notebook, feeling pleasantly like Coleridge Taylor, a sly Coleridge Taylor, because of always referring to my father as Lancelot and to my mother as Morgan le Fay—in case the latter should *again* take it into her head to go prying through my things. And I even thought about turning it all into a poem. But that isn't to say I didn't feel a bit shifty when first confronting my mother over her breakfast tray. More than a bit. After all, she again lay in the very bed from which—blank-eyed and slit from ear to ear— she had so recently been called to meet her Maker. And that morning I seem to recollect I was extra attentive to her; although by evening if not indeed midday my usual mixture of impatience and resentment had probably returned.

Yet the money when it came did partially make up. It couldn't wholly make up because—I don't apologize for this—there *are* things that money can't buy, things like fresh youth to replace the one you've hardly been aware of, things like lost opportunities which might conceivably have led to nothing, but which on the other hand might have led to fulfilment and serenity and new lives and passionate involvement. (Along, of course, with disinheritance!) And human nature being what it is *this* is the version you'll unquestionably believe.

But all the same it was nice to watch the money grow. There was a definite satisfaction in that, an excitement possibly comparable to hearing the first word or to seeing the first step.

It had been a little under £14,000 when it came to me, a sum I'd invested nervously but with some audacity (the lady takes a gamble; the lady indeed takes quite a few!)—at bottom trusting no one, not even my stockbroker. And Sylvia, it hardly needs to be said, had never received the slightest hint.

I wasn't just a miser, though, as was now fully proven—at least to my own satisfaction—for otherwise how could I have been so ready after all these years to raid that cache beneath the floorboards? It was perfectly true, of course, that bricks and mortar make a sound investment; but there was more to it than that. I actually revelled in the submitting of my notice. I revelled in the looks of dazed astonishment, the disbelief, the hurt, the rocking of foundations. I revelled in the fact that while others clearly thought I should have been at my most uncertain, my most worried, most conservative, I was cheerfully looking at heavy curtaining and carpet swatches and books of wallpaper. I worked out my month's notice in a state of well-being and dissociation, floating through my days, feeling very slightly contemptuous of my workmates and letting those feelings, very slightly, show. At least half a dozen of my colleagues mentioned how they envied me. One was a pretty little blonde thing of only nineteen. Another was the office boy.

On my leaving I received a book token for eight pounds fifty and a card that everyone had signed. Though I grew moist-eyed when they presented these two envelopes and felt almost sorry to be going—actually nostalgic already for my long time spent with them, for the little things, the little laughs, the silly accidents and birthday cakes—on the bus home I made the mistake, or took the eminently sensible step, of working out how much on average each had given. It came to thirty-five pence per person, with ten pence added on. As I myself in recent years had seldom contributed less than a pound to such collections—had usually provided twice that sum—I felt for a moment the tears return to my eyes and had to gaze mistily out of the window whilst blinking rapidly and rummaging blindly. But then I shrugged and thought oh what the heck; I didn't need their liking or appreciation, I knew there were parts of me which meant others well, I knew that I had tried to lead a decent life and that I had a value somewhere, in some great scheme of things, whether people were aware of it or not.

But after eleven years in the same department surely I was worth more than 35p a head, with an extra 10p to top it up.

I thought at first I wouldn't spend their book token. At home I took it from my handbag and twice—impetuosity flooding up warmly—wanted to tear it through. But my fingers wouldn't let me.

And I saved the card too . . . yet purely for the sake of the office boy. If *he* had donated thirty-five pence it might have been the most he could afford. I kept it, hopefully, for the sake of that one name.

10

ALL THE same I worried lest I might have given too much of myself away—behaved foolishly. I'd felt a little overcome. After the tea-lady had been up and somebody had handed round the cakes and Mr. Danby had presented me with the card and the book token, it was expected I should make a speech.

"I'm not sure what to say."

Cheers. A suggestion of "Please trot this over to Accounts!" More cheers. I hadn't realized that I had a catchphrase.

"But I'm so glad you all decided on a token. I already know what book I'm going to buy."

"The Kamasutra?"

"*Oh, shut up, everybody!*" That was Mr. Danby. "Let Rachel have her say."

"Actually it's something very newly published. I was reading the reviews. It's a book about David."

I had forgotten that Mr. Danby's name was David. I'd never called him by it, any more than—until just now—he had ever called me Rachel. There were screams of amusement and much foot-stamping and ribaldry.

"*King* David," I explained.

"Dear Lord! He's been promoted."

"No, it's just that it's official, he's been using the royal we for years!"

I laughed. I persevered. I always had this urge to share things with those to whom I felt indebted. "For a long time now King David's been important in my life."

Nobody quite knew what to make of that. Even those who hadn't been listening sensed that others were intrigued. "What did she say? What did she just say?"

"Did you know for instance that somebody once called him a man after God's own heart?"

"*No!*"

I nodded. "And this was despite the fact he as good as murdered Uriah the Hittite so that he could woo Uriah's wife. Yes, even despite this, God still loved him and God still favoured him."

And now there was certainly silence. People gazed at me from every side, either standing like myself or sitting on chairs or tables, their thick white cups in one hand, perhaps a chocolate éclair or a cream horn in the other.

"I can guess what you're going to say of course. You're going to say that he repented."

"He repented!" cried Una, the pretty little blonde. She gave a giggle.

"But what *I* want to know is, would he actually have given up Bathsheba? Would he have changed things even if he'd had the chance?"

"Oh, come on, you lot, let's have a show of hands! Now all who think—"

"So that's why you're going to buy the book, is it, Rachel?"

Mr. Danby had obviously been feeling anxious. But he needn't have worried: the teasing was affectionate and I could take it in good part.

"Well," he went on, "we trust it will provide you with much pleasure, Rachel, indeed we do, and also...er...with much enlightenment. Thank you for telling us."

There was a big round of applause. As the party gradually broke up there were comments of "Slayed 'em in the aisles, Rachel!," "Good for you, Miss Waring!," "Always said you were a dark horse!" I was so relieved. I had unquestionably felt jittery before I'd begun—but because I had tried to tell them what was in my heart it seemed I might have scored a minor victory. Perhaps I could congratulate myself on having provided a leave-taking that wouldn't just blend in with all the rest.

"Do you want to pack up now, Rachel, and catch an earlier bus?"

"Thank you ... er ... David." And then, to cover up my small embarrassment, "Thank 'ee kindly, sire!"

I I

IT WAS a Saturday. Sylvia came to see me off at Paddington.

"And I bloody well hope," she said, "that some day you won't regret all this."

Although I knew she meant precisely the opposite and although I hadn't even wanted her to come I still replied amiably. "I can assure you, you don't hope it nearly as much as I do."

"What a dump this station is."

"I rather like it."

"Oh, God! You're getting more like Pollyanna every day. I'm not surprised they wouldn't take you with the furniture."

I smiled. "You think it wasn't the insurance, then?" Once I might have worried over that. Now I merely observed, "I hope I haven't left the flat too bare."

In fact I'd taken remarkably little—and, anyway, the woman who'd be moving in had a lot of her own stuff.

I added after a minute or so of our walking on in silence: "She really does seem fairly pleasant, doesn't she? Miss Carter?"

But, naturally, we had already discussed Miss Carter. Sylvia had then been quite cheerful; yet you wouldn't have known it now. "Oh, before long we'll probably begin to irritate each other like hell. Give it a month or two."

"Well, that's just being defeatist!"

"Now tell me something truly uplifting," she suggested. "Like, for example, life's simply a snappy little game of pretence—and what fun it is to be a conman! Wasn't that what you were saying at supper last night? I think I'd feel so much better if you could come up with one final inspirational word to illuminate my darkness."

Nevertheless she grumblingly insisted on getting a platform ticket. It seemed well-nigh masochistic.

I found my seat on the train and then remained in the compartment, standing at a window with the ventilator open—because I thought this would save the obligation of a kiss or an embrace; and a handshake would have seemed all wrong.

But anyway, not necessarily as a consequence, she suddenly appeared more manageable. I said, "Don't forget, Sylvia, you're coming to stay with me this summer!" And my enthusiasm didn't sound insincere. Nor was it, entirely.

"Bank Holiday," she mumbled.

"Yes."

Four months away. I almost said, "Make it Whitsun, why not?" I kept remembering we had lived together, breakfast, supper, lunch and tea for nearly a quarter of our lifetimes. A nicer person would have found it harder saying goodbye.

"And before then you'd better let me know," she repeated, grudgingly, "about something you'd like for the house."

"Yes, I will."

Perhaps one reason I was able to say goodbye so easily was that I felt I'd salved my conscience. I had bought her a video recorder. I had given it to her only about an hour before, while the two removal men were still coming in and staggering out. I believed she was pleased—certainly, if pleasure could be calculated by gruffness, she *was* pleased. Be that as it may she'd never again be able to accuse me of meanness.

"Well, then," she said, "be seeing you, Raitch." It seemed the flag was about to be lowered. "Don't forget to ring sometime if you feel like it."

"After I'm connected you'll be the very first I call!"

She stood there awkwardly on the platform. I stood there awkwardly on the train. "Christ Almighty, ten and a half years!" she said.

"I know! Isn't it incredible?"

It seemed a terribly protracted moment, by far the worst of the whole morning, and I knew I had made a mistake. Had I been on the platform I could so easily have thrown my arms about her—I might even have felt glad to—and by making my way back to my seat just before the whistle blew avoided those last desperately long seconds. It would have been natural, spontaneous. As it was, we just stood there powerless, and separated by glass.

She didn't even cough. I realized a short while later—as I was taking my place in the restaurant car—that she hadn't once had a cigarette in her mouth since our departure from the flat. This had plainly been intended as a gesture.

But perversely I felt more annoyed than grateful. It seemed as if she hadn't quite played fair, had cheated a little, both with that and with her final, farewell words.

"It must be nice having something to look forward to!" she had said. "It must be nice having a home of your own!"

Afterwards she hadn't even bid me goodbye; had just languidly raised her arm as the train moved out.

That wasn't the kind of con trick I admired.

12

I FELT now as if I'd *never* had a real home—anyhow not since the age of eight.

The rented flat with my mother assuredly hadn't been a home; it had been a prison. Or at least that's what it had rapidly become, obscuring earlier memories of snugness and contentment and what had seemed unselfish love; obscuring the fun and irrepressible laughter when I was being tickled in my bed or sliding down the back of the bath and making floods upon the lino. Within a few weeks of my father's death we had moved into Marylebone High Street; at that time not the wealthy street it is today. My mother had always been spoilt and somewhat frail—the shock of losing her husband, allied to the fact of our having been bombed out a mere four days after receiving that pitiless telegram; allied to the fact of her having suddenly recognized how relatively poor we had become...these were blows which she unendingly bemoaned throughout the remainder of her life. Add to *them* a reluctance, even an inability, to cope with so many fundamental chores (no husband and—for the first time ever—no maid) and I suppose that in retrospect it's not surprising she grew hard.

But to return to the point. Whether it was a prison or a home, the only time I could remember being consulted on some question of its decoration my opinion had been summarily dismissed; and after that I took no interest.

Admittedly, when she had died and I was sharing another rented flat, this time with Sylvia, I had done my best, we both had, to make the place comfortable; but I had never particularly regarded it as expressing my own personality—Sylvia's had always appeared, up to that odd display of weeping and dependence, by far the more assertive.

Yet now it was different. My homemaking instincts had been aroused. There was something inspiriting about the atmosphere of that house in Bristol, the almost human voice which had bidden me welcome there. It had caused a predominantly cautious person nearly to forget that such a quality existed. I had not only rushed off to Olympia; I had spent fascinated hours in one department store after another, gazing at kitchen units, bathroom fittings, track-lighting—oh, at all manner of things! I may still have been a dull woman but before I quit London and while there were still a few people left to talk to, my dullness had at least gone down a different route. As one slightly overbearing friend had put it when I went to say goodbye—in fact more a friend of Sylvia's than of mine—"Rachel, you used to be such a gentle, timid little thing. Repressed, even. One wonders what's got into you."

"Ah," I said mysteriously, "the influence of a good house. Reaching out in spirit the moment I had stepped inside."

I laughed and opened my eyes wide and held my hands aloft with outstretched trembling fingers.

"Woo-ooo...! Woo-ooo!"

Even if I hadn't been about to leave London I might still have needed to make new friends.

13

BUT FIRST there were the more prosaic things: the damp, the rot, the applications to the council. Rewiring, heating, insulation.

New plumbing. New slates. The removal of the bunkers.

The filling and refilling of the skip. Sometimes it was *this* which seemed the most completely satisfying.

During these earlier stages I compared the whole process to all those years of study and apprenticeship that may finally lead to the work of art, to public recognition and the flowering of an assured, even a flamboyant, personality.

After that, the things that really showed, the fun things: the workmen with their long ladders, trestle tables, tins of paint, buckets of paste; and the woman who was making the curtains; and the man who was re-covering the chairs; and the firm that was fitting out the kitchen; and the shop that was putting down the carpets. Every day had its excitements. "All those years of study and apprenticeship" reduced basically to just over six weeks: one of the few advantages of the recession—the speed with which large jobs could now be undertaken, the promptitude to match impatience. Some of the last tasks were the repainting of the black railings above the area and those of the tiny balcony; the cleaning of the windows; the application of a final coat to the front door. Its deep gay yellow gloss beneath the shining and winking new knocker and letterbox was redolent of springtime and daffodils and seemed to symbolize all the brightness of my own new life.

That yellow was a fine choice, the right choice, even if at first I'd been uncertain. But—oh, naughty, naughty me!—I should have remembered: all things work together for good, to them that love God. Yes, I *was* rather naughty; sang these words to the tune of "I Wonder Who's Kissing Her Now"; only needing to change "love" to "appreciate" to make the lyric fit. I felt like Oscar Hammerstein.

And then too, halfway through June, there was the young student who came to do the garden. He was nicely tanned and muscular and worked without his shirt and though I kept being drawn towards the window of my bedroom I found him almost unbearable to watch; in particular the way he swung his pick when breaking up the concrete. And when I went to speak to him, to settle some fresh point or take him out a cooling drink, I was really afraid of what my hands might do. Fly up to feel the film of moisture on his chest? Fondle that coat of darkly golden hair? Dear Lord! The embarrassment! Whatever would one say? "Whoops! Please forgive me! I thought there was a fly." It was like experiencing a compulsion to punch a baby's stomach in the pram; or to use on someone standing next to you the carving knife you held.

He was only twenty-one.

But despite such unsettling irrelevancies I felt blest to have him there: somebody straight and vigorous and clean who might one day achieve eminence and who would certainly love widely and be widely loved, spin a web of mutual enrichment from the threads of many disparate existences: a beguiling web whose silken strands must soon make way for even me. Indeed, the process had by now begun. He was in the throes of creating my garden. The thread was indissoluble.

Perhaps all this was slightly fanciful but is there anything much wrong with that? The young man worked from a design of his own, so as to obtain, he said, the prettiest town garden imaginable; and I suggested a handful of refinements. What I wanted, I declared, was first and foremost my seclusion: my own small kingdom, where marvellous and curative things could happen: robins sing arias, neuroses go to seed, fear be altogether uprooted.

Then I wanted an air of mystery—and romance: you shouldn't be able to see from one end to the other: it would be nice to have arches and *trompe-l'oeil*s and a path that enticed you with its possibilities. It would be nice to have a fountain, because I loved water, and a bird-table and some fruit trees and an arbour with a wrought-iron bench. It would be nice to have daisies in the grass—daisies, buttercups, dandelions—and lots of lovely things in flowerbeds, most cunningly variegated.

I'd also like a hint of wilderness.

In short—I asked him for the perfect garden: in thirty by a hundred.

"I'm afraid, Roger, it may be a bit of a tall order. Do you happen to work magic?" Our plotting had almost an air of conspiracy: the two of us pitting our wits against nature. It was as though for a fleeting period he belonged only to myself.

He claimed neither potions nor spells, however. "But even without them, Miss Waring, wouldn't you say a tall order is sometimes the most interesting there is?"

"Do you think, then, we can pull it off?" There was even pleasure in the choice of pronoun.

"I've always wanted to find something just like this—and then to start from scratch—just like this—and..."

I understood at once. "Make it your own?" I asked.

"Well, yes...in a manner of speaking."

"The two of us are very similar, I think. We both want the world to be a better place for our having been here, don't we?"

The world of Rachel Waring was certainly a better place for his having been there. He worked in it for ten days.

Naturally my garden wasn't at once what we had visualized. But it would grow. It would grow towards perfection. And even in the meantime it made a worthy extension to the house itself, which if the garden was my kingdom should logically have been my palace.

Yet few palaces could ever have appeared so cosy—unless they came out of a picture book or animated cartoon. (In real life, for instance, could you imagine thorns and trees and brambles and creeper growing up fast and impenetrable around *Buckingham* Palace?) This one, like most of Disney's, even if not quaintly turreted and gothic, was charming, intimate and friendly. In whichever part of it I found myself I never felt troubled or alone. I felt as if I had only to call out—perhaps I'd be downstairs in the basement—and someone would hear me in the sitting room two floors above and send me back a greeting. Elsewhere, of course, I had often felt anxious and unhappy and completely on my own.

This blessed serenity; this conviction of rightness and responsiveness... It was a nice feeling to have about one's home.

AND WHAT had that spiteful and unhappy fairy brought to my own christening? Ah. She dealt in negatives and yet her gift was comprehensive: an inability to make the most out of my life.

But *The Sleeping Beauty* had never been one of my favourite stories and I don't know why I'd even thought of it; Prince Charming's palace would probably have been just as pleasing. I much preferred *Cinderella*. And shortly before the war I'd seen a rerun of *Snow White and the Seven Dwarfs*. I'd liked that, too, and told the little boy next door that someday my own prince would come; at five years old I had genuinely believed it. But Bobby was unkind. "Mirror, mirror on the wall, who's the fairest of them all?" He laughed and pointed a grubby and derisive finger. "Not you, Rachel Waring, not you! Besides, you haven't got a wicked stepmother," he added a little more gently, as though this might actually be a matter for condolence.

Some three years later, after my father had died and all the tickling had stopped, Bobby's words came back to me. Snow White's father had also been dead or at any rate he hadn't seemed to be around. And in the interim, I thought, I'd really grown much prettier. My grief had made me so. Therefore I began hopefully to chant, mainly at bedtime, the mirror incantation. Of course, this hadn't actually been Snow White's role—but was anyone about to nitpick?

In some ways it was almost as well that the tickling had stopped. Handsome princes didn't usually come to maidens who were cosseted.

Not usually. But when I was much older I hesitantly went to a party at which—although I remember it better for another and not wholly unconnected reason—a group of us was choosing the person, living or dead, whom we should most like to have been. "Grace Kelly," I answered shyly, when eventually it came round to my turn.

I then had to say why.

"Well..." It appeared so obvious. She came from a cultured, wealthy family. She was lovely to look at. She'd had a tremendous success in Hollywood; won an Oscar; played opposite many of the best-known and most attractive actors (some of whom, it was thought, had carried on affairs with her) and now, on top of all of that, there were even rumours she might marry a prince.

Champagne and Ruritania combined. Applause; celebration. A honeysuckle path, from cot to marriage bed.

"It just isn't fair," I said.

They waited. Others had made their answer several times as long. I was the one with whom the game was finishing. I fought against providing anticlimax.

"You see, I'd really like to have been an actress. To play interesting roles, have interesting rehearsals, work with warmhearted and truly committed people. As often as possible, I mean, to be part of a close and caring company."

I was talking far too quickly and I knew I'd gone quite red.

"Though I'm not sure if she's ever actually appeared on stage."

There was still a silence but I simply couldn't think of anything to add.

"That's all."

"Well, if you're being serious about wanting to be an actress," someone asked, "what's stopping you? After all you're only twenty. You've still got time." She gave a sidelong glance at those around us.

"But I don't know any of the right people; I haven't got connections." I was aware they thought this very feeble.

"Connections? The ability's no problem?"

"I don't know."

"We must find out," they said. "An audition!"

"What?"

"Recite something. Anything. 'To be or not to be: that is the question...'"

"Don't be silly." I was beginning to panic.

"A poem, then."

"No. I couldn't."

"Oh, don't be shy, Rachel. We think you're probably quite good."

I could see they were never going to leave it. Instead they were growing more persistent. I mumbled desperately for mercy.

"Silence, silence, everybody! Rachel's about to recite a poem."

"No... No!"

I had a choice between rushing from the room, bursting into tears or actually doing what they wanted. I whispered, before the whole party should get to hear of it, "Will just a few lines be enough?"

"Yes, yes," they cried, greedy for at least an ounce of flesh if they couldn't obtain their full pound.

So I said my few lines. I thought that I said them without expression or audibility and definitely too fast. It was the first stanza of *The Lady of Shalott*. From as young as nine I had experienced a fellow feeling for that lady embowered on her silent isle.

And, somehow, this must now have shone through. Apparently I had misjudged my own performance.

"Oh, that was good. Wasn't that good, everyone?"

There was much earnest clapping; they really did seem to have enjoyed it. "You aren't just poking fun at me?" They swore they weren't. Others—presumably because they had heard all the applause—came in from neighbouring rooms.

"More!" they said. "More!"

"What? Honestly?" Still nervous but not like at the start.

"Yes, Rachel. Please."

"You're *sure* you aren't teasing?"

"Of course we aren't. That would be cruel."

I knew I could improve on what I'd done.

Confidence came quickly; the more I recited the better I grew.

> "Or when the moon was overhead,
>   Came two young lovers lately wed;
> 'I am half sick of shadows,' said
>   The Lady of Shalott."

Unfortunately, however, my memory of the poem wasn't perfect.

"Never mind. Just carry on. You're doing great."

> "Out flew the web and floated wide;
>   The mirror crack'd from side to side;
> 'The curse is come upon me,' cried
>   The Lady of Shalott."

Now I really was projecting and making good use of my hands as well. I had known I had it in me to be an actress.

Yet the real test lay in the final stanza—where, recumbent in a stolen boat, she drifts downriver in the moonlight, borne towards the resplendent, many-towered court of King Arthur. In her mirror she had sometimes seen the knights come riding two-by-two. ("She hath no loyal knight and true, the Lady of Shalott.") I wanted if possible to bring the tears into people's eyes. I finished on a quiet and wholly reverent note.

> "But Lancelot mused a little space;
>   He said, 'She has a lovely face;
> God in his mercy lend her grace,
>   The Lady of Shalott.'"

Even at school I had invariably found this a poignant end.

Now my own eyes were so swimmy I couldn't quite tell how my audience was affected. But I certainly caught sight of the odd handkerchief, heard the odd blowing of a nose.

And one triumph led on to another. They wanted other things; just wouldn't let me go. Finally I sang to them. They seemed beside themselves with pleasure. At last I put my hands up to my chest—returned once more to my prep-school days—revived the unexpected hit of my childhood.

> "Although when shadows fall
>   I think if only...
>   Somebody splendid really needed me,
>   Someone affectionate and dear,
>   Cares would be ended if I knew that he
>   Wanted to have me near..."

It was sheer intoxication; a wonderful prelude to what was to happen later that same evening.

15

I WENT back to the chemist's. I wore my red dress, though this was now a little too warm for the time of year. And only the previous afternoon I'd had my hair done. It was a moment I'd been continually anticipating and, squirrel-like, had been hoarding.

Of course, as with nearly all such moments, there was the particle of grit in the shoe, so difficult to dislodge that one almost welcomed a particle in the eye as well: in this case the haunting knowledge of a poor night's sleep, coupled with a touch of indigestion.

But I couldn't have put it off. Having decided this would be the day, postponement would have seemed quite wrong. A giving in to weakness.

I said, "Good morning. How are you?"

"Very well, thank you, madam. Yourself?"

At first it would have been practically a relief if the lumpy, shiny-nosed girl had been there instead but as soon as we spoke I began to feel better.

"I came in last March. You advised me I ought to settle here. Well, I've taken your advice!" I said this smilingly, to make sure he realized he had no need to reproach himself.

"Oh, yes, of course. I remember." It was very clear he didn't.

"I was wearing a light blue jumper with a darker blue skirt. My boat-race outfit as everybody called it! But since it wasn't summer yet (and *ne'er cast a clout till May be out*—or is it may?) I naturally wore a coat over it. Camel hair. And quite a pretty little hat . . . black, you know, and really rather smart." I laughed.

He merely gave a gentle nod, boyish and abstracted; it came as no surprise that he should be the strong and silent type. That was the kind of man I often found attractive.

But I realized I should have to help him out.

"Though who am I to say my little hat was smart? A hostess doesn't praise her own cooking! Besides, good sir, smartness—like beauty—is surely in the eye of the beholder?" I slightly worried that my laughter was beginning to sound foolish.

He said: "Well, well. So you've lately moved to Bristol?"

A man came in behind me.

"Why don't you serve this gentleman? I'm not in any hurry."

The man bought a large box of Kleenex and a packet of corn plasters. I took note of everything. All thoughts of indigestion and of tiredness had completely disappeared now that things were slipping along so merrily. The customer was youngish and his jeans looked clean but he was very down at heel. Literally I mean. It wouldn't have mattered except for one thing. He obviously hadn't heard this: that when there was a shine on your shoes there was a melody in your heart.

Poor man. If he'd recently purchased a tin of polish he mightn't now be needing plasters. There was a definite connection. I pictured him out of work, keeping up a brave front—it was only in that single admittedly important detail he had failed—struggling in something like a garret to produce a masterpiece.

It was a lovely world. I executed a few unobtrusive dance-steps which scarcely moved me from the spot. My own shoes were immaculate: high-heeled red sandals with lovely thin straps, dreamily delicate. This was the first time I had worn them.

I had such pretty feet.

It didn't matter that he hadn't recognized me.

A woman came in. That didn't matter either. She only wanted a packet of sanitary towels.

Corn plasters; sanitary towels. What a funny old world it was. I was so *glad* I could see the humorous side of it.

"Yes, I like it here very much," I said as she put away her change

—and before she should remember, dear heaven, that she needed toilet rolls as well! "I think Bristol must be one of the nicest towns on earth. When did you first come here yourself?"

"Oh, about thirty years ago." He smiled. "I came here when I married."

There was a stillness: the sort of stillness that exists, I believe, right in the eye of the storm. It was like being sealed in a glass cylinder at the bottom of the sea. It reminded me of when I'd caught sight of my name in the newspaper. But that had been different; now only a Houdini could possibly find his way out. With a start I became aware of myself—no expert, sadly, in escape—staring through those transparent walls at a showcard on the counter. Things happened after a Badedas bath. You might be whisked off to Camelot by a lovesick errant knight. There was the picture of a woman staring dreamily from a window, just a towel draped carelessly about her. Well, lucky her. Standing nearly naked in an illuminated bathroom with undrawn curtains she was undoubtedly a floozy; but, right then, I wouldn't have minded changing places with her.

She had to face no brutal truths.

No, not brutal perhaps. Unnecessary. Insensitive. It hadn't eluded me he might be married.

But wait. "Ah, yes, I see. And is your wife still...?" I corrected myself; despite the numbing quality of such a shock I hadn't lost any of my old cunning. "And does your wife enjoy her life in Bristol?"

"Very much so."

I bought a tablet of lavender soap; the same as the one I'd got here previously. I decided the Paracetamol would certainly be cheaper at Boots.

"Have you settled nearby?" he asked.

"Buckland Street." It was the first name I could think of.

"Oh, just around the corner." That, too, seemed an unnecessary scrap of information. I definitely wouldn't be returning here. "Then maybe we'll be seeing something of you. Nice."

It was almost what he'd said before. This time I wasn't fooled. They could make a dupe out of you once ... because, after all, you were only human, you didn't set out to be cynical. But in their arrogance they supposed that they could go *on* doing it, time after time after time.

I thanked him with dignity and in a very natural manner whose slighter degree of coolness such a person could hardly be expected to appreciate. But that was good. I didn't want him thinking his rebuff had been important.

Outside, a few doors along, I passed the marriage bureau through which he'd probably met her. I had never understood how anybody, no matter how lonely, could be sufficiently lost to all sense of pride as to resort to that.

But I wreaked, I thought, a rather subtle form of revenge. I went into another chemist's shop (it wasn't Boots) where the prices were most likely as inflated as his own. And I not only bought the Paracetamol. "Do you happen to stock Badedas?" I asked, with a merry ripple of laughter. "Because, if so, I'll take the very largest size you have."

16

YET DESPITE such inspired retaliation I knew I needed to cheer myself up. I recognized the signs. For the first time since coming to Bristol I felt quite low. Help! I went to the public library.

Where I quickly began to recover. The woman at the desk might have been no older than I was but unquestionably she looked it. Someone should have told her about touching up her hair or even about the invention of contact lenses. I wanted to say, "You know, my dear, men seldom make passes at girls who wear glasses."

I said: "Men seldom make passes at girls who wear glasses."

I tried to convey that it was really neither here nor there but that it might still be as well to think about it. I didn't want to hurt her.

"Excuse me?"

I considered adding that they only caused you trouble for the first week. Contact lenses I mean.

I flashed her a winning smile. "Errol Flynn," I said.

"Oh. Books on the cinema are over there."

I saw that she wasn't wearing a wedding ring. I automatically liked her and despised her and felt sorry for her and was glad.

"Would you know offhand if you've anything on Horatio Gavin?"

"Is he connected with the cinema?"

"Oh! You can't be serious!"

She led me across to the biography section. "I'm sorry," she said. "What was that name again?"

It was all very well—she was certainly not unpleasant but I began to feel resentful. Both on Mr. Gavin's behalf and more obscurely on my own. Probably the fact that I now owned the house in which he'd lived entitled me to some measure of sensitivity.

There was nothing on the shelves. "I'll check the cards," she said.

This was more successful. "Ah, yes, I've found something! Oh? Was he a local man?"

I answered with both relish and severity. "He lived barely half a mile from where we stand now. Why?"

"This booklet was published by a local press. I'll go to check if we've still got it."

After five minutes she returned empty-handed—and apparently they couldn't even acquire it for me.

"Well, never mind," I said. "At least you can give me the name of the press."

"I'm afraid the press closed down. Several years ago."

"This is absurd!"

I felt prepared to make a scene. What had started out as almost an idle enquiry had now become a matter of some urgency.

She said: "I suppose you could try in the secondhand bookshops." But her tone entirely lacked conviction.

"And I could advertise too." I had never in my life thought to advertise for anything. The words just seemed to come to me.

"Yes, indeed."

"I could even go to the council." Goodness, I sounded smug. There was clearly no end to my ingenuity. She nodded a bit uncertainly and I was going to enlighten her but suddenly I didn't want to. It was nice to have one's little secrets; it made one feel superior. This would be something solely between Horatio and myself. Just the two of us. I smiled.

"Well, thank you for all your help. Thank you, at least, for having tried!"

On my way out I passed the shelves bearing the encyclopaedias. There was no mention of Horatio Gavin in *Britannica* but I found a few lines about him in *Chambers*. I felt a tremendous leap of the heart. It was like the feeling you might get on seeing a well-loved face in the crowd when you hadn't believed that it could possibly happen.

> Gavin, Horatio (1760–1793), English social reformer associated with William Wilberforce in his campaign to eradicate slavery; died fourteen years too soon to see the longed-for abolition of the British slave trade.

It was the shortest entry on the page, perhaps in the whole encyclopaedia, but what of that? I rushed back to the desk. "Look!" I cried. "Look!"

I pointed triumphantly, realizing a little too late that I'd pushed in front of two women who'd just arrived to have their novels stamped. They stepped back and I apologized and all was sweetly smiling politeness. But although I knew it was less out of interest than a sense of duty that the librarian read the entry; although she said nothing more than, "Well, fancy—yes I'm glad you've found something!"; although as I walked over to the photocopier I was sure the three women were leaning their heads together in genteelly malicious gossip... none of this seemed to matter. I only felt that in some small way Horatio Gavin had been vindicated.

But frustratingly I soon discovered that I needed help with the photocopier.

For the third time I approached the desk.

"Oh, incidentally, I've found a bar of soap here. I don't know if anyone will claim it."

17

So HE WAS just thirty-three when he died. The same age as Jesus. I was mildly disappointed—not I regret for his own sake but simply because I'd been picturing someone a little older than myself. Yet I quickly adjusted. In the library I had already felt protective. A fine man, his name linked with William Wilberforce. Of course from the beginning I had known that he was good. But the expression "the good die young" now occurred to me with more immediacy, more poignancy, than it had ever done before—even in connection with my father, or with Paul the picture framer.

I suddenly wished I were younger. Well, one wished that fairly often but this time I experienced a feeling of nausea. There were so seldom any second chances. I had now missed out forever.

"Just thirty-three," I said. I spoke aloud. The nausea had briefly brought a fine perspiration to my forehead but now I continued with the preparation of my lunch. "What on earth could you have died of at the age of thirty-three?"

I paused again in the act of peeling a potato.

"Well, at that time I suppose you were one of the luckier ones to live even that long."

And perhaps I was one of the luckier ones too. A survivor. Unexpectedly strong.

After lunch I went round the secondhand bookshops. And just before I stepped into the third, I positively knew that I was going to find it there. I scarcely felt dismayed when the owner shook his head. He was a wizened little fellow who good-humouredly invited me to browse. Yet I did so for barely a minute.

The man stared at my discovery as though unable to believe what his eyes were telling him. "I'd have sworn I hadn't seen one of these in years!"

I felt so pleased. "It was right there in the middle. The shelf was even at eye level."

"Was it now!"

"You know what must have happened? Whenever you had your back turned this wise and precious book made another little jump towards the centre!"

And I couldn't have explained it but I almost believed in what I was saying. Only when he answered, "Yes, a lovely little game of leapfrog!" did I fully acknowledge its absurdity.

But how my heart had bounded—and for the second time that day. Even despite my certainty.

There was no price pencilled inside, no sticker on the thin fawn cover. The man shrugged and said, "Oh . . . 20p." I was immensely moved. He had seen how much I wanted it. He could have asked for ten times that amount and I would willingly have paid. People were sometimes so very kind. I walked home in a glow, almost skipping, almost dancing, nearly as much on account of people's kindness as because I had the book.

I didn't start to read it straightaway. I made myself a pot of Lapsang Souchong and carried this upstairs as I did almost every afternoon. My sitting room looked warmly inviting with its many polished surfaces, its softly filtered light and quantities of fresh flowers.

I set the tray down on a small gateleg table with a red chenille cloth, stood at one of the windows for a moment enjoying the geraniums on my balcony, then glanced appraisingly in the antique mirror over the Adam fireplace—after lunch, before going out again, I had changed into a cooler dress. At last I poured the tea and carried it across to my chair. I didn't want a biscuit. When I had taken a few appreciative sips I placed the cup and saucer on an occasional table by the chair.

I picked up my purchase of the afternoon.

The book had fewer than sixty pages and its print was large. Even then much of the prose was irrelevant, the style long-winded and pontificating. I read the whole thing in an hour.

Nevertheless it was an hour during which I lived intensely.

There plainly wasn't a lot known about Horatio Gavin. The author had probably consulted whatever records he could find but most of the work was surely based on supposition. One paragraph I liked in particular: "He may have thought, that fine Spring morning, as he cantered past the cathedral, of all the faith and hope and backache that had gone into its creation, this immense project begun in one man's lifetime, perhaps not finished even in his grandson's. He may have thought of all the myriad small miseries of daily life, so erosively familiar to anyone in any age, like headache, constipation, haemorrhoids, or family tiffs. Young Gavin may have thought of all these stirring things as he cantered past—yet, on the other hand, it seems unlikely that he did, since his mind that morning must have been very full of what he was about to say to Wilberforce."

A biography like that, even with nothing more to offer, must soon become a favourite on anybody's shelf!

But this one—at least to someone like myself—had a great deal more to offer. It told the story, however fictional, of a lonely brooding idealistic young man, son of a merchant in Bath, who upon his father's death had moved with his mother to live near a widowed aunt in Bristol. It told of his championship of the underprivileged, his entry into politics, his meeting with Wilberforce and of the instant rapport established between them. It told of his tender feelings for a Miss Anne Barnetby and of the great blow when on the eve of their nuptials she eloped with some far more worldly man: a shock from which, averred the Reverend Lionel Wallace, the young Horatio had never quite recovered. The author speculated that when he had died—as the result of a burst appendix—he had not found anyone to take her place.

"I say a burst appendix, where another man might say a broken heart. I claim, however, that that other man would be mistaken.

Hasn't he yet discovered the balm of self-immersion in a noble cause?"

When I had finally closed the book I sat for a long time. I meditated, I conjectured. I wove a brightly-coloured tapestry. I began to picture myself as that shallow fickle woman whom he had so much loved, that sad deluded woman who—incredibly— hadn't appreciated such devotion.

But I decided it didn't suit me to be sad or deluded—any more than I would ever opt, of course, to be either flighty or shallow. For the moment I saw myself, more comfortably, as her successor.

I wondered if despite Mr. Wallace's denial he *could* have found a woman to replace her? The departure of Anne Barnetby was factual; what had come afterwards was nothing but surmise.

I had once seen a play called *Berkeley Square*: about a man becoming his own ancestor and falling timelessly in love before needing to return to the present. Did I believe in reincarnation? I wasn't sure. But what a delightful thought and yes why not? Sup- posing it had been foreordained that twentieth-century Rachel should be returned to the house in which *eighteenth*-century Ra- chel had been able to mend a young philanthropist's heart and lovingly restore his will to live...?

I laughed. Though not by any means through sheer frivolity.

"No wonder I've always felt so very much at home!"

18

SHE WAS a gentle thin-haired deferential lady who offered me a jam tart with my cup of tea. On the telephone I had invited *her* to have tea with *me* but after a good deal of hesitation—and even some apparent reluctance that we should meet at all—she'd finally admitted she would much prefer to stay at home. So I'd taken her a box of chocolates and half a dozen roses and once I was actually there it was pathetic the way she kept on telling me how glad she was to have a visitor, and the way she kept on thanking me—surely five or six times—for those two extremely simple gifts; saying how I shouldn't have done it, oh I *shouldn't* have done it! She was quite endearing but how I hoped that I myself, as I grew older, would be spared from being pathetic.

"There was a painting," I said, "which Mr. Wallace mentions. 'The portrait that now hangs above me as I write.' Do you know what became of it, Miss Eversley?" I had hoped I would see it as she ushered me into the sitting room of her flat (however, her home turned out to be entirely more modest than that: purely a bed-sitter) but this time it had been only a *hope*, nothing stronger.

"Oh, yes," she exclaimed. "That great big monstrosity of a picture!"

I was surprised. "But Mr. Wallace said he had a nice good-natured face with a most intriguing smile." I remembered it precisely: "'A smile that somehow grew more pronounced, increasingly captivating, the better that you came to know the painting.'"

She was nodding even before I had finished. "Oh, I'm not saying anything against it, please don't think that. I'm sure he did have a nice face just like the Reverend Wallace wrote. But somehow it was all so dark; so, I don't know, so..."

"Sombre?"

"Yes! It was all so sombre that in certain lights you couldn't even see it *was* a face. Not if you were standing in the wrong position." She raised her hands. "And the dust it used to collect! But in some ways I wish I was still dusting it today. It wasn't such a bad life. All in all."

I had a vision, briefly, of the past she was remembering. To me it seemed quite dreadful: daily ministrations to some prosy and pedantic old clergyman. Grey, all grey. Yet nearly anything was better, I supposed, than—what?—to be in your middle-to-late eighties. Wrinkled fingers; dewlapped throat. No hope of change. How terrible no longer to have any hope of change. No hope of finding love.

"More tea?" she asked. "Another tart?"

"Not a thing. It was delicious."

I wiped my mouth on my lace-edged handkerchief.

"Do you happen to know what became of it? The picture."

"Well, you'd have to ask Mr. Lipton who came and cleared the house for me. I kept one or two little things of course"—she gestured towards a chest of drawers, a wardrobe and her bed—"just enough to meet my needs in this place, but otherwise Mr. Lipton bought it all; a very fair gentleman, I will say that for him, a very fair gentleman indeed."

"Is he a local man?"

"Oh, yes. The Reverend Wallace said his shop was better than any Aladdin's cave. He bought me this old tin-opener at Mr. Lipton's, the best I've ever had." And she rose with some difficulty, her cup of tea unfinished—expressly, as it turned out, to show me this very ordinary tin opener. "10p," she said. We both stood and admired it.

Then she gave me detailed directions on how to get there. "But if you'll forgive me, Miss Baring, asking you something you'll maybe think *much* too personal...?"

I told her the reason for my interest was that I now lived in Mr. Gavin's house: a fact which seemed to cause her a good deal of gratification. "And I'd love to return your hospitality," I said. "I'm hoping that you're shortly going to visit me there."

But she began to shake her head.

I gently coaxed. "I would arrange for a taxi to fetch you and to bring you home."

"That's very kind," she murmured. "Perhaps...when the days draw out a bit. When it gets a little warmer." We were coming to the end of July.

"I see you've got no television."

"No. I never cared for it. Nor the wireless either."

"I was just wondering, then, if you'd like to come and watch the Royal Wedding with me. Make a day of it. In colour."

I could see that she was tempted. "I'll have to give it a little thought," she told me.

"Shall I phone you next Tuesday?"

"Well, we'll see. I don't know if I shall be able to come to the telephone next Tuesday."

I nodded and experienced a great surging wave of gratitude. Gratitude for being somebody like me, not somebody like her. Gratitude for having so many good years still temptingly in store, so much sheer quality of life!

And I vowed that I was going to make the most of every minute. I was young! I had time! Today was the past I'd be looking back on in another thirty years. Thirty or forty or fifty. And looking back on with such serenity. Such pleasure. I could have hugged her!

However, apart from my sudden desire to express an all-embracing tenderness, I felt relieved that she probably wouldn't accept my invitation. I had no wish to see the Royal Wedding. None whatsoever.

"Well, if you can't come to me," I suggested, "shall I come to you? I don't mean that day in particular. Any time. We could read the newspapers together or simply sit and talk?"

"That would be nice," she smiled—with an expression, I thought, of genuine appreciation. "I'll let you know when it's convenient."

She held her finger to her lips.

"But sometimes they don't like it here if you get too many visitors. They're a bit funny that way. They get jealous and say some very nasty things. One has to be so careful." She was still whispering.

"Who? The other residents?"

"And the wardens. But they're really very fair. On the whole. I will say that for them."

Oh dear.

Yes, it was frightening to see how people's already tiny worlds could contract yet further, into something so engrossing that neither pestilence nor flood nor royal wedding could intrude. And it was as sad as it was frightening since those tiny worlds were in any case so full of whisper and of menace. So immensely far from the haven you'd believe the elderly ought to have found. Despite myself, I had to smile. *The rays of the evening sun reflecting on the water.* Wasn't that how Mrs. Pimm had put it?

I said: "But to return to what we were speaking of..."

For some reason she looked hopeful as if I might supply the answer to a question which either she hadn't dared ask or hadn't known how to.

"I'm also wanting to write a book on Mr. Gavin."

"Ah?"

"Though I don't think it will be a biography, not like the Reverend Wallace's. It's going to be a novel. Don't you feel that's wonderfully exciting?" I had forgotten to keep my voice down.

She returned her finger to her lips. "How very interesting!" she said. "But I was never a big reader."

Oh, Miss Eversley! No novels, no television, no radio. The greyness of her life appalled me. This self-imposed greyness even in a land of colour. No escape. No possibility of escape.

"Yes—all my life I've hoped to write a novel!" I laughed. I was so much wanting to infect her with a little of my own gaiety. "And now it seems I've found my hero!"

She didn't laugh but she certainly did smile. "Oh, I'm sure a lot of people may have seen him in that way."

I was impressed.

"And myself, too—I think of him whenever I look at this tin-opener and remember all that junk in Mr. Lipton's shop."

"Oh, I see, no—"

"But thank you for coming, Miss Baring. And thank you for all those lovely flowers and chocolates you brought. You really shouldn't have."

She was sweet in her appreciation. "I know what I shall do," I cried. "I shall go right out and buy you a jigsaw!"

"A jigsaw?"

"Yes. They're such absorbing things. And you don't paint, do you? You don't work tapestry? Then you simply must have a jigsaw."

"But I wouldn't know what to do with it." She gave her head a puzzled shake.

"I shall get you one with mountains and a lake and a little village nestling on the slopes. And a castle and a church spire and a café. And a woman with a barrow selling flowers."

She seemed a trifle overwhelmed by this.

"And an organ-grinder with a monkey!" (I was trusting I might find something roughly like it in either W H Smith or Woolworths.) "Why, Miss Eversley"—it suddenly came home to me— "you haven't even got a record player!"

"Oh, no, please," she said. "What should I want with an organ-grinder and a monkey?"

I was delighted by her sense of humour.

"Please not," she said.

But when she actually opened the door she had her finger pressed to her lips again. And then we only mimed the rest of our goodbyes.

19

I HAD HARDLY been home ten minutes and was just wondering whether to make myself a *proper* cup of tea when the doorbell rang and I had a visitor. What an eventful day! The employment exchange in the morning, followed by coffee and a scone at *The Good Hostess*, Miss Eversley in the afternoon, my stroll back through the park singing, "Ten cents a dance, that's what they pay me, oh how they weigh me down..." (and doing my best *not* to think of the Reverend Lionel Wallace as I did so!) and now this. A visitor. Or, rather, two visitors. Even three. Standing on the pavement in the sunshine were a tall young man in a smart brown suit and a slim and pretty woman who had in her arms a sleeping baby. The three of them made a charming tableau.

"Roger!" I exclaimed.

"Don't say you recognize me with my hair brushed!"

"What a lovely surprise."

"May I introduce my wife, Miss Waring? This is Celia. And *this*—this normally rather noisy newcomer to the southwest—is Thomas."

"How lovely. Oh, how lovely." My vocabulary seemed limited. "And I didn't even realize you were married. Do come in. I was just about to make some tea."

"What terrific timing!" laughed the young man. "I'm parched." In a moment he was filling the hallway like a glowing Dane. "But perhaps that wasn't very polite. I am sorry. Perhaps I should be saying I do hope we're not disturbing you but that we were just passing and—"

"We *were* just passing," said his wife. "Please, Miss Waring, pay no attention to my exuberant husband."

"I assure you I won't," I said. "Is he always like this?"

"Yes!"

"Oh, how unbearable! But at least you must get him to wear off *some* of his energy by taking Thomas from you—because I'm afraid my sitting room is on the next floor and you can see the stairs are somewhat steep."

He said, while obediently taking his son, "But tell her, Miss Waring, I don't need to be all stiff and formal with you, do I? Tell her we're old buddies."

"We're old buddies, Mrs. Allsop."

"Celia," he said.

But it seemed she was too busy looking about her even to have heard. "Oh, this is gorgeous, Miss Waring. It's delightful. Have you done it all yourself?"

They were my first real visitors to my first real home. I felt very proud yet tried my hardest not to show it.

"Well, I may not have done it all myself but at least I've had it all done ... myself."

"And in the ability to delegate," said Roger, "lies the hallmark of genius."

She exclaimed over nearly everything she saw. So did her husband. It was the most intoxicating stuff. And I too exclaimed: over their bright-eyed adorable baby. We all appeared very well pleased with one another. I went away to make the tea. The baby had awoken on his journey up the stairs and in my absence Celia fed him. She changed his nappy in the bathroom. She seemed so terribly organized and efficient. While we drank our tea and they ate the dainty iced cakes that I'd dashed out to the teashop for, Thomas cooed and gurgled contentedly—this noisy little newcomer to the southwest—and clutched his father's finger. How I wished that Sylvia could have seen us. "Oh, you are such a *strong* little boy, aren't you?" said his mother. "Such a powerful little grasp already!" I visualized that sea of tight golden curls beneath the crisp beige shirt on which his head reclined; and, feeling myself begin to flush, had to look away abruptly.

He said: "Darling, we haven't told Miss Waring the reason for our visit."

"My goodness," I exclaimed confusedly, "does there need to be a reason?"

"Well, *now* I realize not," he answered. He grinned apologetically. "But anyway I was boasting to Celia about that garden we'd created—"

"You created."

"No," he contradicted firmly, "very much a team effort: you the brain, me the brawn. And I suddenly thought how much I'd like to see it again. And I'd like Celia to see it too; to appreciate my cleverness."

"Our cleverness," I cried merrily, aware of having scored a telling point.

"Yes, I swear it. Cross my heart."

"But you're saying you've only come to see the garden?"

I felt like a dreadful flirt but the flirtation came quite naturally, even here under the eyes of his smiling wife.

"The garden?" I said. "Not me?"

He bowed his head. He answered: "I'd forgotten how nice you were."

It was one of those crushing moments when you're wholly taken aback by simple sincerity and you can't think what to say.

"Of course you may come and see it," was all that I did say.

We sat out there for some while close together on the wrought-iron bench—Roger in the middle—and I was most terribly aware of the contact of our thighs.

"I remember you're a student," I said, my voice sounding wholly unnatural to myself, "but for the life of me I can't remember what you're studying."

"Law."

Had I never asked him? I didn't think I had. How utterly remiss. "That must be very interesting."

He nodded. "But another three years to go. That's the hard part. I just can't wait to get started."

"Yes, it must be hard." I leaned forward slightly, looked across him to his wife. "How ever do you manage?"

She replied easily, "Oh, we do manage. Somehow. Roger gardens of course during the spring and summer vacations."

I smiled, not quite so easily. "What it is to be young," I thought. But I hadn't realized I was going to say it right out loud.

"Well, we've got our health," she said. "And we've got Thomas. And we've got each other. Money doesn't really seem all that important."

Yes. And during the night it mightn't seem important in the slightest.

I wondered if he wore pyjamas.

And I wondered how often . . . and how it . . . Sitting there in the balmy evening air I felt momentarily sick again with deprivation and jealousy and the bitterly recurring knowledge that I would never know now what it felt like, that one experience which above all others was alleged to be . . . Oh God, I thought. Oh God, oh God, oh God. For a second I was afraid I'd said all that aloud as well.

But the desperation of the moment passed. We talked some more about the garden. Celia said, "I think in time it will be beautiful. But—and this may sound blasphemous within my husband's hearing—it's the house I truly go for. It's one of the loveliest I've seen. Not only that, it's got such a wonderful atmosphere."

"Ah? So you've really noticed?"

"Well, who could fail to?"

She had gone a long way towards making it more bearable, that retreating minute of desolation. I liked her. I liked her despite the gleam of loving pride whenever her eyes were resting on her husband.

"Then you must come and see me often."

"We should love to," she said. "And you must come and see us, too." She added impulsively: "What about lunch on Sunday?"

But Roger broke in. "Darling, didn't your parents say they might be driving over next Sunday with Ralph or someone?"

"Oh, damn—"

We left it in abeyance for the time being. In all honesty I was just as glad. Although extremely moved to have been asked, especially with so much warmth and spontaneity, I felt there was absolutely no rush. I should get a lot of enjoyment simply from thinking about it.

She made a face. "My parents want us to have young Thomas christened." He was making happy little noises and sucking his thumb while drumming his heels on the plaid rug that I had brought out and arranged on the turf which his father had laid. (How I had liked the way his back muscles had rippled as he was lowering each section into place.) "We ourselves can't see the urgency. But I suppose"—she laughed—"anything for the sake of a quiet life…"

"You know, Celia, I don't think I've ever seen a more contented baby."

"Would you like to hold him?"

FOR VARIOUS reasons I passed a largely sleepless night. In the first place I had fevered, wakeful dreams of having—perhaps—God willing—almost acquired a new family. Roger and Celia Allsop wanted three more children; which on the one hand was a nice notion but on the other a horribly disturbing one. I tried to concentrate on the nice part though. I calculated that by the time I was seventy those four children would either be in their twenties or approaching them. By the time I was eighty they would probably have children of their own. What would they call me? Aunt? Aunty Rachel? I'd be such a sweet old lady. They'd come to me with all their troubles, things they couldn't speak about at home. Aunty Rachel was such a sport! You could always rely on *her*. Her house was such a hive of activity as well, an ever-open door, people coming and going at all times, and everything such fun! Not merely that. She was always so generous. Dear old soul. Nobody quite like her.

My hectic imagination pictured birthday parties, mainly but not exclusively for the children: Christmases, merry traditional Christmases such as I had seldom known: for the most part it had been just my mother and me, or Sylvia and me. I saw myself doing a little song-and-dance routine, the centre of a clamorous admiring crowd,

> Sometimes I think I've found my hero,
> But it's a queer romance;
> Come on, big boy—ten cents a dance,

my pretty, twinkling feet still as pretty and twinkling as ever, my ankles just as slim, my footwear just as elegant. "Oh, I would never let any man drink champagne out of *my* slipper! No matter how he begged. Only think, my dears, of how—for ever after—it would *squelch*!" I would turn into such a character.

And there'd also be weddings. By then I wouldn't mind the thought of weddings; I'd be able to flirt with all the handsome young men—and even, *by then*, with some of the older ones too—and there'd be nothing but sheer wickedness and pleasure and hilarity.

But at some time after four o'clock I fell into a different dream and in this dream Roger—naked—was coming up the stairs towards me. He was dark and didn't look at all like Roger but I knew that it was he. I was waiting at the top of the staircase in a long white garden-party frock and I was aware without any feeling of surprise that *I* had changed as well: I was younger and more beautiful.

Yet the stairs seemed to go on forever—there must have been a hundred flights. It was as though I dwelt in some impossibly high tower, almost as unscalable on the inside as it was on the out. And I became afraid that he would take so long to reach me that all my loveliness would fade. I would not merely grow old but ancient.

Haggard...

The lovely dream became a nightmare—a nightmare directed by Hitchcock but without his penchant for romantic ends.

And when I awoke from it—although, thank heaven, not staying awake for long—I felt disoriented. Drugged. Drained. I tried, as an antidote, to recapture the way it had felt to hold Thomas in the garden.

Unsuccessfully. For some reason what I recaptured was the way it had felt, less than a year before, when my periods had stopped coming.

Useless. Unused.

Wasted.

I recaptured how—when the realization had finally sunk in—I had cried on and off all through one rainy Sunday afternoon. Sylvia had thought I was crazy.

———

But as if all *that* hadn't been enough there was another theme which had run through my restlessness: the book I was going to write: the idea of gradually getting to know another life—a fine, exemplary and altruistic life—of painstakingly removing coats of paint, layers of wallpaper, and working my way in . . . of *feeling* my way in, with a wonderful and enriching instinct for the creation of links. I visualized myself, here too, as being on the verge of a new relationship, one equally important in its very different way. Indeed, the two themes almost merged. It struck me at some point that, after all, the naked man on the stair might not have been Roger. It might have been Horatio. I was in that midworld between wakefulness and sleep where such a notion really didn't seem enormously farfetched.

The face of the man had become a blur. Perhaps this was strange, since my own face remained so vividly in mind. It was the face of Scarlett O'Hara.

Of Vivien Leigh.

And when I finally awoke in the morning—having something as tangible as that to hold on to—it was the image of myself at the top of the stairs which I remembered best. Vivien Leigh in a low-cut white crinoline, with frills at the shoulders and a sash at the waist. Kittenish but strong.

21

WHEN I *finally* awoke, although I now felt thoroughly refreshed and rejuvenated, I was also mildly annoyed that it was half-past-nine—and I had overslept by two hours.

But all the same I didn't hurry. Things had to be done nicely; especially so from now on. My breakfast table with its single rose. My lightly boiled egg, my thin crisp toast, my little pot of real coffee. The housework, my warm and scented bath, the careful brushing of my hair. The application of my creams and makeup. None of it was wasted time.

Far from it indeed. Even while I dusted I looked about me for things that *he* might recognize, for segments of a shared experience.

There was the very shape of the rooms, for instance: the corners, the alcoves, positioning of the windows. The moulding on the ceilings—*that* he would have known, might have gazed at, as two centuries later I myself did, tracing its convolutions with attentive eyes. The mantelpieces—*this* in the sitting room, say. Yes, that was original. And the fireplace. Right here he might have stood, surely did stand, arms resting on the mantel as mine now did, one polished boot upon the andiron, eyes staring dreamily into the mesmerizing, picture-making flames. He had been twenty-one when first he came to this house. I saw the back of his tilted head, its thick healthily gleaming hair, his broad shoulders and narrow waist, the long sturdy legs, the shining leather boots. I imagined, underneath the fitted coat, the play of muscle down that lean back.

Or in 1781 would the fashion still have been for periwigs and shoes? I wasn't sure. Yet details such as this could very easily be checked.

And whilst cracking the shell on my breakfast egg, I had known the chances were good he must often have eaten a boiled egg. His bread would have been coarser, his coffee from perhaps a different bean, but the taste of a softly boiled egg (mine was free-range, very fresh) must have been the same then as it was now.

So with practically everything I did I was preparing myself to see things and feel things—taste, smell, touch and hear them—as nearly as I could in the manner that *he* might have done. I loved every minute of it. It wasn't just an exercise. Time travel, I decided, cried out to become a regular pastime. I should campaign for it. "Infinitely more liberating," I would call from the rooftops, "than all this nonsense about the burning of your bras!"

It was almost twelve when I left home—though not to scale the rooftops. I had a short list of household things I had to buy. But first I went into a stationer's.

There I looked at the ledgers, the account books, the minute books. How beautifully bound they were, how exquisitely tooled! None of the plain exercise books (no, again, "exercise" seemed *completely* wrong) came anywhere near the same standard. Yet there was one, the most expensive, which certainly gave off a nice feel. But was it thick enough? And weren't the lines a shade too close? I replaced it with reluctance. It had to be just right.

I went to Smith's. Once more I hesitated. I made a whistle-stop tour of the city. In the restaurant of a department store I ate a ham salad with a piece of French bread, drank a glass of orange juice, and reviewed the possibilities. In the end I went back to my starting point and bought the volume I had liked originally.

With that decision taken—no, with the book actually bought —I felt a great deal better.

It was a less agonizing matter, marginally, to find the best writing implement. I had thought about a dip pen, being the closest thing to a quill, but memories of how the nibs had so often scratched lumps out of my books at school—and left unsightly and infuriating blobs—directed me towards the ballpoints. I already had several but for this enterprise I wanted something new. And more costly.

I also bought a giant pad of scribbling paper—and a notebook for my handbag.

Then I went to the library, took out a book on Bath and one on Bristol, another on eighteenth-century social history and a fourth on costume. I was glad the woman with the glasses wasn't there.

As I returned home, feeling thoroughly well satisfied with my purchases and borrowings, a light rain was falling. This was unimportant. The gardens would be refreshed and perhaps there'd be a rainbow. En route I popped into the grocer's, bought quickly and extravagantly, without my usual comparison of quantities and prices, and didn't even stop to count my change. When the assistant at the cheese counter complained about the weather I replied, "But aren't you aware, you naughty and ungrateful man, that where you see clouds upon the hills you soon will see crowds of daffodils?" and even though we were nearer August than April I thought it seemed a jaunty, wise and almost witty thing to say, and indicative too of the springtime which had belatedly come tripping into my own heart. And the man said, "You're spot on, madam. I only wish that more folks were a bit like you," and I felt like a combination of Wordsworth, Al Jolson and Walter Huston, only luckier than all three of them, and then I remembered that Huston was connected with "September Song" not "April Showers" but this was also applicable in its own way and I found myself singing it for the remainder of my journey home, not loudly, yet evidently loudly enough to make one or two people glance at me in amused surprise. Well, let them, I thought.

> And these few vintage years I'll share with you.
> These vintage years
> I'll share
> With you.

And at the same time I was careful not to step on any of the cracks. "Bears," I exclaimed merrily—being practically impossible to hoodwink and simultaneously doing one of my nifty little dances, nifty *and* artistic, "bears, look at me walking in just the squares!" I believe that on the second occasion somebody actually heard me—yes, and saw me, too! Oh, Lordy Moses!

I returned to the contemplation of my vintage years and of the way I was going to spend them.

Yet I forgot to look out for the rainbow. That was slightly negligent.

I was still singing, however, as for the second time that day I dusted the table beneath one of the windows in the sitting room. It was here I would sit to write my novel.

I took the book from its bag and placed it on the table; wondered if I should put back the cloth to protect a highly polished surface. But, no, the colours would clash: opposing shades of red. I minutely corrected the book's angle; laid the new ballpoint pen beside it; brought over the Anglepoise and my Chambers Twentieth Century Dictionary (I was so glad that I had Chambers!); also the scribbling pad and my four acquisitions from the library. Lastly, Mr. Wallace's *Life*.

As an afterthought I fetched the tiny vase which I normally kept for my breakfast table and my supper tray and placed it carefully on a doily; tomorrow I would set a fresh pink rose in it.

"There!" I said as I stood back and surveyed the whole arrangement. "All for you!" I glanced humorously towards the fireplace. "I trust it meets with your approval, sir?"

I felt I ought to drop a curtsy but decided against it. No, really, that would be too absurd.

Yet then I laughed. Where was the harm in a small amount of absurdity? One had no wish to be solemn. Serious but not solemn. I had the feeling that Mr. Gavin, like Mr. Darcy, could possibly err on the side of sobriety. A little playfulness might be precisely what he needed.

I dropped him a rather graceful curtsy.

Irreverent yet full of fun.

And for the moment I thought of myself as Elizabeth Bennett not Anne Barnetby. I didn't feel Miss Barnetby would ever have displayed such charming liveliness.

It was four o'clock. I had my cup of tea and petit beurre. I moved my armchair just a foot or so closer to the fireplace. They said that it was better for the carpet, to shift your furniture occasionally.

22

No TELEVISION that night. No novel. No newspaper. I had embarked on my research.

Again I slept poorly. Today of all days I should like to have felt at my very best. But never mind: *c'est la vie*. No doubt there was a purpose. I got up earlier than usual. Broke with tradition and went to the market *before* breakfast to buy myself some flowers, especially my single pink rose. (*His* single pink rose.) It was so lovely to be out in the freshness of the morn.

I had intended to be sitting at my "writing desk" by ten. But in fact I exceeded this modest ambition. I was seated about twenty minutes early; had already dropped the mantelpiece a graceful, laughing curtsy. Probably this would become my signature start to each day's composition. A reminder of the need for levity.

But although ready for work so comfortably ahead of time I was up again and going for my hat and gloves before my watch said even ten o'clock.

This was *not* a bad omen. Nor, despite the fact I hadn't yet thought up my truly perfect opening line, was it in any way an admission of failure.

No, I had suddenly decided that I needed one more thing. It was a signal of victory rather than of vanquishment.

I could have gone to Mr. Lipton's shop the previous day; the thought had certainly occurred to me. But I'd felt scared. Now I saw timidity should play no role in any area of this enterprise. (And it was shameful I should even have to remind myself: *I won-*

der who's kissing her now, I wonder who's showing her how...!) If Mr. Lipton didn't still have that portrait, tucked away in some dark corner and patiently awaiting me exactly as the book had been, and if he couldn't remember or didn't know to whom he had sold it...well then, too bad: at least I could still advertise. And if my advertisements were to prove no more successful... then again too bad: at least I still had the Adam fireplace and my intuitive vision of a friendly dark-haired young man gazing reflectively into the flames. I had seen him there again this morning, just as vividly as yesterday. I even had the distinct sensation, uncanny but in no way frightening, that one day he might actually turn round.

I found the shop without difficulty. Miss Eversley's directions had been entirely lucid. I saw the portrait in the window.

I laughed out loud. I laughed right there, standing on the pavement, a spontaneous burst of laughter that was partly the effect of my ecstatic recognition of *him* and partly an aid to his more sober recognition of *me*: an easy, quite informal greeting, in mature contrast to that clash of cymbals and full celestial chorus which as a girl I had so often imagined would accompany the arrival of my one true love: would announce to the stilled and awestruck world, as well as to our own two selves, the eternal importance of that first meeting of eyes across the crowded room or shop or station concourse.

Nor was this all. For partly, too, my laughter was a message to the passersby that even when you momentarily lost your faith you were reprimanded in the most lovingly gentle and *generous* way.

You see, I had told myself, hadn't I—and without too much conviction—that the picture might be awaiting me in some dark corner *exactly as the book had been*? But had I forgotten already? The book had been awaiting me under strong electric light and at virtually the centre of an eye-level shelf and even, very slightly, jutting out!

And then I had also said to myself, quite doubtfully again,

"Mmm, a whole eighteen months since the bungalow was cleared...?" (Because the deacon who had given me Miss Eversley's address had told me of the date of her employer's death.) But the bookseller had said, "I'd have sworn I hadn't seen one of these in years!" and even after that I hadn't understood. Dear Lord. I was tempted not merely to throw back my head and laugh out loud upon the pavement, amongst those absorbed and frowning shoppers, but even to go down on my knees in front of them, inadequately to express my thanks and to appeal for God's forgiveness.

What's more he was just as I'd expected—with strong clean-shaven features and a faint smile which was already captivating but, yes, would surely grow to be far more so; and with a proud determined chin, broad shoulders and the look of height.

His portrait had obviously been painted when he was in his late twenties or early thirties.

And it was just as Miss Eversley had said: superficially quite sombre—a fact which would make it all the more exciting when those vital grey-green eyes looked straight out at you whichever way you moved—or, at any rate, whichever way *I* moved—as though, almost as though, now that the pair of us had finally come together he had no intention whatsoever of allowing me to get away again.

("Again"? Why had that word so naturally presented itself? Was my subconscious trying to tell me something? Was *he* trying to tell me something? And, anyway, hadn't I already guessed? Besides... How would I have *known*—known even from the pavement and even in spite of the sombreness—that his eyes were grey-green?)

I rushed into the shop.

I saw a man standing by the counter. He was portly, with a drooping moustache.

"That picture in the window," I gasped. It was just as if I had run there all the way from home. "How much is it?" Irrelevant, unnecessary question.

"Madam, I don't work here. You'll have to ask the proprietor."

"Oh, I'm sorry."

Just then Mr. Lipton himself came through a door at the back. He was small, thin and worried-looking, and wore a brown overall. I repeated my question.

His eyes screwed up in a smile that seemed oddly at variance with his tired expression. "The unknown cavalier?" he asked.

"Oh dear, is that what you call him?" Unknown indeed! But on the other hand I liked the thought of "cavalier" with its suggestion of laughter and of gallantry. "Yes, yes," I cried.

"Eight pounds to you, madam."

"Oh—*thank* you!" I said.

I paid by cheque, not because I hadn't got the money on me, and not that I could ever have forgotten such a momentous date as this but because I wanted to have it actually inscribed there on the counterfoil—a monument in black and white—today I met Horatio!

Today I met my destiny.

Met him again!

"What's your initial, Mr. Lipton?"

"Oh, just make it out to Lipton's," he said. "*My* name is Guthrie. I work here part-time."

While I wrote the cheque Mr. Guthrie took the painting from the window.

"Well, I can see he's going to a good home," he remarked.

"I think you must be psychic."

"How so, madam?"

"Just your talking in that way about home. Because you're right, you know. Today's the day he's coming home!"

Yet I left it at that. He didn't look the gossipy kind but even so it was better not to say too much. People could still be amazingly judgmental.

"We're really going to miss him." After Mr. Guthrie had looked quickly at the cheque and also written on the back he spoke directly to the portrait. "This place, old man, won't ever be the same without you!"

I was torn between slightly resenting this easy familiarity (but after all, I supposed, eighteen months did undoubtedly confer on you a position of some privilege) and feeling amused and rather proud that such a display of bonhomie could only have been evoked by a natural propensity on the part of its recipient to inspire friendship.

But, again, the sheet of brown paper which wasn't even new—and the length of hairy string which had been picked up off the floor—seemed wholly out of keeping with the significance of the occasion.

"No, no," I exclaimed, sharply. "Don't shut him in! Only imagine! What a feeling of imprisonment and claustrophobia!"

"Madam?"

"I saw a film once. A woman was buried alive. They finally got to her in time, but—"

"I'd say then, madam, she must definitely have been one of the luckier ones." Mr. Guthrie's tone sounded puzzled as well as amused—*amused*!—yet then he gave his crinkled, kindly smile. "You're really quite sure you wish to take this with you? We could deliver it tomorrow morning before ten."

This? *It*?

And as though I could now bear to be separated from him for twenty-four minutes, let alone twenty-four hours!

I turned to the customer with the droopy moustache who was now sifting through bric-a-brac at a nearby table. "I wonder if you'd be kind enough to hail me a taxi?"

I had asked it with considerable charm and he didn't seem to mind—in any case he had something of the air of a doorman—but Mr. Guthrie made me feel I might have taken a liberty; he himself hurried outside. I apologized to the customer and made some humorous remark about gentlemen vying for a damsel's favour. "Do you think I ought to offer *him* a tip? I would certainly have given you one."

We agreed not, however, and even when Mr. Guthrie had to

come back and *phone* for a cab I received a further small shake of the head—the customer was very nice. They both were.

And less than fifteen minutes later I was back home. In the taxi I'd briefly wondered about putting Mr. Gavin (I should have to decide not only on how to address him but even on how to refer to him) in a spot where we should see each other last thing at night and as soon as I awoke in the morning. But I think I already knew what had to be his rightful position—indeed, what he practically *demanded* as such. Over the mantelpiece, of course, in the sitting room. And, yes, the very moment he'd been hung there by the eventually cheerful cabby—who by then had most definitely received a tip and a pretty large one at that (and who now advised me on the best new place for the mirror and hammered in the picture hook and accomplished the whole cumbersome transfer)—Horatio truly did seem to have come home.

———

Besides I couldn't help thinking that the bedroom, although appealing in many ways, somehow wouldn't have been *quite* the thing. Not really.

———

That morning by second post I received a polite though frosty letter from the bank. I was overdrawn by £15—would I please make good this deficiency as soon as possible? It came as a complete surprise. Two or three days earlier it might well have been a shock, might well have tipped me hard against the bosom of the glooms. (But not once in this kind house had I ever yet encountered *them*.) Today, though, my reaction to the news was more surprising than the news itself. I simply couldn't have cared less. Anyway, I told myself, I had a few shares left to sell—what was all the fuss about? I felt positively gay. Defiant. I was ready to take on the world; and the world, one supposed, included bank managers. I knew that the handsome, strong-faced, utterly dependable man who had been watching thoughtfully as I read the letter would henceforth, without question, make it his job to look after me.

I laughed. My merriment was uncontainable. I had moved my chair even closer to the hearth; now I lifted my feet off the ground and hugged my knees. My eyes never wavered from his lovely face.

"But how does it *feel* . . . to return home after two centuries?"

My question, though, released something unexpected. Along with my exuberance—guilt! I wrung my hands. I remembered how in my heart I had criticized poor Mr. Guthrie for not recognizing the supreme importance of such a homecoming—that dear little man with his sheet of crumpled paper and his piece of grubby string.

But Mr. Guthrie's failing was nothing as compared to mine! How had *I* reacted to this wonderful event? By dashing off to ring church bells? Fire a cannon? Buy a round of drinks in every pub across the city? *No!* It was unbelievable. I hadn't even bought a bottle of champagne.

"But at least I can now put *that* right!" I cried. "No matter how lacking in forethought or how woefully, woefully inadequate!"

I had already leapt to my feet.

"Oh, a fig for Mr. Fitzroy and his fifteen pounds! Thank you so much for coming back to me! Thank you so much for coming home!"

I dashed out of the room, just to fetch my hat. Briefly returned to collect my handbag—and to tell him that I shouldn't be long.

"Oh, it's so *good* to have a man about the house!"

23

HE WAS born after a difficult pregnancy and a long and painful labour to a woman who was then approaching forty—virtually *old* for those times—but who, despite twenty years or more of fearing she would never be able to conceive, had still been so *determined* she was going to do so. After the child's delivery the midwife had gone down on her knees, thanking her Maker, and his, over and over, with hot tears coursing down her cheeks, good honest woman that she was; while Horatio's father, elderly and sensitive, was also much affected.

He said to his wife:

" 'My dear, we nearly lost you. Dr. Smollett says ... that this young fellow here ... our very last attempt ...'

" 'Mr. Gavin,' she answered, 'the good Lord has harkened to our prayer; and what a miracle he has vouchsafed us! So great a blessing as this would make me appear greedy indeed, were I even to *think* about desiring such another.'

"And she smiled up at him with so much simple goodness on her adored and loving features that he swiftly had to turn away, for fear of causing her soft heart a moment's consternation ..."

———

By five o'clock that afternoon, even though I hadn't properly started until two, I had covered over fourteen sides of my rough pad! And by nine o'clock, when I had copied them up neatly—

with not one single crossing out!—I had filled nearly eight pages of the book itself.

(But, oh, how I had hesitated before inscribing my fateful first word upon that awesome snowbound territory: a land which—as the April thaws advanced—might burgeon into richness, a timeless enchantment for both the writer and the reader...As a reader, indeed, I still never embarked on any serious novel without half hoping to find in it the solution to all of life's most pressing queries: all of its problems, mysteries and ills: a story so self-contained and comprehensive it would finally render superfluous the reading of every other. *Yes*. My first word, apart from "Chapter One"—as yet I had no title—was "On.")

When I at last laid down my pen I made a playful feint of collapsing—and how my hand and fingers really did ache! But I felt wonderfully elated by the act of creation; I hesitate to say "re-creation" since it was of course a novel, although "recreation" is what it really was. The *details* might be wrong, for the Reverend Mr. Wallace had in truth mentioned nothing of Horatio's birth, nor had he given me the names and ages of Horatio's parents, nor even once referred to either the absence or superabundance of siblings, but I knew the *spirit* was entirely right.

And even those troublesome details...well, from the word go I had the strongest feeling I was being guided, led on and inspired in the same way (I am aware this sounds presumptuous; but why, when you truly pause to think about it?) that the Gospel writers must have been led on and inspired; my hand, my brain—my Biro—being the media through which some higher agency was seeking to communicate. Oh, yes, I can assure you! It was a grand and glorious feeling.

And how the hours had flown! I hadn't stopped for supper; and even my afternoon cup of tea, would you believe, had been just that, a *cup* of tea, poured in the kitchen and carried upstairs with two ginger snaps balanced on the saucer! I laughed self-reproachfully and declared that never again must art be allowed to get in the way of civilization—but that for this first afternoon (and for this first afternoon only!) I had a special dispensation. And I knew *just* what Mr. Wallace meant: in appreciation of my gentle joke Horatio's smile really did seem to grow a little wider.

At first I had intended to go out for my evening meal; I rather fancied something light and delicate in a stylish Thai restaurant lately opened. In fact I had already put on my coat and was standing before the mirror in the hall adjusting my—rakish, rather saucy—new hat when a further idea occurred to me: how unfair, if there were indeed going to be celebrations (I mean, over and above that very thoughtless, very tardy bottle of champagne), how excessively *selfish* to be thinking of holding them away from home! I took my things off discreetly, as if by acting so stealthily I might avoid having my earlier intentions guessed (what a nincompoop!) and went to look in the refrigerator. I found a little cold chicken and some potato salad and I could open my one small tin of asparagus spears. There was even the last of the Dom Perignon. What luxury! And this time, atoning for my lapse, I should try to be particularly considerate, right down to the second flute set across the table from me and the white damask napkin made into a tricorn: things which collectively, I hoped, would be viewed as a nice forgiveness-seeking gesture. Even the yoghurt looked extra pretty when poured into a stemmed syllabub glass and sprinkled with cinnamon—and of course I had given the silverware a quick polish.

I had recently renewed my makeup but I tidied my hair again, now that I had taken off my hat, and as I went back into the sitting room, bearing the supper tray with humility yet perhaps a touch of bashful pride, I felt in the proper festive mood: glowing, expectant, even a little nervous, just as if this were indeed going to be a party. And from now on, I thought, any true celebration would always be held right here at home.

This was a promise that I made to him.

24

I HADN'T been to church since childhood. What prompted me on this particular Sunday I don't know. It might have been simply to say "Thank you!" but I usually said my thank-yous all over the place and in the main quite unselfconsciously.

Besides, I felt embarrassed as I went in. Was I late? Where to sit? There were already masses of people and I knew that every eye must have swivelled in my direction.

Holidaymaker? Resident? And could it have been in Bristol she had bought that stunning hat?

Yes, yes, I wanted to say: the answer to each of those questions is yes. Yes, unbelievably, my hat was indeed bought in Bristol! And, yes, I'm both a resident *and* on holiday. The whole of life should be a holiday.

I chose a place near the front. That was a mistake. Without turning round I couldn't see most of the congregation.

On the other hand maybe it wasn't a mistake. Most of the congregation—if it strained—could probably see *me*. I was wearing a very dashing sky-blue skirt and jacket. *Summer*-sky-blue, nothing wishy-washy. White blouse and scarf. To get ready had taken me two hours.

But I tried to be self-effacing. I followed through my notion about holidays. Life *ought* to be a holiday. There had been a film with Cary Grant and Katharine Hepburn which said precisely that. Money shouldn't be allowed to dominate. The one essential was having the right attitude. And I agreed with this entirely.

Why, only look at myself: how I had felt about things in London and how I felt about them now!

Confusingly it was in London that I'd seen the film yet it was in Bristol that Cary Grant had been born and raised. But I reflected that I should come to church more often. I had been here merely a few minutes and already I was having deep thoughts.

Yes, thank you—at long last I was truly enjoying my holiday. Enjoying it immensely. I wondered if poor Miss Eversley was in the congregation.

No, of course not. I'd have been amazed. Utterly. Quite as amazed as if...

Well, as if I'd suddenly decided to surprise everyone by rolling up my sleeves (*figuratively* speaking!) and stepping up into the pulpit. The pulpit was close. I could have reached it oh so easily. And wouldn't people get a shock! I should love to see their faces!

"Ladies and gentlemen. What is a storm in the bathwater?" Dramatic pause. "I'll tell you what it is. It's a small tornado, it's a shipwreck, it's a desert isle. Two weeks in a sarong. (And whom would you choose to spend *those* with I wonder?) It's an opportunity to grow. It provides you with a better chance you may have written something good when your Book of Life is finally shut. Something worthwhile. Something fantastic. A success story. That's what the world demands. And every day's a different page—how wonderful is that! So run off home and splash your bathwater! Amen, in the name of the Father, the Son and the Holy Ghost." I supposed I should have to cross myself.

But all this would certainly have added a fillip! Stirred things up a bit!

Unfortunately the service started while I was still thinking about it. A lady had begun to play the organ.

It was a long time since I'd heard an organ. Yet why should it take me back so quickly to the Odeon Leicester Square? A trailer, just a trailer: "Oh, you beautiful doll, you great big beautiful doll..."

When I was a girl I had never appreciated that old Wurlitzer.
Frankly I'd even found it somewhat boring.

What sacrilege!

"The Lord be with you."

"And also with you."

Good gracious, we *had* started. Where was I?

The minister was young and not bad looking in a beefy sort of
way. This no doubt added a spot of pep to the service. No wonder
there were so many women present; I might even come again
myself. He had nicely shaped hands, well-manicured, the fingers
dark with hair. His wrists as well. He'd almost surely have a hairy
chest.

"Almighty God, to whom all hearts are open, all desires known
and from whom no secrets are hid..."

I did my best to concentrate.

As a matter of fact it wasn't Almighty God whom I ever worried about: his knowing what went on inside my heart. Or even
inside my bathroom. It was all the people I had known who had
now died. Or would they by this time have acquired a little more
of *his* nature? I'd have felt shy in front of my headmistress, say,
but not at all in front of God. Wasn't that absurd? I shook my
head and laughed at the absurdity of it.

The minister glanced in my direction.

Oh dear. Now I should have to apologize.

We had a hymn.

> "Dear Lord and Father of mankind,
>   Forgive our foolish ways..."

That was nice. And at least I knew my singing voice was definitely an asset.

"I'm so sorry that I laughed. It wasn't disrespectful. I was simply having fun."

"Miss Waring, that's exactly the kind of sound we want to hear
inside this church. It was like a breath of...well, between you, me

and the gatepost, Miss Waring, I must confess we don't normally get enough of it. The congregation at St. Michael's—perhaps I shouldn't say this in view of such kind hearts and such excellent intentions—has always been, well, quite honestly, a little *stodgy* up till now. And I do so hope we're going to see a lot more of you. I heard your singing by the way. May I ask if you entertain professionally?"

And then he added: "I know I oughtn't to do this—vicars must never grow partial—but I've just got to compliment you on your dress and hat and everything. Breathtaking! Gorgeous!"

Altogether he was a most pleasant young man. During the reading of the Gospel I asked him a few questions. He was delighted by my quick intelligence; by my refusal merely to accept. I told him something of what Mrs. Pimm had said about the man who had thrown himself from a skyscraper and landed on a passerby. "Vicar, do *you* believe in second chances? You see, I keep getting this picture of that...probably by now...rather flat-looking individual being given *his* second chance. Don't laugh. It's the resurrection of a Silly Symphony. He goes loping off down the street like a cardboard cutout with a foolish grin."

He did laugh.

"I say it again, Miss Waring. A positive breath of spring."

"Now, Vicar. You just keep your mind on your business. You haven't heard the rider to my question." I rapped his knuckles with my fan. "Supposing that he *didn't* get that second chance? Would you say then that he was simply in the wrong place at the wrong time or would you actually believe it could have been the right place at the right time? There are other permutations, naturally, but I wouldn't think of troubling you with those."

I smiled.

"I also want to ask about King David...and Bathsheba."

"My goodness! I can see you're going to be a full-time occupation! But listen, Rachel, standing here over coffee isn't really the time for profound metaphysical discussion. You know the vicarage? Well, I'm afraid it's mostly a shambles right now because my housekeeper, dear old soul that she is, isn't quite the world's most dedicated cleaner, nor most enterprising cook. But if you can find it in your heart to overlook such shortcomings as these..."

It was all just agreeable nonsense of course. I hadn't brought my fan.

He was now mounting the pulpit. I prepared myself quietly and without fuss to listen to his address. Firstly I smoothed my skirt out beneath me and, after I'd resumed my place, carefully crossed my legs. There was so little room: even the arranging of one's hem required some element of expertise! Then I smiled with shared expectancy at those around me. (They didn't seem too friendly.) Lastly I cleared my throat and looked all eager and attentive. I even bent forward slightly so that he should realize I intended not to miss a single word. Vicars, after all, were only human: they too unfolded and grew happier with encouragement. "It's just like talking to your flowers," I whispered to the woman next to me. In my own case, however—how should she realize?—it was a good deal more than that.

"We clergymen are always a little behind the times!" he began, quite mystifyingly. (There was a small but appreciative ripple of amusement. I myself laughed—perhaps more audibly than most. "No, no," I declared, "nobody is ever going to believe *that*!") "If you will forgive me I should like to quote from an Epistle we had much earlier in the year." *Forgive* him? For something so immeasurably considerate? Obviously he knew that this was my first time here and had chosen a very tactful way of alluding to it. "Beautiful words can sometimes become so familiar that we almost stop listening to what they mean."

This was true. I nodded my approval. I felt inclined to call: "Hear, hear!"

I laughed instead. "Oh, you're so right!" I observed. "Yes, shame on us! Fie!"

"Though I have all faith," he continued, "so that I could remove mountains...and though I bestow all my goods to feed the poor...and have not charity..."

There was a long and telling pause. He was looking straight at myself.

"It profiteth me nothing," he said.

He spoke the words ringingly, deliberately, with force. I could see his knuckles white upon the rail, those very knuckles which scarcely three minutes earlier had received my playful taps.

"It—profiteth—me—nothing!"

I could hardly believe it. For the sake of appearances he moved his head slowly from one side of the nave to the other; but this didn't fool me in the slightest. I knew full well whose eye he aimed to catch.

"In other words," he said, "without love I would not be worth . . . *anything*!"

No, I just couldn't believe it. He went on to talk about the hunger strikers in the Maze—had I even the remotest idea of the number who had so far died? He wanted to know how persistently I had prayed for any one of them. How many policemen and rioters had been injured at Toxteth he asked. What was the name of that six-year-old child who had been wedged down a well in total darkness for three whole days at the start of June? When was the last time I had passed a hospice or a shelter for alcoholics or even a hospital and thought at all about any of those suffering within? What did I know about either the oldest victim or the youngest who had been killed whilst trying to cross the Berlin Wall?

From there, somehow, he went on to talk about how I might so easily just be whistling in the dark, how I needed to take a long hard look at my priorities, how he felt, for all I know, about *The Man Who Came to Dinner* or *Chariots of Fire* or Shirley Temple—I simply wasn't listening. He stood there looking so pious and dynamic, with his hairy hands and his hairy chest and his hitherto honeyed tongue, and of all the messages of comfort he could have chosen as a loving and warm-hearted welcome he had gone out of his way to pick a text like that. And at only a moment's notice too! How cruel! How unspeakably cruel! To have made me feel he was genuinely pleased to see me there, a leavening and stimulating influence, a rare and charming remembrancer of spring, and then to have demonstrated only too plainly...what could you call it now?...his *jealousy*? Was no one but himself permitted to invigorate?

Well, he could keep his invigoration. He could hold on to his hairy hands. *And* to his hairy chest. I wouldn't want any part of them.

"And now abideth faith, hope, charity, these three; but the greatest of these is charity."

"Some hope!" I said—I thought, quite wittily—staring around me in defiance.

He ended as though he had simply decided to throw this in for good measure: "For now we see through a glass, darkly."

"Do we, indeed? That may be what *you* think! But take a referendum among the rest of us."

There was a pause. I picked up my handbag and gloves and almost walked out right there and then. That, too, might have stirred things up a bit. Yet just in time I stopped myself. People mustn't, absolutely must *not*, be allowed to see how deeply they had hurt me.

But during the next hymn I didn't sing.

Oh, yes, I moved my lips all right; it was just that I let no sounds emerge. I could see him looking at me in pretended consternation.

"Oh, have you strained that lovely voice of yours, Miss Waring?"

"I think I should make it clear, Mr. Morley, that I am no longer fooled by your bootlicking manner. You can now go and practise on the chemist. The two of you ought to found a Badedas Society—compose some suitably ingratiating jingle!"

When the collection plate came round I didn't put in the pound notes I had planned. I almost put in nothing. Yet then, more subtle and poetical than that, I saw I had some silver in my purse and I picked out precisely 35p.

I began to feel better. By the time everybody suddenly and inexplicably started to shake hands (they were evidently a friendlier bunch than I'd supposed) I had sufficiently recovered—by dint of ignoring, blocking out, trying to think only of things pleasant—to be able to participate. Indeed I joined in readily and with considerable aplomb, especially in view of the fact that I'd at first been disconcerted: "How do you do? Don't you find it rather cold in here? I really like your handbag."

What a lovely way of making contact. Now *this* was certainly more Christian!

"Hello. Do you come here often? My name, by the way, is Waring."

Unluckily (how British!) most of my well-wishers didn't seem able—quite—to follow it through. Hands yes, smiles too, yet nothing that went deeper. The overture but not the play. Well, never mind. I found it by far the nicest portion of the service; that and my singing of the first hymn. I had been happy then.

Otherwise the fact that I was based at the end of a row would have been a huge advantage—for it meant I could go round shaking hands long after everybody else had finished. I wanted to show that Londoners weren't the standoffish souls many considered them. Nor were they soft. They possessed character; had tenacity.

One hand I definitely refused to shake, however, was the vicar's—when afterwards he had the nerve, or the insensitivity, to place himself outside the church door.

"No, thank you," I said; and totally ignored his *Good morning I believe you may be new here.*

Oh, the hypocrite.

In fact I seemed to have provided his comeuppance. He looked really at a loss. Piety, dynamism, invigoration—all.

"Er... there's coffee in the church hall if you'd like some."

Because he so clearly didn't expect me to accept I nodded. "Thank you, yes, I think I'd like a cup. But please don't inconvenience yourself. I'm sure I shall be able to find my own way."

So perhaps he wasn't *quite* as bad as I had drawn him. I had always been taught the overriding importance of good manners; I felt that—at least to some extent—I ought to show him what it meant to have breeding.

Therefore, while he was still, I noticed, gazing after me (along with the old couple who'd been just about to speak to him) I went back and said, "Incidentally I forgot to thank you for the wafer and the wine. The wine was good; where did you get it? And you may be surprised to hear that I believe in the idea of transformation. At least I think I do. Not of course that I'm a Roman Catholic."

"Er... no," he said.

I even made a little joke. After all, I wasn't likely to forget our first ten minutes of good fellowship. "And I don't imagine you are?"

"Er... no," he said.

He had no sense of humour and, in reality, not much conversation either. I went in to have my coffee.

The hall was fairly crowded. I joined the queue at a small counter. There was an older woman in front of me who was looking in her purse for change. "Oh, do you have to pay?" I said. "I thought the vicar had invited me. Well, actually it's all of a piece, isn't it? I'm not a bit surprised."

She smiled at me in a way which I was beginning to realize seemed special to Bristolians. "The coffee's just five pence," she said but didn't sound unfriendly. "If you haven't got it no one's going to mind."

"Well, that's a relief; but I think I can *probably* rustle up five pence."

"I hope you enjoyed the service. Oh, excuse me just one moment. I see that little monkey of mine is about to make a pest of herself over there."

But her three- or four-year-old, as soon as she was called, came skipping across quite obediently.

"Well, I can't say," I observed, "I thought a great deal of the sermon."

"No," she agreed, "I'm afraid you hit a bad week so far as the sermon was concerned." She laughed. "*I* was expecting it to be all about the Wedding! Felt so disappointed to find Charles and Diana weren't even mentioned!"

I gave a little shrug. "Well, one must always be philosophical. I suppose that it could have been worse. Look for the good in any sermon and you can possibly find it."

We got our coffees; her daughter had a squash. We stood together, halfway down the room, suddenly not appearing to have very much to say.

"Let's hope the weather will be nice and sunny for next Wednesday!"

I smiled and nodded.

"I do think Lady Di looks such a charming girl."

"Do you?" I asked.

From her expression I might have announced that I'd just left a bomb in the vestry. "Well... don't you?"

"Oh, I daresay she's pleasant enough. But you've got to admit she's very ordinary. Very ordinary, indeed." I sipped my cup of coffee. It was peculiarly revolting.

"Well, yes, in a way, I suppose she is. Yet that's what makes it all rather nice, isn't it? I mean, he's marrying the girl next door!"

"Precisely," I said. "Entirely my point."

At least I had the satisfaction of seeing her think for a moment. But the moment was short-lived and the thinking unproductive. It led merely to her displaying what she must have considered her winning card. "She's undoubtedly *very* popular!"

I was kind. "Yes, you're right. Obviously I'm out of step. But I really don't see what all the hoo-ha is about." It was a relief to be able to say this to a person I should almost certainly never meet again. (If we passed in the street I could pretend to look the other way.)

"Well..." She smiled and seemed to be glancing around for others to support her. "At any rate," she suggested, "far better than some foreigner!"

"Oh, I'm not so sure." She clearly hadn't followed my argument. "An Englishwoman—well, it could have been you or me or anyone. Just picture it." I laughed: to add a little levity, a little reassurance: because for some reason she was starting to look flustered. "Coming out of St. Paul's. Riding through the City in an open carriage. Thousands lining the route, cheering themselves hoarse, waving flags, holding their children up to get a better view. Loving you like the Queen herself. But *why*? Where is the fairness in it all? Why *her*, not you?"

The woman laughed. (Again I'd been able to cheer somebody up; again a victory for politeness!) "Perhaps you hadn't noticed?" she said. "I am a *degree* older than she is." I laughed as well—just as if she'd made some joke.

"But you do see what I mean?" I persevered. "She doesn't even dress well. All those choirboy collars!" I gave another shrug: my good-humoured bewilderment at the folly of the Royal Family. "And Dr. Runcie has asked for the prayers of the whole nation to be offered during the ceremony. Why? Haven't they already got enough without all of us being expected to pray for them as well? But of course"—I smiled—"to them that hath shall be given." It was the old, old story. "Has the whole nation ever been asked to pray for *you*?"

I never got an answer. Before she could supply one her little girl had made an abrupt turn and jerked her mother's elbow. The woman's cup was knocked out of her saucer—and threw its entire contents down my skirt. I screamed.

The next few minutes were chaotic: someone with a tea cloth doused in cold water; half a dozen others offering remedies and opinions, anecdotes and concern; the scolding of the child; the cleaning of the floor.

The little girl cried. No doubt she felt frightened and defence-less, for her mother had been sharp with her. The woman herself was close to tears. In fact the two of them received a lot more comfort than I did.

And it was the first time I had worn it. It was ruined.

"Are you all right?" somebody asked me. "These little accidents *will* happen, won't they?"

"Yes, thank you," I replied. "I'm perfectly all right." I added with a wryness she would plainly not appreciate: "I've had my little bit of fuss."

I noticed that the vicar was carefully keeping his distance. How very typical! In times of joy some people had the Archbishop of Canterbury. In times of stress others didn't even get the vicar of St. Michael's.

So much, then, for the vicar. What about the victim? Oh, well, at any rate the victim didn't cry until she had left the church hall, had walked at least three hundred yards and turned at least three corners. The victim didn't cry until she had got maybe a quarter of the way home, with the damp cloth clammy against her legs and most of the passersby pretending very hard they hadn't noticed. (But she heard one toddler say, "Has that lady done a poo and is that why she is looking sad?") The lower half of the summer-blue sky now showed a spiky dark cloud the size of a Frisbee. You'd have thought it an experience not to be recovered from for days and days.

But here was the unexpected epilogue.

(It shouldn't have felt unexpected.)

The tears stopped the very moment I reached home—literally, as soon as I had opened my front door. The cloud just shifted; blew off to the horizon.

For haven't I said it before: this was a *kind* house, its presiding spirit so expert in the art of healing? How blest was I to have Horatio; how astonishing that, even momentarily, I could have forgotten him. Already as I hurried up the stairs I was humming. My tuneful reminder of God's message. *Oh, you beautiful doll, you great big beautiful doll* ...

Because, as you might expect with God, his message didn't need to be limited to merely one melody.

Oh, no—good heavens, no!

25

THE BEST thing about the Royal Wedding day, apart from my work on the book, was undoubtedly *The Sound of Music*. For the first time I was struck by the line: "like a lark who is learning to pray." It seemed suddenly so applicable, was almost certainly a message. We all need such gentle nods of encouragement.

Afterwards, on ITV, there was another film. Normally I enjoyed the pictures starring Jean Arthur but this one was extremely feeble; I didn't watch for long. Its title was about the only thing I liked. *The Lady Takes a Chance*.

Poor Miss Eversley, though. I felt a little shifty. I hadn't phoned her. I hadn't bought her any jigsaw. Of course it seemed she hadn't particularly wanted these attentions. So perhaps it was all right. But whatever happened I must never become a person who didn't keep her word. Larks who were learning to pray must always be straightforward, free of cant. Creatures to rely on.

Me, especially. Because the thing was, you see, I should never be short of inspiration. I had the perfect example right in front of me.

Over the fireplace.

So if *I* couldn't win through... well, then, who could? Sometimes I felt utterly convinced I had been singled out for glory.

But not always. Far more often I felt I simply didn't stand a chance—even if nowadays I wouldn't allow this thought to get me down. I was the mirror image of the Wandering Jew. I was that other poor lost soul, equally desperate and equally remorseful, lone voyager on board *The Flying Dutchman*.

A charmed life that carried a curse? Or a cursed life that carried a charm?

In short, I knew neither what sort of person I really was, nor how well I fitted in.

Nor, indeed, if I had any true hope of ever finding that place in heaven which, since my schooldays, I had always hankered for.

———

And all through the following weeks he *grew*...though not quite with that astounding fluidity which had been attendant on his birth; and at the same time, obviously, the novel grew.

It was clearly going to be a long one. Before I was done I should need to buy perhaps another *two* of those thick and impressive-looking volumes.

But this didn't dismay me. Not at all. Indeed, I was so far from being in any hurry to finish I thought I might eventually have to ration myself. Even now, with "The End" still maybe *years* into the future, I didn't know what I would do when it finally arrived.

And I wasn't after critical or popular acclaim. If it were given, that would be pleasant of course—and not simply on my own account either. But we weren't impatient for it. Even unpublished the three volumes would still be there as testaments to our existence, would still look immensely distinguished on our mantelshelf, would still provide a constant and a concrete proof of how things were. A proof for posterity. I thought posterity should hear of why I had been placed upon this earth and of the paragon I had been placed here for.

In any case the journey was what counted. Always. I knew for sure that now and forever my life was his—and *his*, mine—as inextricably entwined as Boswell's and Dr. Johnson's.

Only more so.

Consequently, when he went swimming naked in the creek with other boys his own age, I was there as well, enjoying it just as much as they. And when he scrapped, his hurts were my hurts, his victories *my* victories. (I wondered if he heard my voice, a faint and distant echo calling out to him across the centuries, loyally supporting him?) My tears fell like his when he saw beggars dying in the streets or heard about the injustice of the lawcourts or the misery inflicted by the press gangs. My entreaties were added to his when he pleaded with his father for money, with his mother for items of clothing, with Nancy for articles of food: to pass on to the homeless, the crippled, the drunk, the desperate. I had a headache to match his own when he worried over his Latin verbs or his algebraic formulas, or when the sad wife-ridden Mr. Tole got one of his periodic bouts of choler and none of his pupils could ever do anything right. But then also my joy was surely as great as his when he first heard Mr. Handel's music and his heart leapt up in exultation; the experience just as revelatory—for I on my own had never much enjoyed "good" music. This was now incomprehensible. I wondered at my blindness or, more properly, my deafness (one of our silly little jokes; we were gathering quite a store of them) and more especially, more guiltily, at my monumental selfishness. From the beginning it should have *occurred* to me to play the music of Handel and Mozart and Gluck and Haydn... these last two names hadn't come to me immediately, any more than those of earlier composers like Purcell, Byrd and Scarlatti. Even stating it at its lowest it would have seemed a sensible thing to do when one thought about creating the right atmosphere. (Unnecessary, unnecessary.) While from every other point of view...

For the first time in my life I felt ashamed to own no classical music. I couldn't afford to *buy* all the records I now wanted, for although I wasn't worried by the state of my finances I was at least being sensible, but fortunately the main public library included an excellent record section. And no sooner *had* it occurred to me, so belatedly, than I rushed straight over, breathless, without even my scarf or gloves, and brought away as many records as I was allowed. (They almost sent me home for my stylus; I said a little prayer; for this occasion they waived the rule.) And, from then on, the eighteenth-century house was filled with eighteenth-century music. Or earlier.

———

But not exclusively.

"I am coming more and more to appreciate *your* music," I would say, "and I realize that a great deal of this present century's is rubbish; but all the same it won't do you any harm to get to hear some of the best of it..."

And playfully hectoring him in this fashion (oh, how I nagged the poor fellow!—"I feel sure that Mr. Tole would sympathize with you!") I would then put on Jack Buchanan or *Gypsy* or just for old times' sake (a tribute, I had thought when I sent off for it, a tribute both to an over-painted maiden aunt and to an under-valued piece of childhood) a selection from *Bitter Sweet*.

> "I believe...
> The more you love a man,
> The more you give your trust,
> The more you're bound to lose..."

Or even (but not from *Bitter Sweet*):

> "I really must go...
> But, baby, it's cold outside.
> This evening has been
> So very nice..."

And although I half expected it I never once saw him wince. I was pleased. Education should always be a two-way process. We had so many lovely things to impart to one another.

I would often dance a little, too—despite my initial self-consciousness. Usually to the strains of some slow and dreamy waltz. (I could never have done this if I'd kept even a quarter of

Aunt Alicia's furniture.) But before long I grew relaxed and then could easily imagine I was being propelled around the floor by a partner who had a strong arm half-encompassing my waist and a cool hand tenderly enclosing my own. I could imagine that on each occasion he held me just a little more closely.

There were times when afterwards I wasn't so completely sure I *had* imagined it.

26

THE ALLSOPS came back—though not nearly so quickly as I had expected. This didn't matter. I'd had other things to occupy my mind and the thought that temporarily they might have forgotten me had caused me little heartache. Yet when I again saw them standing on my doorstep I felt pleased.

"What can you think of us?" asked Celia. "Saying you must come round and then not getting in touch for almost three weeks."

For almost five.

"What nonsense!" I exclaimed. "You're young. You've got your own lives to lead. I don't expect—"

"Oh, it isn't that," said Roger. "But we've all been down with summer colds and there seems to have been one damned thing after another and what with all my studies and that wretched job of mine..."

He looked more golden and Viking-like than ever.

"Well, I'm sure you know how it is," he ended, with a grimace of utterly irresistible charm.

"Oh, I do, I do. There's nothing to explain."

"Just so long as you don't believe we're insincere," added Celia. "We really couldn't bear that—could we, darling?"

She looked at him devotedly, that same old look of doting admiration, but now I didn't find it so disturbing. Not quite. When I realized this I felt yet happier. I no longer had any reason to envy a soul.

"No, I would willingly plunge a dagger into my heart," he confided, "rather than think you believed that."

"Oh, a little drastic—surely?"

"In fact, madam, it's all your fault," he declared cheerfully, the penitent stepping with ease into the shoes of the accuser. "If like sensible people you only had a phone—"

"Oh, that's unfair," I broke in, with matching gaiety. "The Post Office keeps promising they're going to connect me. I *want* to be connected. Should I go down on my knees and *pray* to be connected?"

For an instant he himself went down on his knees, his hands imploringly uplifted, like Jolson about to give us *Mammy*. "Connect me with the human race! Oh, please connect me with the human race! Somebody—somewhere—must surely want to hear from me!"

"Yes. Sylvia," I smiled. Yet my heart sank. She would be here with me on Friday.

"Who is Sylvia?"

He quickly added, "What is she, that all our swains commend her?"

"The friend I was sharing a flat with before I came to Bristol."

But somehow it seemed disloyal to mention my having doubts about all our swains, or even any of our swains, commending her. I still remembered certain lines of the passage, however—it was another which we'd learnt at school—and I wanted both Roger and Horatio (we were naturally, by this time, up in the sitting room) to know I could quote bits of Shakespeare that weren't boringly familiar to thousands. Therefore I threw open my arms and cried, "Is she kind as she is fair? Oh, bother—something, something, something! Then to Sylvia let us sing."

"That would be charming," he said as he got up, "but I'm afraid that singing to *anyone* mightn't accomplish very much; mightn't actually get you connected. Unless of course you went straight to the fountainhead—no intermediaries—addressed your plaintive song to Buzby. But failing that it would be quicker to become a doctor. Or even, if you must, a solicitor. Or an architect. Or a clergyman."

"Don't listen to him, Miss Waring. Darling, I think it's possible you're being offensive."

"Oh, not at all." I denied it with a laugh. "Only absurd. And anyway..."

I was about to point out that although I mightn't have a telephone I certainly did have a letterbox—but just stopped myself in time. *I* didn't want to make anything out of their not having been in touch; it was *they* who were shaping it into a drama.

"And anyway—enough of all this nonsense. Let's talk about important things. How's my little Thomas? May I hold him, Celia?" (So far, upon greeting them, I had only kissed his cheek.) "And then I'll pop down and put the kettle on."

"How is your little Thomas?" repeated Roger. "He's just about as good and sweet and angelic as...well, I don't know...as his father always is."

"No longer, then, the noisiest little thing in the whole of the southwest?"

"He never really was."

"He's certainly growing heavier."

"Oh, he's going to be so big and strong and bonny. Aren't you, Tom? Just like your old dad. Disgustingly healthy. Never a single day's illness from one year to the next."

"No summer colds?" I queried.

For a moment he actually looked as if I'd caught him out. "Oh, summer colds don't really count!" Then he laughed and gently prodded his son's tummy. "Do you mind if I take my jacket off, Miss Waring? This is the warmest day in weeks!"

"Oh, *please*..."

I added, perhaps a little outrageously, "After all, don't forget I've seen you not only without a jacket but even without a shirt!"

He grinned. "I had forgotten."

Though I didn't altogether believe him I let it go. "I hope it wasn't simply for my sake—again!—that you came here in a suit and tie?"

He seemed about to deny it but then spread his hands. "I think one should always pay one's friends the courtesy of trying to look one's best."

"And I feel honoured by that courtesy, I really do. Especially as I'm surprised to find anyone of your generation still viewing the world like that. Yet all the same, Roger, next time..."

"No," said Celia, "next time *you're* coming to us, no question!"

"Besides," enquired Roger, "why do you say someone of *my* generation? That makes it sound...I don't know...as though we come from different planets, as though you're either Abraham or Methuselah. I honestly don't see it that way. Nor does Celia."

"Not at all."

"That's very sweet of you both, but..." But what? "How long *is* a generation?"

"Oh..." He shrugged. "Isn't it about twenty-five years?"

I spoke quickly. "Well, in that case we don't even belong to different generations let alone planets. Nothing like."

"Who said we did?"

"But the fact remains that I call you Roger and Celia; you call me Miss Waring."

"What was that, Rachel?" He bent towards me, frowning. We all laughed.

"I didn't even realize that you knew my first name."

"Ah. And I bet there are other things you never realized about us."

"I'm sure there are."

He shook his head. "No, that's utterly the wrong cue. You're meant to say, 'Like what?'"

"Oh, your daddy!" I said to the baby in my arms, giving him a merry shake, which made him chuckle. "Oh, your funny old daddy!" But of course I did exactly as Roger asked.

"Like, for instance, the fact that we very much want you—if you would—we'd really be so very happy if...No, *you* tell her, Celia."

"No, *you,* darling."

"Well, if you'd consent to be that little tyke's godmother..."

27

HERE IT was, then: the true start of that other road which—like a spool of yellow ribbon—would soon unwind across the whole of this beautiful poppy-filled landscape. When (at long last) I went to put the kettle on I half danced down the stairs—in the hall holding Roger's jacket out in front of me, a sort of scarecrow partner from the land of Oz, en route to a coat hanger and a coat peg. Celia called down the stairs: "May I come and give you a hand?" "No, you stay there with Tom." Her presence would have spoilt it all.

I hung up—I smoothed out—his jacket. I filled the kettle.

> "Dancing in the dark,
> With a new love;
> I'm dancing in the dark,
> Here with you, love..."

"Caught you!" said Roger. "Caught you red-handed. Or red-footed. And what a pretty voice you have."

"Oh, you villain."

"I wish you wouldn't stop."

"Well, surely you wouldn't expect me to carry on in front of an audience?"

"I'll tell you one thing. You're certainly not Abraham. Nor Methuselah."

"Twenty-one," I said. "Twenty-one, key of the door, never been twenty-one before."

"Really? As much as that? You surprise me."

"Sycophant."

"And that makes us exactly the same age." He became practical. "Now tell me what I can do."

It was fun. He got out the milk jug and the sugar bowl and the silver tongs, though I could have done it all a bit quicker myself, and he shook some more sugar lumps out of the packet and he filled the jug and he sliced a lemon and he went off jauntily across the road .. to buy a selection of jauntily coloured cakes. "But I insist, Roger, you take this!" "And I insist, Rachel, I do nothing of the kind!" While he was gone I went to see if he'd taken his jacket and finding that he hadn't I slipped two pounds into the breast pocket. I buried my nose for a moment in the brown tweed.

Upstairs they spoke about arrangements for the christening and about some of the people who were likely to be there. "It will all be very *dull*, Rachel, but afterwards you and we and a few of our more special friends will have a bit of a knees-up to atone." I could hardly be insensible of the magnitude of the compliment. My hand shook slightly as I poured the tea.

"Are you expecting someone else, Miss Waring?"

"Rachel," corrected Roger.

"Because you may think Thomas *very* advanced but he doesn't yet handle a cup and saucer with total confidence."

I stared at the fourth teacup and teaplate and folded napkin. "Oh, that's your husband's fault. He was so busy playing the fool down there that he got me all mixed up."

"No, I don't think so. I noticed it the last time too."

Then—maybe afraid that it might distress me having to own up to absentmindedness—she hurriedly put another question. It must have been the first thing that came into her head and, ironically, showed that even if my own mind hadn't wandered hers at some point assuredly had.

"Please remind me ... who is Sylvia? You seemed to suggest she might be missing you."

Roger laughed. "Holy, fair, and wise is she." His laugh had relieved any small suggestion of awkwardness.

"I had forgotten that bit," I confessed.

"Ah, but you remembered 'Is she kind as she is fair?' That's pretty good, you know."

"What a patronizing young man!"

I enjoyed being able to insult him, since that naturally gave him carte blanche to insult me right back.

But he didn't avail himself of it. "For beauty lives with kindness," he declaimed.

I was beginning to giggle. "No, don't. Please don't!"

"Why not?"

"Because you haven't met Sylvia and you're going to make it so that I can never look her in the eye again."

He giggled with me. They both did. "Then she obviously isn't *that* close a friend?"

I coloured a little and wondered how best to put things. "Well, let's simply say I don't think she's quite as you've described her."

"But Rachel. You can't quarrel with Shakespeare. Nobody can."

"I do beg his pardon."

(How he seemed to have the gift of drawing from me repartee.)

"It appears, then, there are just two possibilities. Either when in London you saw only through a glass, darkly"—I hoped I didn't start—"or else..." He hesitated.

"Yes? Or else?"

"Or else he got the names muddled. He was describing the wrong flatmate."

Well, if I coloured now, it certainly wasn't on account of any feelings of slight guilt.

"All these compliments!" I managed to get out, eventually. "I'm really not quite used to them. But, 'Thank 'ee kindly, sir,' she said." Had I been standing I might have dropped a curtsy. "Which play does it come from?"

"I think...*The Two Gentlemen of Verona*. It's not a speech by the way; it's a song."

I nodded. Just so long as I knew where to look for it. *Mirror, mirror on the wall, who's the fairest of them all?*

"You'll have to learn to sing it," he said.

Celia may have thought her husband was getting a little too carried away because she again changed the subject, changed it somewhat abruptly, and reverted more or less to where we'd begun. "These are such pretty cups," she said. "I meant to mention it the last time we were here."

"I believe you did."

"Did I? Oh, it must get rather boring. Everything you have is just so pretty. So..."

"Attractive," said Roger. "Pretty is such a milk-and-water word."

"I was going to say perfect. You must excuse us, Rachel." This time she got it right. "It must be very bad form to enthuse all the while; at the very least a bit lacking in sophistication. But the real problem is...I seem to have fallen in love a little with your house."

"Well, you *know* you don't have to apologize for that!" I said. "Who wants sophistication?"

"That picture's new, isn't it?" asked Roger.

I nodded. I didn't trust myself to speak.

"We've been admiring it."

For ten or twelve seconds the three of us gazed at Horatio in silence.

"One of these days I'll tell you all about him," I said.

"Ah, is there a story, then?"

"There most definitely is—and in more ways than one! But not for now. For now, I'm only going to say that if it wasn't for him I myself shouldn't be here."

"You're joking!"

"No. I should have sold the house and gone straight back to London."

Then how they tried to draw it out of me! But they had met their match: I resisted every subterfuge. I had decided not to supply so much as a single hint.

It was far better, I often thought—despite my natural inclinations—*not* to give everything away too quickly.

28

POOR SYLVIA. When I'd left London, August had still seemed a long way off and I'd hoped that after several months of our being apart it would probably be very pleasant to have her spend three days with me and let me show her Bristol. For after all, to begin with, we *had* got on rather well. But when her letter had arrived on the very morning of Roger and Celia's visit, confirming and not cancelling (oh, how one lives in hope!), I had thought then: three days without writing, three days without privacy, three days of weighty talk and ubiquitous cigarette smoke, three days of almost endless coughing, how can I bear it? Three days of profanity and sensible down-to-earth attitudes ... tainting everything. And I had wondered if I could perhaps make some excuse to save myself from such a purgatory. *Any* excuse—how much would it have mattered if she'd seen right through it? But as soon as I'd reflected I had felt ashamed. *He* wouldn't have made one. And did a mere three days really represent such a terrible sacrifice?

"I *will* be good," I promised. "I *will* learn! Please don't despair of me. It's only that I need to have my little grumble."

No, I didn't.

"I shall be gay and full of laughter! No matter what! No one will ever know. Except you."

Yes. Poor Sylvia. After all that foolish trepidation of mine, when she finally arrived, latish on the Friday evening, it proved surprisingly agreeable. I felt quite remorseful and exceedingly relieved. She obviously liked the house—even if her praise was never totally unqualified and usually had to be fished for a little;

she was funny about her new flatmate (although not too maliciously so and in any case when was I ever likely to meet Miss Carter again?); and with everything she said about the intrigues in her office and about some of her adventures on the underground and buses I kept thinking how very blest I was to be out of it all, how very blest I should still have been even if the blessing had been a purely negative one.

But she—evidently—didn't see it in quite the same light.

"Christ! What do you do with yourself all day?" I hadn't yet told her about the book. (I'd decided, since her arrival, that in fact I might.) "Apart from listening to the bloody *Archers*?" she added.

I laughed. "Oh, I really can't remember when I last listened to *The Archers*!"

"Struth."

"It's just astonishing where all the time goes."

"It must be."

"Well, first there's the house itself of course ..."

"All right but don't tell me you've become a woman for going out and *joining* things. I'd never believe it. Do you mind if I smoke?"

My goodness! At least she asked now ... even if from her actions she automatically assumed the answer would be yes. Someday, even, she might become a positively reformed character.

I passed her an ashtray; it was rather small. We'd brought our coffee upstairs—decaffeinated at this time of the evening though I cunningly didn't mention that—and I'd drawn the curtains and quite softly and unobtrusively put on a divertimento ... despite Roger's having told me, almost severely, that this was not the manner in which to play classical music.

"Nice," she said, letting out a long sigh of contentment and, miraculously, not beginning to cough. "Although I didn't know you went in for any of this highbrow stuff."

I only smiled non-committally.

"You'd better eat some of these things," she added abruptly.

"In any case, don't leave them by me. Obviously the time hasn't yet come when *you* need to worry over calories. It's damned unfair."

Besides the box of chocolates—liqueur chocolates—she had given me a roasted chicken and two bottles of wine and a tin of biscuits. I had told her she shouldn't have done it; but had immediately resolved never to use that phrase again.

"At least *I*'ve still got a job," she had said. "Such as it is."

Yet she hadn't brought me any housewarming gift. Of course, I hadn't let her know of anything I wanted. But on the other hand she hadn't reminded me. It wasn't that I was mercenary; something inexpensive would have been truly welcome if I could only have believed that she had chosen it with care. And she *had* spoken about getting me something. So it was rather a shame: despite my unexpected pleasure at seeing her again I still had to stop remembering what that video recorder had cost. Especially since at the moment it was money I could well have done with.

Well, never mind. Now, before they could leave her side too finally, she quickly grabbed one of the chocolates and repeated her earlier question.

"But what on earth do you find to do?"

"Just this and that. I've made some friends, you know."

"Oh yes?" She bit into her chocolate and then tilted her head back to drain the rest of the liqueur. That made her cough.

I smiled, forgivingly. "There's a very nice chemist."

Following her cough she made appreciative sucking sounds and unscrewed the little label she had cast into the ashtray. "I can recommend the Benedictine!" she said, picking up her cigarette again. "Oh, not *tradesmen*, my dear?"

"He says I've changed his life."

"Does he indeed? Good for him. Good for both of you."

"And then there's a deceased clergyman's wife. Widow. I had tea with her the other day. That was nice."

"Did you cap each other's snippets from *The Lady*?"

In earlier days I had found Sylvia's sense of humour one of the most attractive things about her. Notwithstanding its coarseness it had seemed to me at that time the product of an enviable ability to laugh at life. At life. Not just at people.

"Also," I said, "a rather *physical* vicar who compliments me on my singing and intelligence and who all but suggested I drop in to cook him a meal."

"He...what?"

"A sort of candlelit tête-à-tête. Of course I very firmly sat on *that* idea."

"Well, more fool you. And, anyway, what do you mean by physical?"

"Sylvia, you know perfectly well what I mean by physical!" I reproved her with a laugh.

But I had saved one of the two best things till last.

"And then there's a charming young couple, Roger and Celia, who've asked me to be godmother to their firstborn. Little Thomas. He's a darling. And the christening's going to be next week. A rather plush sort of affair so I'm given to believe."

I could see that this time, despite her every effort to conceal it, Sylvia was definitely impressed. I immediately went on to tell her what Roger had said about the probable dullness of this great occasion and followed it up with his suggested remedy. "I swear they think I'm quite as young as they are!"

Sylvia said: "I can see why they're so charming!"

"And extremely nice looking. Him, especially. He's blond, blue-eyed and very muscular. Has a sort of a sheen about him."

"How do you know he's so muscular?"

"Well, you can tell. Besides, the first time that I visited their home, I arrived a little early and he was still sunning himself in the garden."

She stubbed out her cigarette and I got up to fetch her a second ashtray, the only other in the house. She accepted it with a rueful grin. "Yes, I've *almost* managed to fill this one!"

"Anyway," I said as I sat down again, "you're as young as you feel."

"Evidently."

"That's going to be my motto from now on."

Only then did I realize that the Mozart had come to an end. I mentally sang a line or two—though not lines from *Don Giovanni* or *The Magic Flute*.

> Stay young and beautiful,
> It's your duty to be beautiful...

At any rate I now felt I had given Sylvia enough to be getting on with. I had decided to become enigmatic: a woman of mystery. I smiled. Roger and Celia had also been interested to hear about any new friends I might be making; and I had exercised restraint on that occasion, too. I had simply said, "None!" But this had been chiefly because I hadn't wanted them to start feeling sidelined.

I encouraged Sylvia to return to London matters.

All the time she talked, however, that perky little tune was still playing inside my head, making it hard for me not to tap my foot. I hadn't thought of it in a long while. But now I was sure that I'd remember. It would be good to have a theme song. Just like Aunt Alicia had had *her* theme song and had obviously—though in a rather mournful way—found it endlessly life-affirming. (I wondered if she'd sung it as repetitiously in this house as she had sung it at Neville Court.)

And it was perfectly true of course. *I'd* always felt far more positive whenever I'd had a motto.

A motto—even now that I felt so assured of happiness—could only make a very welcome extra ingredient.

> Don't forget to do your stuff
> With some powder and a powder puff;
> Stay young and beautiful
> If you want to be loved...

Sylvia broke off what she was saying—she must have seen me tapping and guessed I hadn't been giving her my full attention. "Oh, I know what you've got on *your* mind," she remarked. "You and your corny old tunes."

I smiled, affectionately. I said: "I remember, you saucebox, how you used to call me the Old Groaner!" But I'd heard presenters on Radio 2 use that same appellation for Bing Crosby.

She smiled back. "Well, one of your most infuriating habits was that way you had of humming under your breath—totally out of tune and nearly always in a monotone. How it could drive me loco!"

I didn't follow.

"Why did you do it, Raitch? That's what I'd like to know. Did it seem to you melodious?"

I laughed. "What *are* you saying, Sylv?" Either she was expressing herself poorly or I was being exceptionally obtuse.

"All those boringly upbeat tunes. Why were you so tediously hooked on them? Still are, for anything I know?" She added: "Yes! I've just been given proof."

I stared at her. There could no longer be any doubt of what she meant.

I said: "Surely it's the right thing to do, isn't it? To try to face life with a song on your lips? Even if it can't—not always—be a song in your heart?"

"Oh, Christ, Raitch! Pollyanna!" She coughed then shrugged—and even chuckled. She had always been incredibly impervious to changes in the temperature.

"Anyway," I persisted, "why on earth do you say 'under your breath and out of tune'? I should think I could sometimes be heard by everybody in the block. I know that Mrs. Crumbling once called me a right little songbird—those were her very words—and *she* wasn't a woman exactly famous for her compliments! And," I went on, "and..."

But suddenly I caught his eye—or, rather, suddenly he caught mine. I looked down at my hands; I looked up again. I made an effort.

"And?" she prompted.

"And...well, I'm sure you *don't* know what boringly upbeat little tune I had on my mind a minute ago!" He was pleased with me for thinking up this challenge and for good-humouredly accepting her assessment. (For *seeming*, good-humouredly, to accept her assessment!)

"You're forgetting, my girl, I lived with you for close on eleven years. For my sins, I might add."

"All right then?"

Clearly she couldn't have expected such tenacity. But Sylvia-like she was determined to make good her boast or at least to go down fighting. The first was an almost impossible assignment. One admired her pluck though. Even whilst being mystified by her choice.

> "Fairy tales can come trew-ew-ew,
>   It can happen to yew-ew-ew,
>   If you're young at heart..."

She added, "Well, I'm no bloody Frank Sinatra. I only wish I was." She gave a caustic laugh. "Not that he should go around getting too bigheaded over that."

Poor Sylvia. Suddenly I did understand. I didn't know who had first called it the green-eyed monster—but they had surely been exactly right. Sylvia's eyes were flecked with the greenest green you ever saw.

"Yes, full marks," I said. "You're really very clever."

I had stopped my toe-tapping. (Of course, long since.) I remembered when I had seen that film and I supposed, on second thoughts, her choice hadn't been in the least bit mystifying.

She let out an incredulous guffaw: triumph and astonishment combined. I wanted to change the subject. I said: "Did you know that Howard Hughes once sat on the lavatory for seventy-two hours? Adventurer, playboy, filmmaker. Unbelievably handsome as well. But later…Three days, three nights, of battling with his constipation. Imagine." I obeyed my own injunction: I imagined. "Furthermore, it probably brought on piles. Could you really call *that* a success story, I wonder?"

Sylvia looked at me a little oddly. But that didn't matter. *She* had certainly stopped crowing and *I* had certainly been able to find a new topic.

"I must remember that as a gambit," she observed, "when I'm next asked out and there happens to be a lull at the dinner table."

But I knew she wasn't asked out very often, whatever she might say, and particularly not to places where you didn't have your supper served up on a tray in front of the TV.

"I had no idea you even used words like that," she said. "Lavatory. Constipation. Piles. I had no idea you realized they existed."

I smiled but said nothing. A woman of mystery.

Indeed, it sometimes did appear to me I had a mildly Rabelaisian streak, which perhaps I ought to keep an eye on. Though on this occasion it could hardly have caused any offence. I thought Sylvia would have felt more vindicated than upset.

I was right.

"I can remember," she said, "when *I* sat on the lavatory for a full forty minutes. And that was bad enough! One gets all sweaty with frustration."

"Oh, *Sylvia*!" I exclaimed. "No, don't! Please!"

"Well, you were the one to bring it up, my dear." She smiled, a little grimly. "Association of ideas maybe? Come on—you'd better tell me all about your romantic chemist. I realize you've been dying to. For a start how old is he?"

I struggled not to take the huff.

"Oh? I don't know. Early thirties?"

"My God, you *are* cradle-snatching. And does he sell love potions not on prescription? If so, I think I'd better have one."

"No, no. He helps the poor."

"What a lot of fun that must be."

I was aware of course that she was scoffing but I didn't mind. Or at least not sufficiently to stop me. It was so lovely to be able to talk about him. I now wondered why—woman of mystery or not—I hadn't in fact done so last Tuesday with the Allsops.

"You see, he's got this idea that because he was born with a silver spoon in his mouth he must always do what he can to help those much less fortunate. He even regards it as a solemn duty. Do you remember by any chance *Magnificent Obsession*?"

She nodded—with a queer little twist about her lips. "Both versions," she answered. "Do you want to say he's more Robert Taylor or more Rock Hudson?"

"Oh, neither. He's himself. Better looking than either of them and with oodles more sex appeal. His eyes are...outstanding. They follow you about the room. They seem to suggest that there's *nothing* he can't understand nor forgive. Above all, he's a sympathetic listener. I talk to him by the hour. And as a matter of fact if you'd really like to know what he looks like..."

"You bet I would! Why, I'm almost wetting my pants, my dear, at the very thought of meeting him!"

"But you can't," I said.

"What, wet my pants?"

"You can't meet him." Foolishly, it hadn't even occurred to me she might expect to. "I mean, he's gone away for the weekend. Gone home."

"Home...to his wife and children?"

"Of course not. Home is always the place where you were born. Home is—"

"Perhaps he isn't the marrying kind?"

Only the emphasis she had laid on the last two words made me understand she wasn't referring simply to a fear of commitment.

Oh, yes, indeed. She was *very* jealous!

But I pretended not to get her drift. "Home is where your parents are," I continued just as if she hadn't interrupted. "Though it's only his mother nowadays. His father died quite young."

"I don't believe a word of it," laughed Sylvia. Yet in my relief at having escaped what might have been an awkward situation I was prepared to overlook her wicked innuendos. "Oh, his father may be dead," she conceded.

I made no reply.

"And I suppose you're one of the poor that this paragon's been trying to help?"

"Don't be stupid."

She suddenly had a prolonged paroxysm of coughing, her first really bad one of the evening.

When she finally emerged from it, still watery-eyed and wheezy, she happened to be looking at the fireplace. "What a bloody awful picture!" she remarked suddenly.

I was dumbfounded.

"I feel like I'm huddled in the dock," she said, "and he's Judge Jeffries and at any moment he'll be putting on his black cap because I've just been convicted of the crime of smoker's cough. And I honestly don't know when I last saw anything so gloomy."

She paused then adopted a more conversational style.

"I meant to comment earlier."

———

It seemed the final disintegration of our friendship. On my side anyway. And there were three more days to get through. It was going to be even worse than I'd imagined.

"Oh, help me!" I implored. "I know that you—being you—will probably forgive her. But I don't think *I* shall ever be able to!"

29

THERE were things that night which I remembered.

(There were things most nights which I remembered.)

I remembered lying awake on summer evenings, for instance, with music floating in through my open window. It came from the pub across the way.

The music was so jolly—even when it was something sad like "There was I waiting at the church, waiting at the church." I pictured everyone standing around the piano and joining in with such gusto.

I remembered my bedroom.

It was a small cream-coloured rectangle, almost boxlike, with a boarded-up fireplace and cheap furniture. But it had my precious window, overlooking the side road and the pub (the side road was called Paradise Street and was narrow and slummy; the pub was actually on the corner of Marylebone High Street), and hanging on my walls were the seven pictures which at various times I had culled from magazines. Almost literally I used to inhabit those pictures; I had homes in seven different countries with seven different professions and seven different sets of parents, family and friends—mainly characters out of my favourite books—and a range of pastimes more or less suited to each locale and frequently lending themselves to either interesting or fabulous adventures.

I remembered the gentle young man in Paradise Street who had a club foot and kept a rabbit in his back yard and who had framed all my pictures for me. Even if he continued to enjoy best the kind of books which I myself did he was still a highly skilled framer.

I didn't quite realize it then but he must have charged me well under cost price.

Paul was knocked down and killed just before I was ten. I never knew what had happened to the rabbit—I was too shy to find out. And I couldn't have kept it, anyway.

I was glad I'd bought him a new edition of *The Would-Be-Goods* two weeks before it happened. E Nesbit was *his* favourite author and this was the only one of hers he hadn't got. I was glad that I'd written something soppy on the flyleaf and included lots of kisses.

Then I remembered how I would frequently sit in front of my mirror—or, rather, lift it down from my chest of drawers and hold it upright on my lap whilst sitting on the bed—and fervently wish that I was beautiful; but how for long periods too I would try to avoid mirrors altogether, like Queen Elizabeth, and live in a blemish-free land of hopeful possibility.

I remembered how when I was older I used sometimes to dream about Gary Cooper or Gregory Peck or—mostly—a fair-haired young second-feature player whose name I've totally forgotten. But in the only film of his I ever saw he spent a lot of his time in a swimsuit or shorts, perhaps because he had such well-shaped legs. When he came to see me in my daydreams, generally as I was just settling down to sleep, he was usually wearing the same swimming trunks that he wore in the film. Occasionally, however, before he ran or dived into the sea he liked to remove them. He said it gave him a greater sense of freedom. I was always waiting for him as he came out of the water.

But I also remembered something else. What I remembered chiefly that night was the party at which I gave a recitation from Alfred Lord Tennyson.

That party and its unexpected aftermath.

His very first words to me:

"Hello—I'm Tony Simpson. I just wanted to say... I thought you did that *Lady of Shalott* thing awfully well."

"Did you?"

"Yes, I thought it was excellent. You know, you've almost... sort of... made history at this party?"

He seemed a bit hesitant though, a little shy, which is perhaps the reason I so quickly felt at home with him.

Yet he was very young, only nineteen, which could easily explain his occasional nervous glances behind him. Almost as though I were the first girl he had ever paid a serious compliment to and he was needing to cut the adolescent ties which bound him to his friends. I liked that.

He was perhaps a trifle too thin for my total satisfaction and his nose was perhaps a trifle too beaky but he was otherwise not bad-looking. He had wavy nut-brown hair and a nice sensitive expression. And he was certainly no mean hand with those compliments. "As a matter of fact I think you ought to be an actress."

"That's what I want to be." The flush of success was still upon me. For the moment such an ambition seemed practically within reach.

"Not just because you recited that thing so well"—he appeared to be growing more confident every time he spoke—"but because you also remind me a lot of Vivien Leigh."

"Really? Do you mean that? But Vivien Leigh is *beautiful*."

"She's my favourite film star. I've now seen *Gone with the Wind* four times."

"I've seen it twice."

"I would go again tomorrow if it were on."

"So would I."

There was a pause. I was suddenly terrified he might simply nod and move away.

"Do I *honestly* look like her?"

"Hasn't anybody ever told you?"

"No. Nobody."

"Well, I think that's strange. I really do."

Another pause.

"What did you mean when you said I'd sort of made history at this party?"

"Oh, nothing much." Again that nervous glance across his shoulder, that search for reassurance from a phalanx of his pals; he didn't even realize he was doing it. "There's a kind of catchphrase going around," he said, less easily again. "I'm sure you must have heard it?"

"Catchphrase?"

"Mm. I don't know why."

"What is it?"

He hesitated. "The curse is come upon me..."

"...cried the Lady of Shalott!"

"Yes."

"Oh, what fun. You must be right. I do seem, don't I, to have made a bit of a hit?"

He immediately sounded happier. "It's like a password. If you know the password you gain entry into any group."

"I must try it!"

It was fast becoming the loveliest evening of my life. In every way possible. Now I even liked his beaky nose.

But incredibly it was to grow yet nicer. (Who said that selfish prayers are never answered?)

"I have a car," he told me. "Would it be all right if I took you home after the party?" Suddenly so decisive. Suddenly so very much his own man.

And a little later when Tony had gone off to the little boys' room I found he hadn't been exaggerating. Although I wasn't quite brave enough to employ the password myself I soon heard somebody else doing so. It was a man, though, which for some reason actually made it sound a bit absurd and no doubt accounted for the screams of laughter, both masculine and feminine, which instantly arose to greet it. But the man definitely gained entry to the group and I was delighted to think that it was

I who'd given him the key. Well, Lord Tennyson too—to some extent. We clearly made a good team.

Perhaps Tony Simpson and I would also make a good team. In the car he said, "And maybe it *is* on somewhere!" I was glad his friends had all been left behind: no more defiant or panicky or jubilant glances over the shoulder. Umbilical cord effectively severed.

"*Gone with the Wind*?" I asked.

We were marvellously attuned.

"Yes."

"Maybe it is."

But I wasn't taking any chances.

"As it happens, there's another film I'd very much like to see. It's called *Young at Heart*. Supposed to be excellent. It's showing at the Astoria in Charing Cross Road."

"*Is* it?"

"Last week it was at the Tivoli in the Strand." I felt that this somehow clinched it.

"You know, I'd really like to see that." Oh, God *was* in his heaven.

The following morning my mother said:

"It must have been a fine party—in spite of all the fuss you made beforehand! Aren't you grateful to me for insisting that you went?" She sounded quite jaundiced.

"Yes, it *was* a fine party. How could you tell?"

"You've got a sparkle. You look almost pretty."

Praise, indeed!

"Who is he, then?"

"A man called Tony Simpson. He's going to take me to the pictures."

"Why?"

"What do you mean, why? Because he wants to, I suppose."

"Well, just don't let him make a fool of you, that's all." She poured my cup of tea and pushed across the toast rack.

"Why should he want to make a fool of me?"

"Oh, for heaven's sake, Rachel! Don't pick me up on every word I utter!"

Young at Heart would have been a special film under any circumstances. It was charming, funny, tender, sad. About an ordinary middle-class American family to which anyone in her right mind would have wanted to belong. Doris Day was one of the daughters, Ethel Barrymore the amused no-nonsense aunt, Gig Young the good-natured newcomer whom the whole family fell in love with; Frank Sinatra, the self-pitying music arranger whom Doris eventually married. Added to all of this there were some first-rate songs.

It was so enjoyable, in fact, we saw it again the following night. My mother was *astonished*! And even when—less than a week later—we went out for the third time she still seemed at a loss to understand it.

And didn't I relish her amazement! Didn't I wallow in it! Each date was utterly wonderful—despite that tiny crumb of disappointment I invariably experienced when first I saw him: a feeling which lasted maybe a full minute. But the third time was the best of all, even though the film, *The Bridges at Toko-Ri* (notwithstanding the presence of Grace Kelly), was much less entertaining and even though, at the very end of the evening...

Well anyway. In the cinema we held hands for a lot of the time and even when we didn't our arms were close together on the armrest—it was early summer and we both had on short sleeves. Afterwards he kissed me in the car. It was heaven.

Before the film oh how we had talked! Of all sorts of things, I can't remember what. After it we had supper and simply went *on* talking! We agreed on almost everything and although when we spoke about what we most wanted out of life he never actually mentioned children, nor even marriage, and although as yet I couldn't quite be sure he loved me and had to keep on telling myself it *might* be a mistake to wear my heart so openly upon my sleeve... still, I thought, it really did seem that he was growing in affection. Indeed, I was almost certain of it. We had to be turned out of the café when they wanted to close; it was just like one of those romantic comedies in which the members of the orchestra are starting to yawn in protest because the starry young lovers don't even realize that they're the last couple on the floor.

And when he reached my home, instead of stopping the car in Marylebone High Street, in front of our drab main door beside MacFisheries, he turned into Paradise Street and drove down to the end, where there was a public recreation garden. Here I often escaped to read—and read to escape. The garden had cherry, laburnum, hawthorn; it had decaying gravestones, an eighteenth-century mausoleum and the statue of a small street orderly: a boy of about ten who sat looking pensively at his hands, his face a picture of calm acceptance. When I'd been about that age myself I'd often stopped to speak to him—and tried hard to learn from his example. Even as a young woman I continued to smile at him as I passed.

Tony now pulled up before the locked gate. It was well after midnight and the streets were deserted.

"I really ought to be going home," I said unconvincingly. "My mother never turns her light off until I get in."

"Oh, just another five minutes won't make any difference though. If you liked we could get into the back. It might be more comfortable."

His voice held that same discomfort, combined now with dryness, almost a brusqueness, which had drawn me to him in the first place. Poor Tony. He sounded such a very long way from casual.

"Just another five minutes?" I said, then adding brightly, "You sound like Tessie O'Shea! But you mustn't get me wrong—you don't look like her, not one bit!" He wouldn't see that I too was nervous.

"Yes."

I wasn't sure if it was the time period he was agreeing to or his partial resemblance to Miss O'Shea.

But before I stepped out of the car I sang:

"Five minutes more,
    Give me five minutes more,
    Only five minutes more
    In your arms..."

We cuddled on the back seat. His hands were everywhere. For the first few minutes I was more than merely nervous, I felt positively scared and could only sit—or lean—a bit inertly. Yet at the same time I was thrilled. I thought, "Rachel Waring, a real live man is doing these things to you! Never again will you be the person you just were! When your feet next touch the pavement you're going to be a complete woman!" And gradually I relaxed. I told myself this was a moment that could never ever be repeated—and that I really had to savour it. Create a memory. Take a photograph. Most of my apprehension departed and my breath quickened. By the time his tongue was licking one of my breasts, my skin pearly white above my pushed-down bra, I felt quite weak with longing. I heard myself moan and was so happy: such a reflex must absolutely mean that this was the proper thing, it wasn't just because I'd *read* it was the right reaction. And I began to writhe (well, so far as I was able to, the car not being a large one) and my hands began to fumble with his clothing, moved caressingly beneath his shirt—what did it matter if his chest was smooth and bony? They then moved along his trousered thighs, even as his own hands fumbled their way under my skirt and kneaded a little, suddenly pulled at, nearly tore, the garment that I wore there. Oh God. It was such bliss. A man's hands—warm, hard, questing, unpredictable—where a man's hands had never been before. We didn't talk, we only moaned—yes, actually the pair of us; it now seemed *doubly* right. But when I realized that one of those hands was simultaneously trying to get his flies undone I did just say, "Oh, do you think we ought to? Have you any...?" because in every book I'd ever read in which the young heroine was unmarried she unfailingly became pregnant as the result of a single encounter. Or—no, in fact—*did* I say it? I wasn't sure. Perhaps I had only thought of saying it, because I can also remember thinking that a new life resulting out of such a moment would be the most fantastic thing imaginable. I had no wish to be conventional. Besides, a baby must surely mean he'd marry me. I waited—there was a brief hiatus, a giddy moment of suspension—feeling more alive than I had ever felt, tingling with sheer expectancy and love and a sense of culmination. It occurred to me suddenly, with both my hands upon his chest, that I couldn't picture, wouldn't want, any chest more beautiful.

There was, unexpectedly, an exclamation. And a second later I was aware of something rather warm, felt its warmth even through nylon, a fluid which spurted along one of my thighs, slipped down the inside, copiously, some just above the stocking top, dripping and growing cool between my suspenders.

"Oh, *God*!" he said. "Rachel, I'm sorry! I am so sorry. Oh, *God*!"

It took me a moment to realize what had happened but the first thing I recognized, even perhaps before the fact of my own disappointment, was the pure misery of his. "It doesn't matter," I cried, "it's all right! Oh, my darling, it doesn't *matter*!" And I soothed his damp brow, tried to ease away its creases (that I could sense rather than see), ran my hands around his ears, stroked the back of his head and neck, endeavoured to comfort him in any way I could. "Oh, my darling, it doesn't matter at all! And I enjoyed myself, I really did. Was it...was it...was it fairly okay for you?" I think he gave a sob.

"It was a farce," he said.

"Oh, no, don't call it that. It was fantastic. It was a truly wonderful experience."

"I couldn't even get it into you," he said. "Here's my handkerchief. You'd better clean yourself up and then I'll get you home."

I took his handkerchief: it was larger than my own. He began to readjust his clothes. He told me, still tonelessly: "I'm sorry for the mess."

"But you mustn't be. Not for anything. I honestly don't mind the mess."

I added after a moment—it didn't strike me as being crude:

"In fact I'm *happy* to have it. Shooting out like that. All devil-may-care and imperious. You know, in some ways it's a big compliment that he got so excited, just couldn't wait, young Mr. Thingummy..."

Then I laughed—no, I assured him, I hadn't forgotten his name. "I'm not calling *you* young Mr. Thingummy!" I tried to make an even better joke out of it. "All nicely chambré-d, too. The perfect room temperature."

I even capped my own pleasantry. I so much wished to see him smile.

"The perfect womb temperature!"

I felt inspired.

"It didn't get there," he said.

He moved into the driver's seat. It took him less than a minute to drive the length of Paradise Street, even allowing for his having to turn the car around in a seriously restricted space.

"I'll wash this out," I said, "and give it back to you."

He shook his head. "Oh, don't bother. There's a bin over there. I'll just get rid of it."

"But it's a *lovely* handkerchief. I wouldn't let you!"

I got out of the car. I didn't feel a complete woman. He crossed the pavement beside me. We stood at the front door.

"Rachel?"

"Yes, darling?"

He faltered. "If you should ever meet any of the others... and any of them should ever allude to this in any way... well, I mean, you'd never let on, would you? That it all turned into such a bloody farce?"

"Of course not, Tony! What do you think I am? Besides—how could any of your friends ever *possibly* get to know...?"

But I wasn't annoyed that he had asked me. I had read about

the tremendous vulnerability of male vanity in matters such as this—and he was obviously upset and not himself. Oh, it was such a dreadful shame!

No, I wasn't annoyed. What afterwards annoyed me more— long afterwards—was the thought that I'd once been so very close to a man, almost at the very root of him, and yet I'd never... had never...

So close and yet I'd never even touched it. Never placed my fingers lovingly about it.

Nor was that all. What somehow seemed worse... what made me on several occasions actually want to cry out with the bleak awareness of an opportunity wasted...

I had never even seen it.

———

But that was for the future: that bleak annoyance or regret. For the time being I was still extremely positive; and what had made me especially happy was the way he suddenly seemed to cheer up. After he'd taken my key and opened the front door he stood facing me for a moment. A long moment. He had a hand on each of my arms and was looking at me as though in some strange way I was indeed a different woman.

"Rachel, you've been very sweet about all this. Shall I tell you something? I think perhaps I've been a little blind."

"Really, Tony? In what way?"

"I've got to say you're quite a girl!"

Even his kiss felt different.

"I'll give you a ring tomorrow night," he said.

"Really? So soon?" I was delighted. "Though haven't you forgotten something? Tomorrow night you'll be in Edinburgh."

"Yet people tell me that, by now, the telephone may even have reached Scotland! Incredible, isn't it? But if they're right...yes, then, definitely tomorrow night!"

I had it ringing through my dreams: if they're right, tomorrow night, if they're right, tomorrow night. And the dreams I had during those very few hours' sleep before my breakfast—I was called extremely early, as I now knew would always happen if I stayed out late with my "persistent young suitor"—those dreams were among the best I'd ever had.

30

I FELT almost from its beginning that the August Bank Holiday represented a travesty of hospitality. For the first time in that house I lost my inner peace.

To make matters worse it rained through most of the weekend and Sylvia—never at the best of times an outdoor person—didn't seem at all disposed to come out and explore. She sat around and read the newspapers and looked at television and did the crosswords and the air appeared to get thicker and bluer by the hour. I opened as many windows as I could but along with the rain there had sprung up a driving wind and I seemed to be faced with the alternatives of either getting everything drenched or of having all my cushions and furnishings smelling pungently of tobacco. Though—in reality—there was no alternative. Sylvia enjoyed a fug.

"Is it *always* like this in Bristol?" she asked, with quiet satisfaction.

"No, just the opposite. We've had a lovely summer."

She laughed, derisively. "Strange—when the rest of the country seems to have had one of the coldest on record."

Also she liked to belch; she was a loud and inveterate belcher. "'Whoever you are, wherever you be,'" she had formerly been disposed to quote, "'always let your wind go free. For not doing so was the death of me!'" She claimed it was a factual epitaph.

"I still don't see why you have to be *quite* so flagrantly earthy and natural about it," I used to complain, whenever I felt driven to it—and once, wittily, "But *your* letting it go free will probably be the death of *me*!" And this weekend it appeared she was extra intent upon remaining alive. Or had I just forgotten?

In any case, during the whole of those three days until the Monday evening, I hardly raised my voice in song. And even when I did, the attempt was only tentative and couldn't be sustained.

Fortunately the television was on the ground floor—in the breakfast room—so for much of the time I was able to get her downstairs. ("*Some* of us still have to make do with black and white," she announced with the same somewhat gloomy satisfaction. "But then, of course, I'm not one of the gainfully unemployed, am I?" Well *really*, I thought, remembering the video.) Yet though the radio was there as well and I kept on returning the crumpled newspapers, folded as best I could, to the table where we ate our meals; and though I left one bar of the electric fire on, *all the time*...still, it seemed that nothing could keep her from drifting up the stairs again, as though even she, despite her blindness and bad manners, was somehow drawn uncomprehendingly to be often in *his* presence.

Indeed, as I saw that she appeared to be quite fascinated by the picture—because she couldn't ever leave the room if I was there without making at least *one* casually disparaging remark—I did, a little, begin to soften towards her. After all, who had hated Christ more thoroughly than Saul of Tarsus? And I started to think that even for slovenly Sylvia there might come her slightly soiled Damascus. Notwithstanding my carefully suppressed sensations of resentment and my unwillingness (now) to share anything important, I began to be intrigued to see if it might possibly happen by train time: that opening of the skies and great blinding flash of revelation. "You *could* do it!" I thought. "I know that you *could* do it. If you wanted."

During Sunday breakfast Sylvia said, "Won't you be rushing off to church this morning? To ogle your responsive and—what was it now—rather *physical* vicar?"

"No, not with you here. It would scarcely be polite."

"In fact I wouldn't mind rushing off with you, to do a bit of ogling on my own account. Inspecting the field, as it were. Studying form!"

"Sylvia, don't be crude. Anyhow, at present he's away. Vicars sometimes go off on retreats."

"Bizarre! This is clearly the weekend for a mass exodus from Bristol! Can he, too, be visiting his widowed old mum?"

I didn't answer; but a bit ironically, hurriedly looking for some sort of distraction on the radio, happened to catch a few moments of the morning service. "Tom Lehrer once said modern math was so simple only a child could understand it," was the preacher's first comment that we caught. "Well, it's precisely the same with prayer and trust. So simple only a child can understand them! Which is exactly why Jesus said we must all become like little—"

"You can't really want to listen to this muck?" said Sylvia. She reached across and switched it off.

"I was hoping it might entertain you."

"I don't *need* entertaining for Christ's sake! I'm your best friend. You shouldn't have to *work* at entertaining your best friend."

Then, inexplicably, she flipped the radio back on. The preacher was winding up his sermon. Hymn number something-or-other was announced.

"'Christian, seek not yet repose,'
  Hear thy guardian angel say:
  'Thou art in the midst of foes;
  Watch and pray.'

"'Principalities and powers,
  Mustering their unseen array,
  Wait for thy unguarded hours;
  Watch and pray.'"

Presumably she had meant to be considerate, had been thinking more of me than of herself. But her kindness wasn't up to it. "Oh, no, you really *can't* want this!" she cried a second time. "I shan't allow it! It may be okay for infants and loonies but as us two don't happen to be either...at least not yet..." She turned it off, and this time very finally.

"No, I'm honestly not so convinced you *could* do it," I said to myself—or, of course, not at all to myself—with possibly quite praiseworthy humour.

And I continued to remain cheerful, as I had promised him I would.

I even relented so far in my attitude towards her ("I'm your best friend," she had said) as to suggest she might like to come and help me window-shop for a christening present.

But I was greatly relieved when she declined.

"You go if you want to. You can leave me here."

"No. I'll have plenty of time during the week."

I was somehow reluctant, though it would have given me an hour or two of welcome respite, to leave her in the house alone. I don't know quite what I imagined. Certainly she wouldn't have done anything to harm my picture. No, that was too preposterous.

Perhaps I thought she might have snooped and come upon my precious book—in the drawer where I had hidden it. That would have been as bad as any grubby-fingered burglar rifling through my underwear.

(There had recently been a spate of burglaries. The police had issued a warning to every householder in the vicinity. It was one of my greatest worries; but not of course for the sake of my underwear. Fire worried me for the same reason. So did ants. I kept fearing ants might eat up my manuscript—ants or some other hoard of tiny nameless insects, less visible, that feasted on paper like woodworm did on wood. Each night I blew between the pages and laboriously inspected for the onset of attack. But none of my precautions could ever wholly rid me of anxiety.)

Besides, through jealousy and malice, she might decide to change things. Well, suppose she contrived it so skillfully as to utterly defy detection? What then?

So we stayed indoors and somehow managed to pass the time.

("My God, you're a compulsive polisher! You were never like this at home!") We talked desultorily. I would almost have welcomed some of those earnest topics I had formerly been dreading: apartheid in South Africa, our responsibility towards the animals, our ceaseless consumption of junk foods. (Yet hadn't she brought me a battery chicken and biscuits and a box of chocolates?) Even on the Saturday evening when there had been little to watch on TV and when we had opened the second of her bottles of wine "in an attempt," she had said, "to cock a snook at the President of the Lord's Day Observance Society" (for the first few seconds it simply hadn't occurred to me whom she meant) "and hopefully stir him into some sort of action with a show of debauchery and bacchanalia!"—even then our conversational flights had remained obstinately earthbound. There was only one exchange in any way worth recounting—and that, certainly, not for the sake of its intellectual content. It came a minute or two before she decided she would probably do better to go downstairs and watch the cricket.

"I've been thinking recently," I said, "that I might start to wear a brighter shade of nail polish." I held out my fingers as I spoke and regarded them reflectively.

"Yes," she said, "I saw it mentioned in the paper."

"In London I always wore clear; since coming here I've worn pink. Now I'm wondering about something deeper...scarlet, maybe? My toenails, too? Or does it all sound—still—a bit too jazzy and Bohemian?"

"My dear Rachel," she answered. "Bristol may be a bit of a backwater but I daresay it can just about stand the shock of scarlet nail polish."

Suddenly she stopped.

"No," I said, "you're right! I don't care if it *does* sound too jazzy and Bohemian."

"You know—something's been bothering me. I've only just realized what it is. At times it doesn't even sound as if you're actually talking to *me*."

"What on earth do you mean?"

There was a pause. She shrugged. She gave her characteristic snort of laughter.

"Oh, search me. I don't know. I think *I* must be going round the twist even if you're not."

She heaved herself to her feet.

"Or perhaps it's that romantic chemist," she added, inconsequentially.

———

Late on the Monday afternoon I was clearing away the tea things while she, I supposed, was packing her suitcase. But suddenly I heard her heavy tread on the staircase and she came into the kitchen holding a cut-glass bowl.

"Ah ha! Bet you thought I'd forgotten!"

"Forgotten what?" Early indoctrination dies hard.

"Housewarming present," she said.

"Oh, Sylvia!" I quickly wiped my hands and took it from her. "But, Sylvia, it's *exquisite*! It must have cost you a week's wages!" I wondered what she had done with the packaging it would have come in.

"Not quite the £39,000 bowl that Charles got from the Reagans!"

"But not far from it." I laid it down with great care, put my hands upon her shoulders and kissed her fondly on the cheek. I imagined her spending her lunch hours browsing attentively through John Lewis or Selfridge's, or else some pricey little place in an arcade, until she was totally satisfied she'd found the right thing to please me. "I shall treasure it for ever," I said.

"I wish it was still you I was living with, not Lucy!"

Oh dear. What could I possibly say to that? Was there already more friction between her and Miss Carter than there had eventually been between *us*?

But I knew, anyway, she hadn't meant to say it; that she had embarrassed herself quite as much as she had me.

"I hope you won't mind," she hurried on bluntly as I turned back a little awkwardly to looking at the bowl. "I used the box and the carrier bag for something else and I really couldn't be bothered to wrap it."

"You could never have done it justice."

"It had my nightie and cardigan and things wrapped round it in the case: a new kind of presentation pack..." We laughed companionably at that; that moment of awkwardness left mercifully behind. "But I bet you *were* telling yourself that I'd forgotten! Or that I was just too mean to have done anything about it!"

"No, really. I hadn't given it a thought."

Yet suddenly I smiled and nodded.

"Yes, you're right—actually I did believe you might have forgotten. You see now? A new way of life. I'm aiming at telling nothing but the truth!"

"Oh Christ!" she said. Not because I had been honest but because I had told her I wanted to be.

"Is that so terrible?" I asked.

"Yes."

"Why?"

"It's infantile. And nauseating. And bloody dangerous."

I wasn't sure if she was making a joke or not but sadly by the time we set out for the station some fifteen minutes later I was having consciously to hold on to my feeling of reawakened affection and the hope that after all there might just be something left between us to blow on and resuscitate.

Then, still more sadly, as I was locking the front door she seemed to notice for the first time my darling's plaque. (Surely it hadn't been that dark when she'd arrived on Friday? Though to be fair there *had* been something of a deluge and her large black umbrella—"bloody-minded article; want to bet it's because I was stupid enough to lend it to Lucy?"—appeared to have sprung a leak.)

"Politician!" she scoffed now. "Philanthropist! Busybody! Aren't there still enough around today without our having to commemorate all those sententious old buggers who preceded them? Do-gooders it seems to me have always been such a complete pain in the arse!" She shifted her suitcase to the other hand.

This was scarcely—in view of the magnificent obsession we had spoken of at the beginning of her visit—the most tactful thing she could have said.

No, I thought, as far as the outward signs went she hadn't received a vision. And on the whole (I do have to admit this) I was glad. It would have been a confirmation of his powers, yes undoubtedly, but why should I ever require that? And on the other hand it might subtly have spoiled something if Sylvia had indeed been vouchsafed any intimations. I'd felt almost pleased to hear her final words to him. "Goodbye, old sourpuss. I can't say I've exactly grown accustomed to your face."

In effect they were also her final words to me—even without that business on the doorstep.

Had she acknowledged him at all it could well have been different (although I didn't *want* a fellowship) but as it was I felt little compunction about saying to myself as the train drew out, "Well, maybe that's the last I'll ever see of you, my dear best friend." Naturally this decision was not untainted by the shadow of regret; principally in view of that lovely present.

I walked back—still beneath a light drizzle—despite the evening's being calm and mild and despite it seeming that the sun might soon break through again. I felt carefree. Almost refreshed. I felt that although the remains of a particularly dreaded and mostly awful party still had to be cleared away at home this was obviously a negligible price to pay for the restoration of our peace and privacy.

Oh, hallelujah!

From now on we should be blessedly free of trespassers.

31

WHEN HE was twelve Horatio got lost, not in the Temple but in the Assembly Rooms in Bath, as the result of a dare, and caused *his* parents too a vast amount of worry. But that was nothing of course to the worry he occasioned them a few months later when he nearly died. He'd contracted a chill whilst swimming with his friends and boy-like had neglected it. Pneumonia resulted. But this time I identified with the mother. The fact that every church-yard in the country was filled with the graves of babies and chil-dren—sometimes one after another from the same family—did nothing to accustom you to the idea of loss; or rather, resign you to it. I imagined how it must feel to watch the relentless decline of a child who'd been denied to you for years and years but who when he'd finally arrived had been everything you could have wanted: healthy, good-humoured, intelligent, caring.

I myself had never borne a child but now I felt a steady ache of fear and wild rebellious grief—one couldn't, wouldn't, *wouldn't* let it happen! Not to him! Not to Horatio! Was there no God?

Yes, naturally there was. Then didn't he *know* what type of be-ing he'd created; couldn't he *see* his value for the future? Had he only given—and after such prayerfulness, such patience and tra-vail—so soon to take away? She wasn't Sarah. She couldn't bear to be thus tested. Oh yes, if she *had* been Sarah, then perhaps she could have; but if she was to be only Eliza Munday or Anne Arm-strong or Eleanor Jenks, each of whom had stood at more than one pathetic little graveside in the past few years—well, *then* she couldn't bear it.

And she had always been led to believe that God was good. All-powerful. And a conscientious listener to prayer.

Oh, she didn't question it—she *couldn't* question it, for down that path lay only despair, surrender, madness—but where in that case was His mercy? A twelve-year-old child was essentially so innocent.

Oh, God, where *are* you at such times?

So you see, although I had no children, I *knew* what it was like. It would be like someone taking from me my book, my purpose, my power to start again; my portrait, my hope, my belief in the marvel of mankind, my belief in the marvel of life itself.

And I was more than simply mother; I was wife as well. It was as if she saw, Rebecca Gavin, that not only would she lose her son, she would lose her husband too. Jeremiah Gavin was over sixty. He was far from robust. The son's death would also be the husband's.

But God *was* merciful (in this instance). And although with one part of my mind I had plainly known all along what was to be the outcome . . . still, the enormity of her relief, of her thankfulness, the blessed sense of *calm* following all the tumult and the terror, was nevertheless nearly as much the reaction of Rachel Waring as it was of Rebecca Gavin—it seemed we had both stood to lose real flesh and blood and heart and soul, along with the miracle of innocence and trust and unreserved devotion. The two of us had known something of the same desperation; the two of us now felt the same exuberant return to life.

For I had not at all enjoyed the days wherein I wrote that section of the book. Possibly these had followed too close upon the Achilles' heel of the bank holiday and possibly the strain of Sylvia's visit had pulled me down rather more than I had realized.

Perhaps it was that.

But I just couldn't forget, you see, the fate of poor little Alfredo. Little Alfredo Rampi. (You notice, dear Mr. Morley, I *was* concerned; you had no right to tell me otherwise. I had gone out to the library just the following day and asked for their back numbers and read up all about it. I had also read up as fully as I could about the Maze prisoners and about Toxteth. I had borrowed a book about the Berlin Wall. And I had actually taken the bus and stood outside St. Lawrence's and *prayed*—only briefly ducking behind a tree when I saw Mrs. Pimm come out of a side entrance. So that really did prove it, didn't it? I wasn't just whistling in the dark and I was not, repeat *not*, uncaring!)

So I couldn't quite get it out of my mind, all the while that I wrote about Horatio. I heard him sobbing in terror down there in the darkness, that little six-year-old, crying out and whimpering for help, wedged fast but not so fast apparently that he couldn't still slip a little further, trapped there during three unimaginably slow and dreadful days of hell... until he died. And I kept reliving the moment when a volunteer cave explorer, slim himself like a child, who had forced his body head first down the narrow well, had managed to drop a handcuff round one of Alfredo's wrists, a handcuff with a rope attached. It must have seemed such a breathtaking moment, with success practically assured and the prayers of thousands almost answered. (Ask and it shall be given you; seek and ye shall find.)

And *yet*...

Small though the handcuff was, the child's hand had been smaller. All that earnest supplication, all that straining effort, all that anguished clinging on in hope... Vain.

Completely vain.

Oh, God, where *are* you at such times?

And while we struggled for Horatio's life I tried very hard not to listen to the prayers of Alfredo's parents; and not to be dismayed, either, by the attack of nervous indigestion from which I had been suffering all that week.

32

THE DAY of the christening came. It wasn't to be held until the afternoon but even in the morning I did no writing. I spent a long time soaking in the bath, then giving myself a beauty treatment. After all, I was going to be meeting many of Roger's and Celia's family and friends; I had to look my very best.

I'd considered buying a new outfit for the occasion, had even gone back to my special shop. But they had nothing there that really took my fancy. Except, that is, the sweetest, loveliest, darlingest wedding dress you ever saw—oh, it was so delectable!—with hundreds of tiny roses embroidered all over its bodice and skirt. But perhaps a wedding dress wouldn't have been entirely suitable for this occasion! Well, not entirely! The assistant who'd been there the first time (it had been another who had served me with my sky-blue) must have seen me gazing at it and even gently touching it—like a penitent in Palestine reaching out to touch the robe of Jesus. She crossed and stood beside me, confidingly.

"Yes, isn't it gorgeous?" she said. "It seems to have that effect on nearly all of us." I don't believe she recognized me.

"What effect?"

"Total captivation. It's a real heirloom. The sort of thing you would hope to hand down to granddaughters, great-granddaughters, everyone. It rather makes you want to weep."

I smiled politely. I thought about handing it down to everyone.

"But you know one of its really most delightful features? It's so simple that without the train your daughter could easily wear it as an evening dress. The effect would be quite ravishing! Even at the smartest do it would turn all the other ladies into frumps."

"How wonderful," I said. "Will that be stated in the guarantee?" We continued to stand there gazing at it. It occurred to me that in March I had liked her rather more.

"So, you see, after the wedding it wouldn't even have to be put away into mothballs. It could still have a long and a *very* exciting life ahead of it!"

"You mean, as a real heirloom?" I said this a shade ironically but she didn't seem to notice.

Perhaps it was just as well.

She couldn't see my hands of course; my gloves were hiding them. I was gratified that I should look married. But at the same time I could scarcely feel surprised.

"And the truly remarkable thing, madam, is just how low the price is!"

"Tell me."

"Under £200!"

"Really?"

"Yes indeed." It was a whole penny under £200. She nodded beatifically. "May one enquire, madam, when your daughter's. . . ?"

"Oh, the date hasn't been decided yet."

"You'll have to bring her in," she said. "But I'd certainly advise against your leaving it too late."

"Yes. Well, thank you." I bade her farewell with—apparently —great sincerity. But through the window I saw her looking pleased with herself and I laughed as I walked away. I considered that I had most decidedly outwitted her, that over-keen rapacious saleslady. I felt mischievous, clever, triumphant, sad—though perhaps the dominant emotion was really this last. I felt like a mildly melancholic Mrs. Machiavelli, already ashamed of her duplicity.

But I liked the alliteration. I chanted those four words as I went along the street, wondering how rapidly I could say them without stumbling. Thus employed I unthinkingly passed the chemist's shop.

Well, not *completely* unthinkingly. I must have noticed it peripherally. And my reaction would undoubtedly have pleased the late Professor Pavlov.

"Badedas!" I said.

Oh dear. Like an irrepressibly wilful child I had such an impulse just to open the door, put my head through the doorway, cry out "Badedas!"—and then run! That would be so glorious.

At first I resisted it. I walked on a few steps. But then I stopped. Where honestly would be the harm? It might even cheer people up; provide them with a hearty laugh. It would certainly provide *me* with one.

There were five customers—and himself, thank heaven, not the girl. Yet maybe I should have done it sooner. Then I mightn't have had time to grow nervous.

But no admissions of defeat, please. "Badedas," I shouted, as distinctly as I could. There was an instant and very satisfying silence. All heads jerked round to look at me.

Still, I think perhaps I should have practised it at home. I realized, sadly, that I hadn't managed to inject the word with the full richness it deserved. It ought to have been heavy with the distillation of experience, the kindness of constructive comment. It ought to have been almost *dripping* with importance.

I simply don't believe it was.

So I knew how actors must feel when they give an under-par performance on a bad night.

In one sense I had obviously picked a good time: there were several people waiting at the counter. A young man and his girlfriend were standing by the door. The young man was the first of all of them to speak.

"And bananas to you too!" he said cheerfully.

His companion giggled. A pert little blonde, she reminded me of Una at the office.

I withdrew—having first, with slightly feigned high spirits, blown my chemist a kiss, on the assumption that if at the beginning he had been labelled romantic it couldn't in all fairness have been totally for nothing.

Yet I have to admit it wasn't one of my all-time successes. I didn't even argue when the young man suggested I should just go home and make myself a hot toddy. Properly nurse my bad cold.

Well, never mind, I thought. Better luck next time. Back to the wedding dress.

No, good gracious me! The *christening* dress.

Anyway I couldn't really have afforded a new outfit—especially since on the day after Sylvia's departure, the day before I'd started on that chapter relating the illness of Horatio—I had spent far more than I'd meant to on young Tommy's christening presents. I had chosen him a silver napkin ring and a lovely little eggcup to which I would add one of my own silver egg spoons, and a boxed collection of Winnie the Pooh with all the original illustrations.

(Whilst in the jeweller's I saw a wedding ring so much prettier and more delicate than those you normally see. My heart quite ached to hold it, never mind possess it! I joked to the jeweller, "Things always happen in threes! I've seen the dress—and now this—what do you think will be the third event? I suppose it *ought* to be an engagement ring, even if the order's a bit skew-whiff!" He was by no means a beauty but he was such a pleasant little man, immediately and unquestionably on my own wavelength. "Yes," he answered, clearly in total agreement. "Would you like to see *our* selection of engagement rings?" "Oh, yes— what fun—why not?")

But even that wasn't all. I thought my godson would get scant pleasure for the time being out of a napkin ring and an eggcup— even though they *were* doing a rush job to have them both engraved for me, ungrateful little monkey!—and if he couldn't yet handle a teacup and saucer with aplomb it might still be a year or two before he could really appreciate A. A. Milne. I was fully aware of this. So I got him, too, a large and wickedly expensive cuddly: rather appropriately a cheeky-faced monkey in a natty checked waistcoat! I was sure he'd get costly presents from his grandparents and godfathers and aunts and cousins and all the rest of them; but his *godmother* certainly didn't mean to be outdone, either now or later. Maurice the Monkey had more sheer character and impudence, a far greater potential for growing into a lasting favourite and a reverently-handled and much-loved member of the family (perhaps, even, a real *heirloom*, madam?) than any mere common or garden teddy bear or golliwog or woolly lamb.

Come to that I shouldn't even mind too much if *my* little monkey gave *his* little monkey the name of Rachel! The chequered waistcoat didn't necessarily have to make it masculine—not in this day and age. "I mean, if he really is set upon it, the insolent young pup!" as I was later, laughingly, to say to Roger.

But to return to the morning of the party. I finally decided I should wear my green. My green was very soft and smart and people had frequently said it became me, although in London, strangely, I hadn't always felt it suited me so well and Sylvia had actually pronounced it a mistake. (*That* seriously overweight and self-styled fashion guru, herself without a single shred of clothes sense or originality, had maliciously asked for my assistance: "It's the last damned clue in the crossword—infuriating—just can't get it! Two six-letter words—the first beginning with R, the second with W, 'intimating the birth of a laughing stock . . . this cautionary tale of mutton dressed as lamb?'") All these months later, however, when I first tried it on I saw it in a wholly different light: one that had almost the freshness of revelation attaching to it. Some premonition must have made me keep the frock, for either *it* had changed or *I* had. Or maybe both of us. But if the picture of Dorian Gray could do it in an attic the dress of Rachel Waring could definitely do it in a wardrobe.

That was a joke, obviously. The portrait of Dorian Gray was inherently evil whilst both my wardrobe and my world were thrown wide open to the begged-for influence of good.

Prior to my bath I coloured my hair. I suppose I took a risk: switching without trial before an important occasion such as this from Brasilia to Naples. But I'd suddenly felt like a change—it was only a very small one—and what better time for changes than before some great event? (At least if the risk turns out to be justified—as this one most certainly did!) I'm normally someone who wouldn't colour her hair *and* bath all in the same morning— actually, I'm not sure why—but there are few things so pleasant as breaking with tradition even in absurdly minor ways. It gives you the sensation of turning over new leaves and defying dullness and remaining resilient and youthful.

Yes, predictability, not age, is the antithesis of youth. Predictability and the death of hope. An end to seeking.

It was a happy morning full of pleasant anticipation; and this, despite the fact that I made what would at one time have been a most mortifying discovery and one which—even as it was— needed the summoning up of all my resources to handle adequately.

No, not merely adequately. Rather well.

On the back of my left leg, just above the knee, I had several tiny swellings; and further down, now that I had made myself *really* look, little lines of blue—and these were also visible on my right leg!

Oh, sweet heaven!

Young as he was, my father had apparently suffered from varicose veins which he had inherited from *his* father. (In wartime this hadn't been enough, necessarily, to keep you out of the army. Not that anyway he'd have wanted to be kept out.) And ever since my mother had first mentioned it—needlessly, perhaps even spitefully, her being well aware of my propensity to worry—the idea of that inheritance had never left me.

And now never would.

But I was sensible about it. I admired the fortitude with which I coped. I admired and was surprised by my philosophy. I was becoming quite a girl.

"Rachel, you are becoming quite a girl!"

It was just a pity there was only myself there to say it.

I shook my head a little sadly, *humorous* in even such a situation. "No, it's no good, I just can't hear *you* using any expression of that sort!"

And I laughed brightly.

In any case there was no real reason why they'd get worse. Hadn't I even heard that vitamin E, regular doses of it, could sometimes eradicate varicose veins?

Besides there were clearly ways of disguising such things: makeup or a slightly thicker denier—not *thick*, for heaven's sake, just a degree less fine. And my skirt lengths would never be above the knee. And I'd never wear a swimsuit.

"Oh, I don't know. They must have said things like that in your time. Our time? And of course you *have* been listening to Bing Crosby!"

This was ridiculous. I wasn't even in the sitting room.

Yet what better approach was there than by way of the ridiculous? The whole of life was ridiculous. Varicose veins were *incontestably* ridiculous.

And to illustrate this I did a little Charleston right then and there in my petticoat.

> "We dream about,
> We scheme about,
> We have been known to scream about,
> That certain thing
> Called the boyfriend."

Oh, what a hoot it all was! I added a final *Vo-di-o-doh*.

"Yes, I think you *could* say that you felt proud of me."

I listened for a moment.

Then I dropped him a curtsy.

"Thank you, kind sir."

I didn't *need* to be in the sitting room.

"'Life without him is quite impossible—quite devoid of all charms...'"

Oh, how you could ride anything when you were gay: not just the *big* challenges but the petty, unworthy, often sordid little things as well—like, in this instance, wanting his approbation but not wanting him actually to know the cause of my deserving it. One's blemishes weren't something one was ever keen to advertise.

Though veins, of course, had nothing to do with age. I knew of a woman who'd had an operation at only seventeen. Seventeen! Why, it could happen to a child.

I must admit it though: my body had always been something of a problem. But that's what came of having looks. They left you with expectations—even with responsibilities—and naturally with fears. Is it better never to have had, you may begin to wonder. For it could actually strike you on occasion that *body* was more important than *personality* and that having a nice shape automatically equalled being found desirable; and worked very hard to keep my nice shape. I was terrified my dainty breasts would one day start to sag.

(In London just the thought of this had sometimes been sufficient to depress me. But there are certain things you simply *cannot* quite own up to. The doctor would say: "Have you any idea what might have been the cause of this depression?" "Oh, yes, Doctor! I think my dainty breasts have now begun to sag.")

I reached for the nail polish. "*Red-Letter Day*...for that extra glow of excitement, that extra bit of colour in your life." And I certainly had that. I somehow felt no doubt that he too approved of it, this more exciting shade.

I looked up sharply; thought for a moment I had caught a glimpse of him in my dressing-table mirror and—as befitted such zaniness—wagged my finger at him, playfully. "No, *not* in the bedroom, please!"

But then it crossed my mind: And yet, why not?

This *is*, isn't it, the latter half of the twentieth century?

When my fingers were dry I started on my toes. Was that the wrong way round? Well, never mind. I was such a beginner. In all things. I would simply have to learn.

Oh, pretty feet, I said. Pretty feet. I sounded like a parrot.

Did varicose veins ever move down to your feet? Oh no! *Quite* out of the question! Definitely not permissible!

> "Stay young and beautiful;
>   It's your duty to be beautiful.
>   Stay young and beautiful...
>   If you want to be loved!"

Young and beautiful and with a Marcelle wave in your hair. No, on this occasion I might just do without that—forgive me. But how do I look? Let me pirouette! Have you considered your verdict yet? Do I look almost as if I could possibly be...just possibly...one day...(not everybody has to think me so)...*When you go dancing you look so entrancing they call you the belle of the ball*...Do I?

Well, do I?

Thank you, Roger and Celia, thank you both so much—thank you for inviting me to your son's christening. For inviting me to be his godmother. For inviting me to stand by the font and cuddle the baby and be practically the star of the whole show.

Practically its leading lady.

Practically the belle of the ball.

Oh, my! How *scary*!

33

AFTER the church service, we all went back to Celia's parents' house. Indeed, I had the place of honour, in Colonel Tiverton's own car. "Isn't he angelic?" exclaimed Mrs. Tiverton—she meant her grandson, not her husband. "And wasn't he *such* a good baby?" (Even during our five-minute journey she asked me this three times; it was as though she had no other conversation whatsoever—couldn't even comment on the lack of fashion in the front pews. She seemed a bit *perplexed*.) "And that lovely way he gurgled at the font!"

There was one slightly embarrassing moment when I was standing near her in the lounge and somebody said, "You must be feeling very proud!"

Well, *I* was holding the baby when he said it. It seemed only natural that his words were meant for me.

"Oh, I *am*," I answered—with a lot more conviction, actually, than Mrs. Tiverton herself, who was a half-second behind me and must have worked off some of her enthusiasm by telling me what a good baby he had been and what a lovely gurgler at the font.

We all laughed but I did feel a little foolish and even Mrs. Tiverton didn't look enormously amused. The only way I could fully recover my composure was by thinking in what a lively manner I'd be able to retell the incident at home, along with a few witty character sketches and a full account of what we'd eaten.

Celia's family *was* a bit stodgy. Does it seem a little rude to say so? And even Roger's wasn't a great deal better. How did someone so very much alive—and wicked—and amusing—spring out of such a thoroughly conventional background? Was he outrageous only in order to shock: I mean, to shock his and Celia's relations: retired military, stiff Civil Servants, even a rather stuffy younger generation? (It appeared almost as if they were mounting a demonstration of block solidarity... to keep outsiders out; initiated babies in.) Roger shone golden through the midst of them. His very vitality seemed almost an affront.

Perhaps, I thought, this was a takeover bid from outer space and he and I would be the world's joint saviours.

But then of course there were his friends, his and Celia's—I mustn't lump *them* in with the rest—although surprisingly they weren't quite so easy to distinguish as I'd assumed that they were going to be.

"Friend or foe?" I asked a tall and rather handsome young man whom I considered to be one of the likelier contenders. "In place of a Masonic handshake," I genially explained.

"Excuse me?"

"I mean, friend or...?" "Family," I had nearly said. Luckily at the eleventh hour I remembered my diplomacy. "Well, let me propound it to you in another way: if this were an invasion of the body snatchers would you be one of the bodies or one of the snatchers?" I laid my hand on his sleeve. At parties—well, *especially* at parties—it was always one's duty to be as entertaining as one could. "Of course, it does occur to me I'll have to examine your answer *very* carefully! For would a snatcher admit to being a snatcher? Wouldn't he try instead to palm himself off as a body?"

"Er—I'm sorry—I don't quite..."

I nodded. "It *is* rather a conundrum! Oh, what am I to do? And who is there to save me?"

"...understand," he said.

I took my hand off his sleeve. Despite his nice face and reasonable build he clearly wasn't one of *us*. "Oh, it doesn't matter. Please don't worry. Allow me to recommend one of these surprisingly tasty vol-au-vents."

He wandered off with a vague smile and a slight shake of his head (perhaps he didn't care for savouries) and I was glad that at least I hadn't put my foot in it. A moment later I was casting around for another contestant. Or did I mean—candidate?

But before I could greet one I myself was greeted.

"Good afternoon, Miss Waring. What an unexpected pleasure!"

"Why, it's...it's Mr. Wymark!" I was so pleased I had been able to recollect his name.

"I'd no idea you were related to the Allsops," he said.

"Oh, I'm not. I'm not. I'm just a friend." I tried to keep my tone casual. I laid no stress upon that final word.

"Ah...I see." He nodded amiably and—much to my relief—didn't look surprised.

"And Thomas's godmother," I added, realizing he must have missed the service. "Well, actually, I don't know if that does make me a relation of some kind. But are you...are you a member of the family?"

"No, no," he said.

"And *I* can't *really* claim relationship either!" He might have thought I was being serious.

"Then from now on, Miss Waring, you and I will always know how it feels to belong to a most seriously outnumbered minority group!"

We laughed. I felt we shouldn't have but we did. We laughed with gathering momentum. I hadn't suspected he had this naughty side to him.

"Mr. Wymark," I said, "I think you're being a touch wicked."

Now this was something a bit more like it!

"Heaven forfend," he answered, "yet *friends*, in this situation, are a little like those orphans who brag that they had to have *you* but that they really wanted *us*!"

I had heard this joke before, though it seemed to make no difference—it must have been the champagne. "Oh dear. Please don't. You'll make my mascara run."

He reassured me. "At the moment it looks most perfectly in place. In fact, may I take the liberty of saying, Miss Waring...?"

"Rachel."

"...that you look extremely nice? By far the best-dressed woman here."

"Belle of the ball, might one put it?"

"Oh, definitely."

I didn't do anything to try to hide my pleasure. I felt his compliment was extravagant but perhaps not *so* completely wide of the mark. And it was certainly a very pretty shade of green. It occurred to me that Roger should have a shirt made up in precisely this colour.

Green and gold. Gold and green. I wondered whether I stood out as strikingly as he did. Well...the best-dressed woman here! Was I at last worthy, then, to take my place beside him: saviours of the world from large-scale planetary invasion?

Damp golden curls across the chest. And running down from chest to navel. And probably beyond.

What *was* sure though...if they could only read my mind... they'd undoubtedly find me every bit as shocking. Did I too shine with expectation? With a refusal to look dulled and muted and resigned?

Oh, I hoped so. I did so hope so.

But such a deal of nonsense! What need had *I*, any longer, to take my place beside *him*? That wish would now be on the other foot. I saw him looking at me and I turned away.

Oh dear. Should I have done it? I wouldn't want him to think me coquettish. He didn't know yet about Horatio; I hadn't told him I was unavailable.

Rachel—you—are—quite—a—girl!

"Well, thank 'ee kindly, Mr. Wymark. Thank 'ee kindly, sir." I treated him to my usual graceful curtsy; then instantly decided I had better not mention *that* when I got home.

He accepted the tribute with a grin. (Yes, he was certainly well qualified to be a member of the company: the fun-group, the life-enhancers, the anti-stodge.) He said: "Well, you know—among friends—if you're Rachel I'm Mark."

"What! *Mark* Wymark! Oh, no, I can't accept that!" If I'd had my fan I would have rapped his knuckles (raps whose sweetness, *this* time, would not have been wasted on the desert air). "In future I shan't believe a single word you say!"

"But I'm afraid it's true. You've only got to ask Roger or Celia."

"No, I think you're all *co*-conspirators; I think you're all in this plot together!"

"You see, it must have been some misguided little joke on the part of my parents. Silly people! Or perhaps they—just—never noticed!"

My mascara was in jeopardy again.

"But have you never asked them?"

"And if you like I'll tell you something else they say about friends! They're God's way of recompensing you." He paused. "For families."

I said, "I wish I'd known that you were like this on the day we first met! We'd have had a so much jollier time."

"I wish I'd known that *you* were like this!"

"You wouldn't come for coffee."

"That can only be a source of immeasurable regret."

He was a clown. He had a charming personality. He hadn't the looks of either Roger or Horatio but he was certainly a clown.

"Did you know," I asked, "that Petula Clark got a fifteen-minute ovation last month for *The Sound of Music*?"

"Really? I shouldn't have thought that she could spare the time. After all, she's *already* a bit long in the tooth for it, isn't she?"

He was a gem.

"I say, you must let us in on some of this merriment! We've been dying to know what's going on." Family.

"Oh," I cried gaily, "just a series of absurd but entertaining jests. Little things please little minds. You must know what I mean."

"Such fun!"

"Godmother's Follies," I explained.

Obviously the eyes of the whole room had been upon us.

"*Not* Grandmother's Footsteps," I hurriedly pointed out—having suddenly realized that I could conceivably have been misheard. "Grandmothers are sweet doddery old things. Whereas godmothers..."

Briefly I thought about it.

"Godmothers can still be full of Eastern promise!"

But unfortunately Mark Wymark had now been taken over. (By the body snatchers!) I later caught his eye and he raised his hand in salutation from a group across the room just as Mrs. Tiverton, a most conscientious hostess, was purposefully approaching me once more. I'm afraid I got the giggles.

It was no reflection on my godson. He was indeed a remarkably good baby—and had continued to be so throughout the party.

But..."*Mark* Wymark," I said to her. "Can we permit ourselves to be so taken in? Shouldn't we start a ladies-not-for-the-fooling-of society? With you, dear Mrs. Tiverton, as our duly elected Member?" (I had thought she would be flattered.)

"Pardon?"

"Or do I mean...chairwoman? You see, I've even had letters from him; oh, two or three times—chiefly, though, before I came to Bristol—so wouldn't you think I might have noticed? Yet possibly he never signed his Christian name, only its initial. Yes, I feel satisfied by that."

"Oh! I think I can see my husband trying to attract my attention," she said.

"The mark of Zorro!" I replied. "The mark of Wymart!" That was an American superstore I'd heard about; but my good hostess, apparently, knew neither solicitor nor superstore.

I was probably confusing her. Afterwards I learned that the place was actually called Walmart.

Oh, well!

34

AND THEN something rather awful happened. It had all been so extremely nice, with Roger and Celia so charming, so very pleased to have me there.

Yet—suddenly—it all just sort of fizzled out.

Up in the air one minute; nose-diving the next.

Roger came over to me and put his arm around my shoulders (I was bad: I *still* felt the electricity zooming straight through me) and said, "Well, Rachel, it's been great!" Then, with appealing timidity, as if almost seeking reassurance: "It has been, hasn't it?"

"No other word for it," I answered happily.

"Thank you for making it so swell."

All these Americanisms!

"Swell?"

"Yes—swell."

I joyously concurred.

"Celia and I are awfully grateful. And so's young Thomas of course."

"And so he should be. I shall expect nothing but gratitude for the next half-century."

"Fine. A deal. Look—what I wanted to say—is it all right if my father-in-law sees you home? Celia would quite like to get back to the flat—after all this excitement, you know—to have young master into his jimjams and into bed."

"Yes, *naturally* that's all right. It's very kind of Colonel Tiverton."

"Good. Well, then..."

I imagined this was all for show. I expected him to add a lot less audibly that they would pick me up a little later. Or else give me directions on how to get there. I waited to be told of the arrangements.

Instead he leaned forward and kissed me on the cheek. (Now there wasn't quite the same high voltage.) Celia, who had come up just then with Tommy in her arms, also kissed my cheek. She held up my godchild, warmly squirming and reluctant, to administer something of the same treatment. But that was all. It was over. No mention of a knees-up.

And I had no right to complain, naturally—none whatsoever. After all, I'd had a very lovely time.

Yet even so.

That was the part I'd most been looking forward to. This afternoon, I'd thought, had been merely the warm-up. The prelude.

"See you," he'd said.

"We promise to be in touch *very* soon," Celia had added.

No chance, then, even to give the little invitation I myself had been planning. In the car with Colonel Tiverton I felt a trifle flat.

But I'd seen Roger again just before we left. He had waved to me with a broad smile and a bit of jolly clowning and not the slightest idea in the whole world that anything could possibly be wrong.

Well then, I reasoned, when we were about half the way home, a poor memory in one's friends was definitely an inconvenience but not something one could truly blame them for—not with any real conviction, let alone resentment. And they certainly *had* provided me with a brilliant afternoon and an opportunity to shine.

"Young Thomas is a grand old chap," said Colonel Tiverton. "Wouldn't you agree?"

Something else that surprised me though: why had Mark Wymark thought I might be related to the Allsops? Could he have forgotten that *he* was the one who had given me Roger's address? "A friend of mine...an undergraduate. Name of Allsop." And had Roger never told him I'd be at the party; or that I was going to be the baby's godmother? No, patently he hadn't—"What an unexpected pleasure," Mark had said.

Well, just talk about people having poor memories! And such very young people at that! Clearly they were both as bad as one another.

35

AND, AFTER all, it was good to be home.

It really was.

I flopped down in my usual armchair. I kicked off both my shoes. Displayed my newly painted nails—hardly visible, however, beneath the reinforced stocking tips. I wriggled all my toes.

"Yes, be it ever so humble," I said.

I frowned—though not with impatience, obviously. Merely with surprise.

"Oh, surely you know it? 'Be it ever so humble there's no place like home.'" And then I realized my mistake. "Oh, I'm a fool! That's only nineteenth-century, isn't it? My father used to love those sentimental ballads. I think I can remember him singing it!"

I smiled nostalgically. I felt utterly relaxed.

Indeed, the sense of anti-climax after the party, succeeded now by this feeling of tranquillity at home, had made me rather drowsy. I yawned, my hand across my mouth. "Oh, do excuse me." I began to sing.

> "Flow gently, sweet Afton, among thy green braes,
>   Flow gently, I'll sing thee a song in thy praise.
>   My Mary's asleep by the murmuring stream,
>   Flow gently, sweet Afton, disturb not her dream."

I went on: "Oh, isn't it strange? I'd have said I didn't know a single word of that, apart from its title."

My Mary's asleep by the murmuring stream . . .

"Doesn't that sound just so tender and protective; so considerate and trustworthy?"

I smiled. "But on the whole you can't really trust people, can you? Not deep down. Not in small things. I suppose the truth is—we're all thinking more of ourselves than of anybody else."

In saying that, I surprised myself a little—in fact, may have surprised myself more than I did him. "No, I don't want..." I gave another yawn.

"I suppose your Rachel's half asleep as well. That's why she's burbling on like this. 'O, my love is like a red red rose, that's newly sprung in June...'

"No, I really have no wish to grow cynical. And, anyway, when people are married and they have each other it may be rather different. I mean, a *good* marriage. Presumably they really do care— the death of one could almost be the death of both. They lie at night locked in each other's arms, entangled in each other's legs, heartbeat close to heartbeat, and they tell each other how passionately they care. And sometimes—frequently—it must be true. How lovely to be loved!"

I looked up at him wistfully. I remembered Roger's tiny but amazing revelation of his need for reassurance. I seemed to get a nod.

"And also parents care for their children, don't they? I mean again, good ones, a mother like yours, a father like mine...

"But apart from children...and people in love...and sometimes, I suppose, a sibling or a parent...I'm rambling, aren't I? Am I making any sense?

"I was in love once. Yes. He told me I reminded him of Vivien Leigh. Oh, you won't know Vivien Leigh. She was an actress. An extremely pretty one. Next time I go to the library I'll look for a book that has a photograph. She..."

———

At breakfast, surprisingly, my mother wasn't cross that I'd got in so late the night before. She hardly questioned me as to what we'd done. Instead she informed me that my grandfather was ill—she'd had a call from my grandfather's housekeeper who'd been speaking from a phone box—and that we'd be leaving for Winchester that very morning.

"But I can't!" I was aghast. "I've got my exams in another month."

"You can study there just as well as here," my mother said. "We shan't be gone for longer than a week and you can telephone the college before we leave."

"But can't I stay here, Mother? Wouldn't it be simpler? Besides—who's going to water the plants?"

He'd said he would telephone me that night from Scotland.

"Mrs. Fowler will water them. And if I really thought, Rachel, that either the plants or even your examination results meant more to you than your own grandfather, who is clearly dying..."

And Tony himself wasn't even on the telephone at home; and if he had been it wouldn't have done me any good. He was already on his way to Edinburgh and none of his family would have known where he was putting up—he'd never been to Edinburgh before. And his firm was called Smith & Son and other than its being in London I had no idea of its location. I just couldn't reach him.

"It isn't that," I said, "but I'm expecting this very important phone call, you see, and—"

"Oh, from Mr. Heart-Throb?" Her tone was unexpectedly sympathetic. I felt a moment's hope.

I nodded.

"Well, look, darling, so much the better. It's *fatal* always to be just sitting by the telephone and waiting—take it from somebody who knows!" (For a moment I was sidetracked: I wondered how she knew.) "If you seriously want to hook him you've got to let him have a few anxious moments. Play a little hard to get. That's the thing which always brings them running."

It was funny she should have said this. I certainly hadn't mentioned my fear that I might be too openly showing him my heart;

I'd scarcely mentioned his name in her presence. (To anyone else who would listen, or even on my own, I must have spoken it on average twenty times an hour.) And an enforced absence was assuredly the one thing that would enable me to keep him guessing. If I stayed in London I shouldn't have the strength.

It would only be a week.

And I could write to him.

"Of *course* you can write to him. Though I'd suggest you leave it for a day or two."

But Grandfather seemed no worse than usual. He'd been bedridden now for several years and he'd always been hypochondriacal; even Mother said so. Indeed, I almost suspected that our abrupt summons had been nothing but a ploy on the part of Miss Wilkinson to get herself some help. Yet when I said as much to my mother she only answered, tiredly, "Look, write your letter to the boyfriend and I'll go out and post it for you. I could definitely do with the air."

The week turned into a fortnight. When I hadn't heard from him after ten days, ten days of hope and disappointment and living on my nerves, which had put *me* into bed as well as my grandfather, she recommended that I write again. She was really rather sweet. "After all, it's just possible it could have gone astray. Letters do, you know. Why not suggest he come to see you here? Tell him you've been ill."

In the end we stayed in Winchester for three months. I didn't even take my exams: typing and shorthand and business management seemed completely unimportant to me now—in fact they always had—both to me and, less foreseeably, to my mother. Grandfather recovered; or at any rate appeared to. "Dying?" repeated the doctor when I met him one day in the town. "That wily old fox? He could live another fifteen years! Longer!"

"That isn't what he said three months ago," Miss Wilkinson

later protested. "Oh, dear me, no. No, not at all." It was a strange look that I intercepted between her and my mother.

And I seemed to recover, too, after a fashion. But I had certainly lost that sparkle which had made me *almost* pretty.

I met Tony just once more—within a week of our return to London. By then he was unofficially engaged: to the schoolfriend at whose party we had met.

Letters? No. He hadn't received any letters. He said he'd tried to get hold of me each evening for a week; had eventually been informed by a plant-watering neighbour that we'd gone away for the remainder of the summer, were moving from place to place on the Continent—she'd no idea where. In the end he'd had to tell himself I wasn't interested. Despite appearances. I was probably having *far* too good a time of it in Italy and Greece. Never trust a woman, he'd added with a smile.

It didn't matter now of course but the only other person to whom I'd written from Winchester had been that same schoolfriend, Arabella. I knew *her* letter hadn't gone astray because I'd received an answering short scribble addressed to the flat for some reason but sent on—with all our other mail—by Mrs. Fowler.

———

Many girls, naturally, would have got themselves a job, left home and had a life of their own. During those early years there wasn't a day when I didn't consider it. But what could I do? I was unqualified, had no experience, had no inclination to return to college. As a shop assistant I *might* have earned £6 a week—hardly enough to make me independent. Besides, I *wasn't* independent. I lacked both character and know-how and had always been unusually timid. Frightened of the unknown. Frightened of the jungle that grew outside our door.

But, blessedly, coupled with the fear there had at least been the hardenings of a discontent, which would later hone themselves into a sharp-edged desperation and help me hack my way through.

Yes, a sharp-edged desperation and a sudden resurgence of the will to survive... plus, of course, the letters.

For at that time, post-Winchester and post-Tony, I had believed I might always be frightened; and of course, basically, I suppose one nearly always is—there are degrees of trepidation. So I stayed with my mother. And she and I experienced a mainly joyless and destructive relationship of hopeless interdependence. God knows why she needed me: she was perfectly capable *then* of sweeping her own floors and making her own bed; of seeing to her own washing and shopping and cooking. (And I'm not suggesting that it *all* devolved on me; until the last year or so we used to share it more or less.) Perhaps she had some prescience of the incapacity to come—she had never been strong and oh how my father would have pampered her!—or perhaps it was simply a question of *anyone*'s company being better than none. (We often went to the cinema, occasionally to the theatre; I daresay it wasn't all gloom—we generally made conversation.) But more dominant even than her need for a companion or a nurse or a servant, so I believe now, must have been her need for power. She had to have her daughter to manipulate.

And I—for all of my envying looks towards the outside, my reading of advertisements, my reading of romance, my secret play-acting ("I'll tell you what I want. Magic! Yes, yes, magic! I try to give that to people. I misrepresent things to them. I don't tell the truth. I tell what *ought* to be truth. And if that is sinful, then let me be damned for it!")—*I*, for all of my obstinate resistance to it, ostensibly obstinate resistance to it, must have needed to be manipulated.

Until it became too much and—if the desperation hadn't finally kicked in—might well have led to madness.

Perhaps already had!

So it was a bleak kind of life we led together throughout my supposedly best years. A perpetual petty seeking for retaliation. Almost a game.

But in the end it was I who had the higher score. The verdict was a simple one of Misadventure.

Lucretia was the daughter of Lucretia.

The day before her death I discovered the letters. I don't know why she'd kept them. Had she wanted to gloat at me; intending, eventually, to tell me something from beyond the grave?

The first letter was the one which really rocked me and hurt me and released the tears.

My dearest Tony,

Were you thinking I'd deserted you? I hope you didn't ring and ring and stay awake all night. Or, rather, perhaps I hope you did, a little! I've hardly slept a wink for worrying about you and picturing all the uncertainty you must be going through. "You walked into my lonely world, what peace of mind your smile unfurled!"—recognize it? The rest of it is just as true: "My love is ever you, my love, now and forever you, my love..."

Talking of love, don't laugh at me, my darling, but I'm so very glad I kept your handkerchief. I keep it under my pillow at night and bury my face in it a dozen times a day, thinking exuberantly that your nose has been exactly where mine is—well, I don't know too much about the laws of chance and probability but I imagine that at some time it must have been, don't you?—I sort of work my way from end to end. Also, of course, the other night this precious handkerchief absorbed your love (perhaps "absorbed" isn't entirely the right word—poetic licence!) and I really felt so loath to wash it. (I did wash it though!)

I keep remembering the way that your hands just went wandering all over me—so possessive, so proprietorial; upstairs, downstairs, in my lady's...whoops! I can't wait until I feel those naughty scampering fingertips again! Or perhaps I shouldn't say that—am I being too forward? But we don't want ever to have to hide our true thoughts and feelings, do we? No matter how intimate? Except for one or two little white lies we're only ever going to tell each other the truth.

And as an earnest of my good faith...it doesn't worry you, does it, that you're just a degree younger than I am?— only a year and a half, nothing much, hardly worth the mention. (That little joystick of yours certainly didn't seem to be too worried about it!) And, in any case, just through knowing you I shall probably grow younger by the day! You'll have to watch out—they'll say, "Who was that child I saw you with last night?"! I'm so happy by the way that that was the first film we happened to see together, aren't you? I'm sure it must have been meant. Symbolic! Thank heavens it wasn't *Gone with the Wind*!

This is, of course, the first love letter I've ever written. Just fancy! I'm enjoying it so much. (It almost makes our separation seem worthwhile! Almost, I said!) But now I suppose I'd better get down to some rather boring facts for the time being and tell you exactly why I couldn't be at home when you rang—has it been a little naughty of me, all this while, to keep you in suspense? My most heartfelt apologies, good sir! And how I wish my silly old granddad had a silly old telephone down here...

I couldn't bear to read it all; there were more than a dozen sides. Towards the end I simply skimmed. Some of the words were badly smudged—most likely my Biro had been running out. A comma, for instance, had smeared across three lines; one full stop looked like the hangman's noose. I imagine I just hadn't cared. I imagine I'd been feeling much too pleased with myself, with life, to fret over anything so pitifully mundane.

———

I told Horatio all of it; *all* of it; though in a funny way I had the feeling he already knew.

And understood.

After I had made myself a sandwich we finished with some more songs.

> "Gin a body meet a body
> Coming through the rye;
> Gin a body kiss a body,
> Need a body cry?"

I said, "I once read the book of that. I liked it but I couldn't quite—not quite—see what the fuss was all about. Not like when I first set eyes on James Dean... in one of his films, I mean. Now *that* was an entirely different affair. And it didn't even happen— would you believe this?—until about a year after his death!"

At first I could have bitten my tongue off. And then I thought: But why? Just be natural. People aren't so easily hurt as you'd imagine.

(I smiled... Except, perhaps, by vicars and by chemists.)

I felt like singing him a song of my own choice.

> "After the ball is over,
> After the break of day..."

Nothing strident or bouncy or out of keeping with our mood —even something a little melancholy: a lament for lost innocence and artlessness and for the fragile, gossamer, everyday little hopes that people carry with them throughout the early part of their life. Maybe through every part of their life.

"Many the lie that was spoken,
　　If you could count them all;
　　Many the heart that lies broken ...
After the ball."

And as I sang I danced ... to that sad and wistful, dreamily
haunting little tune ... and while I did so I was very much aware
of the presence of Aunt Alicia—and Bridget—and Miss Havisham—and Sylvia: poor disappointed ladies all who had each in
one fashion or another been left waiting at the church, waiting at
the church, waiting at the church ... I could have cried for them;
my heart was overflowing. Because there, I knew only too well,
there but for the grace of God ... the most wondrous and bounte-
ous grace of God ...

"Oh, the days of the Kerry dancing;
　　Oh, the call of the piper's tune ..."

It was a gentle, pleasant, homespun evening; comforting, companionable, snug.

Better far than any knees-up.

36

THAT NIGHT I dreamt that I killed Celia. Like my dream of many years before, the one involving my father's repressed dissatisfaction, it should have been a nightmare but instead it was something I didn't want to wake up from. I stood with her on the suspension bridge and pointed to the beautiful reflection of a star upon the water. And then as she leant over...

I watched her plummet and waited till she'd gone down for the third time. ("Un—deux—*trois!*") Then I straightened my shoulders, briskly brought my hands together as if—no, not to clap—simply to indicate a job well done and an obstacle disposed of. I pulled the collar of my ermine cape more snugly round my neck and strolled back to the carriage in which Tommy sat waiting patiently to take me to the palace. He said not a word but he gave me a nod and a reassuring smile (I knew it wasn't wind) and then he drove me hell-for-leather through the starry night.

In my ball gown and glass slippers I ran up six flights of marble stairs. Both the stairs and the ballroom were open to the sky, although many chandeliers hung blazing in the void and at each corner there was a Corinthian column, presumably intended to support a roof. The dance floor was deserted.

But almost immediately a solitary resplendent figure emerged from the outer darkness of—perhaps—a terrace and came towards me with his arms outstretched. As we joyously reached one another the cape slipped from my shoulders and he gathered me into his embrace and kissed my waiting lips, tenderly yet passionately and long. Then we swayed together, almost as a single organism, to the most lovely lilting waltz you ever heard. But the words inside my head weren't quite in triple time: "If you want to be a big success here's the way to instant happiness: stay young and beautiful if you want to be loved . . ." He said, "Oh, my darling. Tomorrow, the coronation . . ."

I said, "Roger, I knew perfectly well who you were; you didn't have to give me that hint. You're the Crown Prince Rudolf."

"And you, my own beloved Flavia!"

Next minute we sat together in our coach—it was daylight—regally acknowledging the cheering of the crowds; I with a dignified uplifting of the hand, Roger (or Rudolf) merely with a gracious inclination of the head, which conveniently if rather wickedly allowed *his* hands to set out on a right royal progress of their own. More of a walkabout really.

"Darling," I said gently, "I don't think that you should. Not here. Not in the coach."

"Give me one good reason why."

His head continued its solemn nods; my hand its gracious waves.

"Oh, that's unfair," I answered. "You know of course I can't." I smiled. "All right. I've always been like putty in your hands."

Well, as I say, it was very far from being a nightmare: the bells ringing, the populace cheering, the Archbishop waving us Godspeed from the cathedral steps—and all the while those merrily cavorting fingers . . . oh mmm, just there, oh *yes*, that's it . . .

Even when the coachman turned round to reveal the smiling face of Celia it was still all right. "Don't worry," she said. "Horatio stepped in at the last minute and wouldn't let you do it. You only *dreamt* that bit about my fall."

"Oh, Celia, I'm so glad. Such *very* welcome news! But all the same, dear, if you can, please try to keep your eyes to the *front*!"

Celia laughed. "Oh, darling, what a rascally old daddy you have!"—for one of the footmen turned out to be Thomas, a little older than the night before. "So it's probably just as well, isn't it, that nowadays Flavia can truly be thought of as one of the family?"

Horatio, it transpired, was there as well. He was always there when needed. I nodded at him with sweetly serious gratitude. (I was still nodding at everyone when I remembered.) "Thank you," I mouthed. "Thank you for stopping me. I'm so relieved you did."

And yet he shook his head.

"Rachel, it really had nothing to do with me. It was you who made the ultimate decision."

"You see?" crowed Celia. (I suppose she considered that—as a person who had so very nearly plummeted—she might have had *some* right to pontificate.) "In the last resort you are always alone!"

"What nonsense," I cried. I looked quickly at Horatio. "*We* know better than that, don't we, my darling?"

His answering look was full of confirmation. Sometimes, I find, there are few things more sexually arousing than pure unadorned kindness. Both Rudolf and Celia looked on in outright jealousy.

***

I've said I wasn't intending to hurry through my book and I meant it. But in the May of 1781 Horatio attained his majority and although I wasn't anxious to hasten the death of his poor father it must be admitted I *was* rather looking forward to the time when he and his mother and Nancy should arrive in Bristol. For despite the fact that much of the next twelve years would inevitably be spent away from home—and generally in London—the first period of his life with which I was so happily dealing, indeed almost two-thirds of his entire allotment, still represented little more than just a prologue to the main events. And the bright mid-September day on which the small family was eventually to move into *this* very residence, No 12 Rodney Street, then a recently built dwelling in a recently developed area, was the day on which I believed the true story was about to start.

By then he was a grown man, of course, with a lithe and well-formed figure and an altogether striking appearance.

Exactly ten days after my coach ride, at about nine o'clock on the evening of Wednesday 16th September, just as I was thinking of going downstairs to watch the news (dear Mr. Morley, art thou listening down below?), I had a fine opportunity to judge something of this from my own firsthand observation. He was standing at the mantelpiece.

I knew he must have stood there on countless other occasions but now I realized that by standing beneath his own portrait he was probably making some subtle reference to the Ouspensky theory of time; I can't pretend I understood it. He had his back towards me and—just the way I'd always pictured him—was gazing pensively into the flames. Luckily I'd had the chimney swept a few days earlier and since then had lit a fire up here each evening.

I wanted to get up and touch him. I wasn't sure I dared.

Then I must have glanced away an instant, without realizing I did so. For when I was next conscious of looking at him he still stood there in the same position. But now he was naked.

It might have been shocking; somehow it wasn't. As I had known he would, he had a lovely muscular back—broad shoulders tapering to a narrow waist—a dancer's buttocks; strong and graceful legs. Such handsome feet. I'd also been correct about his hair...because obviously he wore no wig. It was dark brown, almost black—and short—with a natural healthy sheen. His skin looked healthy too; Roger's by comparison might have seemed a fraction over-tanned. And I so much wanted to touch him.

I was suddenly aware of his eyes in the portrait: you know how it is when you feel you're the focus of somebody's attention—you immediately glance up. There was no hint of embarrassment. Nor even of amusement. I wouldn't have wanted either. But was there—yes?—a look of somehow even greater attachment?

I felt that anyway he always watched over me and protectively followed my every move. Yet was there now something marginally more pronounced about the quality of his concern? Marginally more profound?

While I met his look unwaveringly—unsmilingly as well yet with a smile about to burgeon—his other self disappeared. But that was unimportant. I understood it would come back; I mean, that *he* would come back. (In fact I knew he hadn't even gone, not essentially.) And the eyes continued to express at least the same degree of tenderness.

37

SUDDENLY... I became so good. I had something to live up to and I realized that my actions inside the house were no more important than my actions out of it. He could see me everywhere, knew just what I was up to. I distributed largesse. I did the one thing I reckoned he would want especially: I helped the poor. I was down to my last twelve hundred at the bank but even this didn't worry me: a little here, a little there: I felt convinced that in some way he'd provide. It was as though he'd actually told me that the more I gave the more I would receive.

But it wasn't only money that I gave. I gave away my time as well: writing time, probably the hardest kind. I talked to old ladies in the street and, more importantly, I listened. I suffered fools gladly. Sometimes I carried their shopping for them or helped them onto buses. I had no fear. To think *now* about my nervousness as a younger woman could frequently amaze me. I would rush into any situation without a shred of inhibition. When a man fell off his motorcycle I was the first to be beside him, administering first aid and comfort—similarly when some poor woman had an epileptic fit. Indeed, I almost welcomed all such incidents.

I travelled specially—and often—into poorer areas of the city, with twenty or more pound notes folded neatly in my purse, each carefully separate. And marvellously I seemed to attract people who said, "Excuse me, lady, any chance you got the price of a cuppa?" and I felt so glad. It made no difference even when I suspected it was more the price of a pinta they might be hoping for; I had little patience with anyone who said never give money to an alcoholic, they'll only drink it—weren't they as entitled as the rest of us to their brief moments of escapade and flight? I practically advertised for hard luck stories and from the young just as much as the old—from students in snack bars, or dropouts and drifters, just as much as from hoboes lounging on benches by the cathedral or from tired housewives standing at their own front doors. The employment exchange made a first-class venue. Likewise the social security office.

Oh, people often gazed at me quite strangely but I didn't care. I didn't give a hoot. I always tried to look my best, my motives were only of the highest, I had no cause to feel ashamed. So let them gaze; a cat may look at a queen. I always stepped out with my head held high, with my prettiest laugh and my most radiant smile, whenever I believed I was the object of attention. They could only have admired me.

And felt envy.

Not that I wanted that. (Oh, of course I wanted that but I was always trying my damnedest not to.)

And of course, too, my writing did suffer; but even that was unimportant. (Well, arguably.) Horatio was a man now—he was twenty-one—why should there be any rush? (In fact there was every reason why there shouldn't be.) I had the strongest feeling I was standing on the brink of something, heaven knew what. I only knew it must be something good.

38

I MADE an appointment to see Mark Wymark. "This *is* nice," he said, as he walked into the waiting room. "Come to invite me to that cup of coffee?"

"Yes. But first there's something slightly less important. I've come to make my will."

We went through to his office. "Then you haven't already got one?"

I shook my head.

"In that case very wise," he remarked, "even though it won't be needed for another fifty years."

"You have a crystal ball?"

"The best in the business."

It was a happy occasion. No, of course it would have been that, anyway—I mean, it was a lighthearted one. "In the past," I said, "I've never had anyone to whom I wished to leave my millions!" At one time, it was true, I'd vaguely thought about Sylvia, although there wasn't any reason at all why Sylvia should outlive me—*I*'d never been a smoker! "It wouldn't have worried me too much whatever happened. A charity—a dogs' home—even the government." I shrugged.

"That's what I—"

"That's what you what?"

"That's what I call sad. It sounds really sad."

"Does it? I suppose it does. But that was in the past; and now it's like my past was lived out by a total stranger. Does that seem odd?"

"Not in the least. It only means you've changed."

"Yes! I've come into my own. It's the reverse of sad."

"Now, *that* sounds absolutely splendid! Although I'm not sure what it means."

"Nor am I." We both laughed.

"And whom are you going to leave it all to now?" As he spoke he was looking out the appropriate documents. "Apart from me, obviously?"

"Well, in fact you may have to forget about all those millions I've just mentioned. I'm afraid there mightn't be *any* money to leave. Not unless I hit the jackpot. There may be just the house and its contents. And if we're really going to have to wait another fifty years . . . then even you may have trouble making it up to the top floor!"

That was a rather pretty compliment, I thought, but he hardly seemed to notice. "No money?" he repeated.

"Not a bean!" I replied happily. "Not at the rate at which I'm currently spending it!"

He also smiled, though *his* smile seemed less spontaneous than mine. "Still more improvements to the house?"

"Oh, you materialist," I chided. "Man cannot live on bread alone! Nor on bricks and mortar." I wagged my finger. "Mr. Wymark, you must try to raise your mind above such very worldly considerations. Lord Jesus will provide!"

"That's kind of him," he said. But on this occasion he somehow failed to hit the right note. His eyes weren't in accordance with his comment.

Or perhaps I was mistaken? He now acknowledged the compliment I had paid him.

"In any case," he said, "difficulty with the stairs . . . what a feeble excuse for ruling *me* out! Who do you know, then, who *won't* be having difficulty with the stairs in fifty years' time, who'll still be bounding up them with a roistering cry?"

I hesitated for about ten seconds, wanting to prolong this most truly fulfilling moment.

"Shall I tell you whom?"

"Please."

"Can't you guess?"

"I haven't a clue."

"Then . . . very well! My godson Thomas."

But I think he *had* guessed. He showed not the slightest hint of surprise.

However, he leaned back in his chair and regarded me approvingly.

"That's a nice thing to do, Rachel."

"Nice? I'd say it's natural."

He shook his head and smiled at me with all the charm he'd practised at the party. "Do you know what they're going to write on your tombstone, Miss Waring? In some fifty years' time?"

"Just so long as it isn't 'Good!'"

On the other hand, I reflected, I wouldn't mind that—provided they put no exclamation mark.

"No, far from it," he said. "Something like: 'She was a true lady.'"

"I'd rather they wrote: 'She was resilient. And she looked about her.'"

"All right," he said. "I'll make a note." And he pretended to do so.

How pleasant it was to be sitting here by his window, with the sunshine pouring through, and to be putting the world to rights like this; to be discussing eternal verities. I didn't yet take it for granted—my feeling so thoroughly at home in every new set of circumstances. I didn't wish to, either.

"Do the Allsops know of your intentions?"

"Not yet. I'm planning a sort of Mad Hatter's tea party. I may announce my intentions at that."

"Mm. Sounds fun."

"Not sad any longer?"

"Definitely not sad."

"Perhaps you'd like to join us?"

"Yes, please."

"Well—we'll see. I may have second thoughts. It may have to be another time." I laughed at his mock disappointment. "Did you know there's an old superstition that crocodiles weep while luring and devouring their prey?"

"And I believe it to this very day!" he told me solemnly. "Spiders as well."

This *was* a jolly conversation. But suddenly he glanced at his watch—a little ostentatiously, I thought. (Perhaps he was proud of his wrists. He did have fairly nice wrists as it happened. Clean-cut.)

"Now then," he said, "reluctant though I am to be so dull... Back to business, Miss Smith!"

"We were talking of my party."

"Yes, I know, but—"

"My big surprise party! Or do you think it would be better *not* to break it to them? It's such a very lovely house, isn't it? Perhaps even the *nicest* people might start to get a bit impatient. Start ticking off the days..."

"What!" he exclaimed. "Roger and Celia?"

"No, you're right, of course. Oh dear." I gave a little chirrup. "Please don't tell them that I said it!"

39

AND I DID break the news to them. Naturally. When you've got a wonderful gift to make—indeed the best, materially, that lies within your power—and to someone whom you more than like...When you stay awake at night anticipating his pleasure and thinking how deeply, how *permanently*, it's going to affect his whole attitude towards you, his whole already warm attitude... When you've always so much wanted to be a part of almost any loving family but never thought to find one *quite* so magical as this...When, finally, following a lifetime of generally forced and fruitless communication, you now feel drawn towards a way of holding nothing back...Well, then it's well-nigh irresistible, the mounting urge there is to tell.

Maybe I could have resisted it. I could have gone on hugging myself with the knowledge of the joy they'd get when I was dead.

"If only we had known!"

"Life's going to be so bare without her!"

"Oh, when you think of all the time we had her with us and of all the opportunities we wasted...!"

"Where has the enchantment gone...?"

Oh, yes, I thought. Some firm assurance that I'd be present at my own funeral, perhaps as a gaily-coloured butterfly fluttering prettily around the graveside—maybe *that* would have been enough not only to encourage me to keep quiet for the time being but even to make me consider...!

No, that was just a pleasantry. (I do believe in pleasantries.)

What, an early death—when nowadays there was so very much to live for!

But on the other hand how *agonizing* if you were truly able to hear the nice things people said about you at your funeral. To hear them while being well aware they weren't justified and knowing that if you could only have heard them in advance you'd have done your utmost to make sure they were. One of the first real intimations of hell?

Anyway, thinking about it, if I were honestly going to participate in my own funeral I'd have no wish to be dependent on just the impact of surprise legacies.

(Besides, I wondered if the will would even have been read by then. And the bond of silence between solicitor and client was surely as binding as that between doctor and patient, priest and penitent, and few of us would want to go round canvassing on doorsteps: "Oh yes, just take it from *me*! I can't exactly be specific about this and I most certainly wouldn't want to start blowing my own trumpet but all the same...!")

Oh no! How soul-destroying!

So I told them.

Roger and Celia.

Of course I did.

I'd invited them to dinner, not merely tea. It was to be a very special evening. And Thomas was to be there, safely asleep in his carrycot, not left at home with some stupid or indifferent babysitter. (And I'm certainly not alluding here to Mrs. Tiverton, who wasn't—no, not by any means—indifferent!) It wouldn't have seemed right for *him* to be excluded.

Next in line to the throne? Or at any rate to the succession? I felt unhappy even about excluding Mark Wymark but to exclude *Thomas*...

I bought caviar and duck and we had *sauce à l'orange* and green salad and homemade meringues and ice cream. I bought two bottles of wine and a magnum of champagne. (I already had some sherry in the house and an ancient bottle of liqueur.) Yes, I *had* been cocking a snook at Mr. Fitzroy: telling him, in my own small way, that heaven would provide—would provide abundantly. And that very afternoon, in fact, I had written him a note on more or less this subject.

Dear Mr. Fitzroy,

Thank you for all your recent letters and for your obvious eagerness to stay in touch. Appreciated! But please don't worry about my overdraft; that really isn't important and if you're in the mood you can always send me a postcard when you go on holiday. But I don't feel easy about your frittering away the bank's resources: stationery and postage stamps aren't free, you know! Besides—unless Horatio reads me the riot act or I'm feeling a soupçon skittish—I always toss away your envelopes unopened.

But you mustn't repine, dear sir. I remain your obedient servant and I promise you I won't forget.

And, indeed, hoping this will find you—as it leaves me—in the pink.

Yours sincerely,
R. Waring

Self-evidently I had known that my farewell wish was a smidgen over the top but somehow I hadn't been able to resist it. I had always wanted to write to my bank manager—*all* of my bank managers—in just such an appropriate vein. But as a refinement I had lightly crossed out "pink" and substituted "red"—although I hadn't really meant that: I bore the poor fellow no malice and felt sure he would appreciate the joke.

But what I *did* mean, of course, was my carefully considered postscript. I hoped he would work hard at that, God willing, and be encouraged to shake his sieve—yes, like the real forty-niner I felt sure he was at heart—to extract its precious nugget of pure gold.

"Oh, you beautiful doll, you great big beautiful doll..."

I had only set my initials to that, however, and afterwards fretted he might simply dismiss it without paying it due attention. I might have to telephone him.

Let me put my arms around you. I'm so very glad I found you...

Anyway. *Anyway!* Returning to the dinner table...

I had decided I would hold back my announcement until we were eating our dessert. Roger had opened the champagne—and how we'd all laughed while we were hunting for the cork. "Finders keepers!" we had cried, competitively.

"Losers weepers!" I had thought—unavoidably—but it didn't seem quite suitable to mention that.

It was Roger of course who found the cork.

We had all sat down again. "I shall take this home and treasure it!" he said. "Darling, shall we put it in the place of honour on the mantelpiece—on a little stand with an inscription?"

Celia laughed. "I think we ought to give it to Rachel. She wanted it too."

"She doesn't need it as a memory of her own loveliness."

"Oh! Oh! Oh!" I raised my hands. "I don't think *you* had better have champagne!"

I could feel my cheeks burning.

"Nor as a memory of a meal which—I honestly believe—has been the most sumptuous I have ever eaten," he continued unashamedly.

"It *is* only the wine, Celia. He really doesn't mean it."

"Oh, that's all right," she answered with a smile. "Cooking was never one of my major strengths. You'll see what I mean when you finally come to visit. I don't enjoy it very much."

But Roger ignored the pair of us. "My one regret," he said, "is that we're not all wearing evening dress."

Possibly that was my own one regret. I'd been tempted—oh, how I'd been tempted!—while I was out spending all that money, while I was still in the mood for one last extravagant fling; one last *ridiculously* extravagant fling...

Perversely Roger wasn't even in a suit and tie. He was wearing jeans with an open-neck shirt and sweater. "You see, I've taken you at your word," he had said when they'd arrived. "Tonight I'm at my most relaxed."

And I'd replied: "You feel you don't have to impress me any more?"

"*Exactly*!"

Now he said, "But if only we had known...!" (Ha!)

Well, at least Celia wasn't wearing jeans and—like myself—looked a lot more *comme il faut*. "I must say, Rachel, you always do everything so beautifully. I take my hat off to you!"

"Is it a pretty one? Be careful if it is. I shall probably want to keep it."

"And I *do* like this very sweet custom of yours of the extra place-setting. The unexpected guest. It's almost biblical."

"Well, now...," I began.

"It's certainly hospitable."

I raised my glass. "In fact," I said, "I'd like to propose a toast. The forerunner of many! Let us first drink to the unexpected guest."

"To the unexpected guest!" We all drank solemnly. To myself of course he was neither unexpected nor a guest; but obviously one never wants to *spring* things on people! One always aims to be subtle.

"In any case," said Roger as though the question were still under discussion, "I mean to keep this cork." I think he *was* a trifle tipsy.

"But I insist on having it," I said. "I'll tell you why. I've got a better memento for you to keep—not merely better, a lot bigger!"

I smiled at their air of mystification. "I only wish that Thomas was awake."

"Then wake him!" exclaimed Roger and before either Celia or I could do more than halfheartedly protest he was beside the carrycot and had scooped up the baby—was already lifting him towards the ceiling! It was nearly as if he had some idea of what was to come.

"Oh, Roger!" cried Celia. "He's not even properly awake. Only imagine! If it were you!"

"Yes, my friend." I shook my finger at him sternly. "It could be a lesson you would profit from: we should make you walk a mile in another man's bootees!"

And quite certainly, sitting next moment on his father's lap, Thomas did look a little dazed. Dazed but—yes, we had to admit it—distinctly interested. Roger dipped his finger in champagne and put the tip of it into his firstborn's mouth.

"Like father like son," sighed Celia.

"Come on, Rachel," he said. "We're all agog. What can it possibly be?"

"Don't be so impatient," I said. "Actually it isn't even for *you*. It's for Tom."

"What is?"

"This house."

Well, now. You can imagine the hoo-ha: all the hugging and the kissing and the carrying on. The further pouring of champagne. The tears. The talk of fairy godmothers.

It was all so lovely. So exceedingly lovely.

"I don't know what to say," declared Roger, at last. "There doesn't seem a *thing* one can say."

I smiled at Celia. "For someone who couldn't think of anything to say he doesn't appear to have done too badly. But set my mind at rest. You don't think he might be mildly disappointed the gift was for Thomas, not for him?"

Yet Roger answered for himself. "Rachel," he said, his hand upon mine, "life is full of disappointments. One has to be brave."

"Though that's more easily said than done," I replied, in the same light tone. "So much depends upon your constitution and the way you've slept the night before."

"Agreed."

"But in any case there's a little something else I might have up my sleeve."

"Something else?" They said it in unison. If you hadn't known them it might have sounded ... well, let's simply call it eager.

(And I'd never wish to be judged on some of the impressions I realize I myself may give on occasion. Well, I ask you! Who would?)

"Nothing but a proposition," I said. "I hesitate to call it a consolation prize."

"My goodness! What?"

"Something I want the pair of you to think about both long and hard."

I again looked quite severely at Roger. He was the one more likely to be impulsive. "Yes," I repeated. "Both long and hard! *Very* long and *very* hard!"

"Go on," said Celia quickly. "It isn't kind of you to keep us in suspense."

"Well, first, if it doesn't seem bad-mannered of me ... ?"

"Rachel, be as bad-mannered as you like!" suggested Roger.

"May I enquire, then, what rent you have to pay for your small flat?"

"A hundred and twelve pounds a month," answered Celia, after a pause. "But why?"

"Well, I don't know. I've been considering. This house is rather large for just one person. And when I think of you two having to pay good money for a flat you don't even like—and, Lord knows, hard-earned money you can ill afford—well, it seemed to me I simply had to mention it, that's all."

"Mention what, Rachel?"

"Why, the notion of your moving in with me! Hadn't I made that clear?"

Paradoxically they seemed more surprised about this than about my previous revelation. There was a silence lasting several seconds. "Phew!" said Roger.

"But you mustn't suppose I'm being purely altruistic. It would be very nice for me as well."

I smiled and started to push back my chair. Roger jumped up immediately.

"Yet, as I say, I don't want either of you to utter a single word before you've had a chance to sleep on it. For instance! Celia mightn't at all like the idea of having to share the house with another woman. Someone, I mean, who isn't precisely old and ugly. Well, I shall leave you to argue that one out between yourselves. Consider every angle. But for the moment—thank you, Roger dear, how lovely it is to receive these small attentions—if you'd like to go up into the sitting room I shall shortly join you there with coffee and Grand Marnier."

40

HOWEVER, despite my every attempt to preach caution, we hadn't even finished our first cup of coffee before they gave their answer. If I had really meant it, they said, they genuinely couldn't be more delighted. Overjoyed. Ecstatic. Their gratitude would know no bounds.

"Roger," I remarked, "I think you've got French blood flowing through your veins!"

"Why?"

"Because the French also exaggerate."

"Then—not a drop! I swear it!"

We drank to it: to his protested lack of French influence, to his innate abhorrence of exaggeration, to our approaching *ménage à quatre*. ("Well, for the moment, anyway," I hinted coyly—delighted to discover that nowadays I could talk so very easily about these things.) Oh, it was going to be such fun.

"A commune!" I said. "'All for one and one for all!' We could name ourselves the Co-Optimists—like that old concert party in the...Well, many years before my time."

"Why not the Musketeers?"

"We don't want to fight. We want to entertain. To sing and dance beside the sea forever."

"Naturally we must pay you," said Celia.

"Naturally," I smiled. "But only in laughter and in song."

"Rachel," declared Roger, "you can have no idea of what you're letting yourself in for. The only place I dare to sing is in the bath."

"Then you must bathe often," I cried gaily, "and throw the casement wide."

"We must obviously share the bills," persisted Celia.

"We'll have to see."

"The whole point of a commune," pointed out Roger, "lies in the sharing!"

I felt so happy.

"I shall teach Tommy the dangers of electricity," I volunteered.

Tommy had gone back to sleep.

We finished the bottle of Grand Marnier.

"Rachel, do you remember? You were going to tell us the story of that portrait."

"Yes." I smiled at her. "I certainly hadn't forgotten."

"Well, then...?"

There was a pause. I took a deep breath. "I've often thought, you know, that in my next life I shouldn't mind returning as a cat."

"But is this telling us about the picture?"

"Cats are such very comfortable creatures, aren't they? Wherever they are, they can always make themselves at home."

"In that case," said Roger, "I'm surprised you haven't got one."

"Oh, I'm not really much of a cat lover. It's silly, isn't it: possibly I'd rather become one than own one?" For an instant I considered this. "Although Mrs. Pimm *did* tell me a cat story which I wouldn't quite describe as promising."

"We don't want to hear it," laughed Celia. "We want to hear about the portrait!"

"And so you shall, my dear, yes so you shall! But when I was a child I used to think I'd like to be a little red hen—imagine that! I had a picture on my wall of a sunlit garden on a drowsy hillside... half a dozen chickens roaming far and wide; I could sometimes hear their peaceful clucking, catch the smell of the eggs in the straw. If I woke in the middle of the night I could even get back to sleep by imagining myself curled up on a shelf in the coop. And I remember once saying to my father, 'I wish I were a little red hen! I'd lay an egg and sit on it and keep it warm and be forever happy!' And afterwards he called me *his* little red hen. I enjoyed that. Isn't it ridiculous?"

"It sounds idyllic," said Roger.

"Yes, it was."

We were quiet for a moment; they must have thought I was lost in tender reminiscence. I played a prank on them. I laughed. I said quickly, "The cats—there were nine of them—turned out to be cannibalistic. *And* human-flesh eaters! There! I got that one in, didn't I?" But they both looked slightly more disconcerted than entertained. "I warn you," I told them. "From now on there'll be lots of little japes like that. One thing you'll find, I hope, is that I'm not...particularly...predictable!"

"Oh, I believe we've discovered that already."

"Thank you, Roger." I inclined my head. (Which suddenly reminded me about my dream. I felt both guilty and amused. But I decided not to tell them of it—not yet at any rate.) "Now then, Celia. Next time around, what would *you* like to come back as?"

"Well, candidly," she replied, "I don't think anything. This once is probably enough for me!"

"Oh, you poor thing..." We laughed—she a shade uneasily, myself deriving a certain shameful pleasure from the insight I'd received.

"What about you, Roger?"

"Oh, I'm not fussy. Rockefeller—Vanderbilt—Onassis. King Midas..."

"I don't think they led very happy lives; not the last two, anyway."

"I'd teach them how."

"Did I tell you about Howard Hughes?"

"No. What about Howard Hughes?"

"In that case, whom *did* I tell? Oh, yes...perhaps it was in church. A nice, quiet, slightly *stodgy* congregation. But attentive. I preached them a sermon."

"You did? You preached them a sermon?"

"Yes, but only a very short one. Yet did you realize there are foxes in Bristol and that at night they come right into the centre of the city? They scavenge from the rubbish bins. People sometimes feed them."

"Yes," said Roger, "we did realize that."

"Don't you think they're such a lovely colour—foxes? Such beautiful and rippling things? So graceful?"

"But what on earth put foxes in your mind?"

"I don't know. Maybe God did. So why is it insulting to call a person foxy?"

I paused. They didn't answer.

"Anyhow, Celia, before too long you should honestly give it some serious thought. Though that's really a case of the pot calling the kettle black! I realize that I never did; not even after *Berkeley Square*. Except that I was then a lot younger than you are now. Anyway," I continued, "you're both very well aware, aren't you, of the gentleman whose name is commemorated on the front of this house?"

"You mean," said Roger, "the plaque?"

"Yes—it's strange." This hadn't occurred to me previously. "You've never asked me about him, have you?"

"Haven't I?"

"No, not once. I wonder why?"

Still. I was prepared to be charitable; prepared to put it down to nothing more than pure jealousy; prepared to help him get over it. (Well, at least, get over it to *some* extent.) I rose to my feet and went towards the portrait. I gave Horatio our secret little smile. With my right hand I made a gesture of presentation.

"Well, I think the time has now arrived to introduce you all." (I heard Celia hissing at her husband to stand up; felt slightly saddened he should have needed such a prompt.) "It is with great pleasure," I went on, "that I present my dear friends Roger and Celia Allsop. It is with great pride and pleasure that I present my dear friend Horatio."

There! I had done it. It was a shame that I had felt a little piqued with Roger—I had been fully meaning to introduce him, and therefore Celia too, with *pride* as well as pleasure. Now I could only hope they hadn't noticed. (But why is there always *something* to mar these great occasions? Why?)

"You mean ... Mr. Horatio Gavin himself?" asked Roger in wonderment.

"Yes. Yes!"

"But how fascinating! How fantastic! Really, that's tremendous." He turned back towards the picture. "How do you do, sir? What a rare and extraordinary privilege to get to meet you!"

This was everything I could have wished for. My little *faux pas* obviously hadn't mattered one little scrap.

"Rachel," he said, "was the portrait painted, do you know, during Mr. Gavin's lifetime?"

"Oh, yes—certainly."

"And it's an original of course? I'm sorry. I know almost nothing about art."

I gave a small forgiving shrug and a smile of fond indulgence.

"Who was the artist?" he asked.

"Well, that, I'm afraid, I really couldn't say."

Somehow this had never seemed to me of much importance. Somehow I had never actually thought of the painting as being ... well, just that. A painting.

"It's so very dark," said Roger. He was standing at the fireplace, with his fingertips upon the mantelshelf, gazing intently upward. "So hard to make out any signature ..." After a minute, though, his heels came back to the floor and he half turned his head towards me, his eyes bright. "But where did you pick it up?" he asked excitedly. "Or was it always here?"

It was an excitement which I loved him for.

I laughed. "What *are* you suggesting? Pick it up, indeed! Yes," I said, "he was always here."

"May I take him down?"

"Oh, I ..." Surprise made me awkward. "No, I'd prefer it if you didn't! I'd much prefer it if you didn't!"

His hands were already halfway there; they didn't stop. "Roger!" cried Celia.

He lowered them at once. "I'm sorry. Just wasn't thinking. All that booze! All that excitement!"

And almost as if rebuking himself—well, certainly as if preoccupied—he abruptly brought his head down and looked into the fire. He rested his right elbow on the mantelshelf. He raised his left foot and placed it on the andiron. I clutched the back of a chair and thought that I might faint.

The instant passed. At least, the worst of it. And Celia hadn't noticed; I was sure of that.

Roger turned round. It *was* Roger. He was smiling again and with all his usual amiability. But just the same I had to look away. I felt as if there'd been some violation.

"Do you know," he said, "I really think this picture might be worth a pound or two. We ought to have it looked at."

I stared at him; perhaps a little blankly. Celia made some comment. I was under the impression she had made it practically at random—as seemed to have happened once before. (Or had I grown confused?) I suddenly became aware she must have asked me something.

"What?"

I turned my head towards her, slowly.

"Well, you mentioned previously that if it hadn't been for him—for Mr. Gavin, I should say—then you yourself wouldn't be here in Bristol. What did you mean by that?" "Oh," I said, "I don't know. Nothing—probably nothing! I've forgotten."

She was tactful. She didn't press the point.

"Roger, I think it's time that we were on our way. Oh, incidentally...who is Mrs. Pimm?"

She gave me a faint smile.

"The fact is, Rachel, we feel we want to get to know everything about you. *Everything!*"

41

I DON'T know when the following dialogue took place. Somehow it seems cut adrift from time, like a rowboat quietly loosened from its moorings, while its occupant, entranced, oblivious to each hill or field or willow tree upon her way, lies whitely gleaming in her rose-embroidered silk, trailing a graceful hand and sweetly carolling beneath a canopy of green.

The question I put to him required courage. I had hesitated for a long time. But I knew it was important. "What about Anne Barnetby?" I said.

At first I thought he wasn't going to answer. (Oh, no! Not you! Don't join the club of those who won't respond!) And I couldn't have enquired a second time.

But then he did reply, and very simply, just as I had hoped he would. "Anne Barnetby? I loved her."

And now it was easier to go on. "And she? Did she love you?" I prayed for an affirmative.

"I believed so. I believe she *almost* did."

I held my breath.

"She toyed with me," he said.

Yet I detected no resentment. "So what became of her?" I asked.

"She married. Anne Barnetby married the man of her choice."

"And regretted it, I know."

"I've no idea; I never heard from her again. Nor from him. He'd been a friend of mine at school."

"One of those you swam with naked in the creek?"

"Yes."

His voice was no longer as casual as he might have hoped. But that was good. Even after all this time he couldn't speak of her and wholly hide the fact that he still loved.

Yes, that was good. It was wonderful. For what did it matter if he hadn't recognized me yet?

"A clean break is always for the best." I sensed it might help him if I drew out the conversation for a while. I wasn't simply talking tongue-in-cheek or just for the sake of it. I wasn't merely fishing. "Surely," I said, "it must have hastened the whole process of forgetting."

Silence.

"You *did* forget?"

"I..."

"Never?"

"When I began to think I was recovering," he said, "I soon realized how absurdly mistaken I was."

"My poor sweet love. My dear. I *know* she must have come to hate herself."

I don't believe he heard me. In any case he plainly missed the message I was meaning to impart.

"This may sound fanciful," he smiled, "but later she returned to haunt me."

"Her ghost?" I'm not sure what my feelings were just then.

"No, no, it's not as bad as that!" He laughed—yet not with any mirth. "My mother always claimed I was theatric. She said my rightful home should be at Drury Lane alongside Mr. Garrick. No, I was haunted less by *her* than by the *idea* of her; or by the idea of the two of them together: the realization of everything I'd lost. Even when I could no longer—quite—visualize that much-loved face, the thought of all that I was missing might have had the power to..."

"Yes?" I asked.

Though I shouldn't have prompted. My voice reminded him he had an audience. His eyes regained their focus.

But I led him forward gently—well away from all those former thoughts of self-destruction I knew he now recalled.

Oh dear! Could *I* have been the one who had driven him to the brink of that? (If only Anne Barnetby *had* had a successor who had restored Horatio's faith in love, and if only I myself—as I had briefly fantasized—could have been that beautiful and fortunate woman. But life is far too testing: that easy route would not have done.) I felt unbearably ashamed; yet at the same time unashamedly overjoyed. *I* knew of the wondrous ending we had both arrived at. Now Horatio must discover it too. What a reunion *that* would be! How I would atone for all my many failings!

"Her face," I said, "that lovely face, the one you cannot *quite* visualize? Have you never been reminded of it?"

"It's strange that you should ask me that. Because... and not so very long ago..."

"Do *I* remind you of her?" I put my hand to my breast and looked at him wide-eyed, all charmingly aflutter. "Oh pardon, sir, I interrupted."

He said: "Perhaps at odd times, yes, you do. Some fleeting expression which... But what I was going to say was... not so very long ago the image suddenly returned in all its clarity. In all its dreadful clarity." He added quietly: "I had forgotten how unsettling such a clear remembrancer could be."

I nodded, commiseratingly. "Well, I don't want to speak out of turn; yet I don't feel that reminder could have come from anyone but me!" I smiled. "Well, after all, it couldn't have been Celia, could it? Oh, I know she possibly strikes people as being fairly sweet and even almost pretty—although, admittedly, in a rather frigid sort of way..."

"No, it wasn't Celia."

"And I don't feel it can have been Sylvia?"

"No, no, not Sylvia." We laughed together over that.

"And it surely couldn't have been Roger or young Thomas. So it *must* have been—"

"I'll tell you when it was." My, my, such manners! (Had I set a bad example?) But he *was* rather masterful. "It was when you showed me that book."

"Book?"

"Yes, you'd been to the library. Don't you remember? There were several pictures in it; you'd said there was an actress you wanted me to see. There was one picture in particular, in which she posed beside her husband. You showed me many times."

"Because you asked me to."

"Yes."

It had been a little ceremony, a little act of adoration. For over a week we had performed it every day. Until, with an expression of unmistakable pain, he had pleaded with me not to continue.

The thing was this. Although he hadn't recognized me yet (but, as I say, the time was drawing close), although as yet he hadn't made that final joyous leap . . . still, of course, whenever he had seen the book, it was naturally I who had been holding it. It wasn't strange that he should feel perplexed.

42

THAT NIGHT of my dinner party.

I began to feel better. Later—after my guests had gone and Horatio and I had the house all to ourselves again—I totally got over it. I truly did. Excitement reasserted itself, came flowing back exactly as it should have done. I *wasn't* like the child who knows what he wants while he wants it (they could hand you the moon—you'd grow tired of it soon). Oh, but I'd really started to believe I might be. Just when I had almost everything I wanted . . . Just when I could see it all so nearly coming true . . . Oh, what a terrifying thought, that I might be intrinsically fickle, spoilt, impossible to satisfy!

But I quashed it. And as I say, thankfully, so thankfully, intoxication caught up with me again. As I undressed I sang. Yes of course! My theme tune. "Oh, if you want to be a big success— pom, pom!—here's the way to instant happiness—pom, pom! . . ." And I *was* young and beautiful. I must be. Otherwise none of this could possibly have happened. They didn't *know* that I had varicose veins (even though mere children sometimes got them!) —they never would know—that was the great big glorious confidence trick. So what on earth did a few silly veins matter? Where was *their* importance in the vast eternal scheme of things?

And then I stopped. I stopped singing. I stopped performing my little musical striptease. (So tantalizing to the gentlemen!)

I suddenly thought . . . how stupid I was. It came over me so strongly. Jesus had said, "Pick up your bed and walk." He had cured the blind, the paralytic, the mad. Just like that. Rise from the dead. Chase out those devils. Open your eyes. Walk. So easy. I really felt—I really did feel—that the next time I ran my fingers down the back of my left leg they would encounter... only smooth flesh. I really did feel that.

———

In fact I tried it. No, not "tried"—just did it. And how right I'd been! My fingers found nothing but smoothness: lovely silky smoothness. No bumps, no blemishes. I was a whole person once again.

Fit to be a bride of Christ.

———

Really a whole person.

That night he came back.

No, I express myself badly. Not for a moment had he ever been away.

What I mean is—he came back as I had viewed him only once before. Unclothed.

And he came with love.

I'll tell you how it happened.

I hadn't been able to sleep; and after what appeared like hours of tossing and turning, half-dreaming but continually jerking awake, my mind still racing and delirious, I decided to get up and go to make myself a hot drink and a sandwich (it seemed preposterous I should be hungry after such a meal; yet actually I'd felt rather too excited to eat)—then listen to some music. It was a mild night and with my young and silky, firm, unblemished limbs I had no need of any nightdress. I threw it off, luxuriously—and felt so free, so unencumbered. I floated down to the kitchen, remembering how we had laughed and fooled about and sung over the washing up and made it almost the loveliest part of the whole lovely party. The kitchen seemed so full of happy ghosts, my own very much included. I glided upstairs to the sitting room—it felt equally alive, maybe even more so—and selected a record, sat down and ate my sandwich, drank the milk; took a pink carnation out of a vase and joyfully threaded it through the hair of my maidenhood. I made a small garland of daisies (I had picked them just the previous day; had them right beside me in a honey jar) and carefully set it down in that same hallowed spot... how sweetly it added to the charm. I may have fallen into a reverie; lulled by the Water Music I had put on the player. I saw myself searching for bluebells in the moonlight, feeling the dew-damp grass between my toes... I wanted to run straight out and find some; had begun to leave my chair. But then suddenly he was there again, at the fireplace, and even as I completed the action—having forgotten the bluebells and determined this time really to hold him if such a thing were possible—he turned round and smiled and extended his hands to me. And he said:

"I've been waiting for you for so long."

He admired the fine, upstanding quality of my breasts—even before he started stroking them; the flatness of my stomach, the smallness of my waist—"Surely," he laughed longingly, in a tone of wholly undisguised wonder, "my fingertips could almost meet around it? And oh my one true love... I can't believe in so much excellence and grace. Tell me this isn't just a dream! Tell me you won't fall to pieces in my arms! Tell me that you're no mere fragment of a starved imagination—and of my endless years of waiting and desire!

> "Then to Rachel let us sing,
> That Rachel is excelling;
> She excels each mortal thing
> Upon the dull earth dwelling...

"All this outer loveliness," he said, "*and* a heart that's filled with poetry, sweetness and delight." He clearly marvelled at such a glorious combination. "My Rachel, my darling, my all. You have fresh flowers in your cunt." He bent, and watered them with tears.

43

"Ah. I see that madam has come back. It is *so* lovely, isn't it?"

"I'd like to take it," I said.

"You would?"

"Yes, please."

"I'm sure you won't regret it, madam." Yet was it my imagination or did she sound a jot uncomfortable? "Your daughter will be coming in too?"

"No. That won't be necessary."

"But any small adjustments which might be thought desirable...?"

"We can see to those at home."

This time I wasn't wearing gloves. It didn't matter. Indeed I had left them off on purpose. She'd be able to gawp discreetly at my wedding ring.

"In fact I want to tell you something. My daughter and I often get mistaken for sisters. Even for twins. We have precisely the same measurements."

"Then you're very fortunate, madam." She began to gather up the dress. "Extremely fortunate."

"And I'd state with complete confidence that this gown is the correct size. Wouldn't you? But please don't ask me to try it on. Not here. It wouldn't seem appropriate."

"I must admit," she said, "I should feel happier if I could only see the young lady herself."

I laughed. "Oh, ye of little faith!"

"Madam?"

I hastened to reassure her. "And that remark applies almost as much to me as it does to you."

"Besides," she went on, "I'd naturally feel interested to see her. We all would; it's a very special dress. We'd like to wish her luck."

"Luck?" I said. "Oh, no! You mustn't pin your hopes on *luck*! Nor on experiencing life at merely secondhand. No one should ever feel content to live vicariously."

"I beg your pardon?"

"Poor woman—I sensed immediately that you were under stress. What can I do to help? My dear, you should try to relax a little more. Try to let go, lean back, give way. That's the great secret of it all." I smiled encouragingly.

Or was the trouble really something else, I wondered—something far less easy to prescribe for? In seeing me, was she perhaps seeing a younger version of herself, a heartrending image of what she, too, might once have been?

> I can endure my own despair,
> But not another's hope.

Oh no. That was the last thing I wanted—to become a punishment to others, purely an object of envy, a knife-twisting reflection in some enchanted looking glass. I wanted to become so much more than enviable. I wanted to be viewed as an example. A pattern of what anyone could hopefully aspire to.

Radiant.

Charismatic.

Irresistible.

"Tell me your name, dear?"

She didn't answer. She appeared flustered. It seemed I'd got there just in time—oh, thank God, thank God! She called through a curtained doorway for somebody called Doreen.

Doreen! Doreen couldn't possibly be the name of the

manageress. Doreen could only be the name of an assistant, a rather lowly one at that, quite probably a temp. Oh my! That made my flustered friend the woman at the helm?

"Are you?" I asked.

She didn't answer that one either. I began to understand the full nature of my problem.

Issues over privacy in particular; communication in general.

But at least she *tried*. You've got to give her that. "Your daughter's getting married, then?" A start—of sorts—no matter how inept. Or superfluous. Or borderline grotesque. A bit like Judy Garland tottering onto the platform in smeared makeup and peering out across the footlights at all those suddenly hushed thousands. (Oh, Judy! Whatever happened to Baby Dot?) "You say the wedding date's been set?" I hadn't spoken of any wedding date. "How nice. The young man. Is he local?"

Chillingly unnatural but, as I say, potentially encouraging. And of course I did what I could to reciprocate.

"Oh yes. He was local long before all others whom you'd see around today."

She didn't quite know how to deal with that. It *was* complex. "He's thirty-three," I added quickly, to make it all much simpler. "Naturally, he's a little older than I am."

(Anyway, she couldn't truly have supposed I had a daughter of marriageable age; she must have seen it was a jest—would surely have ascribed it to shyness, though, rather than a sensitivity to the longing of others and a determination not to flaunt.)

Doreen finally arrived, really little more than a schoolgirl, pale, freckled, endearingly anxious to please. I was thinking she might have been the one who'd sold me my sky-blue but probably this shop had to replace staff every week . . . patently understandable. I wished her a smiling good morning—merry, magnetic, inspirational—although obviously it wasn't only her I was thinking of as I did so.

The older woman laughed. I'm afraid it was a harsh and none too pleasant sound.

"Then in that case you'll still be seeing a lot of them." (She was getting muddled.) "That's good."

At her mother's knee, I thought, she must have learned the Ten Commandments: make conversation, keep up pretences, never lose a sale, your conversation doesn't need to make much sense... (Well, yes, I had to change my mind: that was *one* form of communication.) But even so I still wanted to say, "Oh, please, don't strain! If it doesn't *flow* just fill your reservoir in peace." But I couldn't of course; not in front of her subordinate.

Instead I told them the story of Howard Hughes sitting on the lavatory for seventy-two hours.

"Now to whom do I make out the cheque?" I hadn't really forgotten though—it was all a part of the therapy.

The woman told me.

"Ah," I complimented her, "much better! That truly is...much better."

Her little helper could have given her a lesson or two in *flow*. She asked: "You live in Rodney Street, don't you? I've often seen you."

"Yes, yes, I do. Next time make sure you wave hello."

"My mum has the teashop just across the road. Sometimes I help out."

"That makes us almost neighbours!

> "Hey, neighbour, say, neighbour,
> How's the world with you?—
> Aren't you glad to be alive this sunny morning,
> Can't you see the sky above is showing blue...?"

Laughingly I went back to their desk to complete the writing of my cheque. "How foolish! I ask you! Where else would the sky be if not above? Yes, it's foolish...but it's fun. Oh, no, for heaven's sake—*please*—you mustn't try to start me off again!" I concentrated on the cheque.

"Is that young man, the one with the fair hair, going to be the bridegroom? He's ever so handsome."

"Yes, isn't he? Like some sun-dappled Scandinavian god. He's got a beautiful physique."

"My!"

"You should see how all the muscles ripple in his back."

"My boyfriend's got a back like that. He goes to weightlifting."

The other woman said sharply: "Thank you, Doreen. That will be enough! *I* can manage now."

"He just came in to buy some cakes, Mrs. Pond." The girl had gone a little red. I felt so sorry for her.

"Yes, that'll do, Doreen, thank you!" The woman almost shrieked. *Mrs.* Pond. (I'd been wondering if the wedding ring might have belonged to her mother.) Undoubtedly divorced then or separated or widowed—or else the wedding ring must have belonged to her mother. Oh dear. I felt quite sorry for her too. I didn't mean the mother—although she also, on reflection, could probably have done with all my sympathy.

I said to the departing Doreen: "Why don't you pop in sometime for a cup of tea? We could talk about your boyfriend."

"That would be nice." She disappeared behind the curtain. "Don't lose your spontaneity," I called.

I thought I would extend the same invitation to Mrs. Pond. For on no account must she feel ostracized and the visit might do her good, poor thing—although I myself, naturally, could hardly be expected to look forward to it with *avidity*.

"These school-leavers...!" she said after a pause. "I'm afraid she still has a great deal to learn."

"Haven't we all," I agreed. "'And if it ever come to pass that I inherit wealth I'll eat and drink, and drink and eat, until I wreck my health...' Those old songs can be remarkably comforting, don't you think? They show us that *other people* do it too! We're none of us alone, Mrs. Pond. No, dear—you've just got to believe this!— there is nothing new, nothing new whatever, under the sun."

I added merrily: "Apart from this lovely silk and rose-embroidered wedding dress."

"Oh, it's futile," she said.

"What is? What is? Dear lady, it doesn't *need* to be wrapped up quite so beautifully as that. You mustn't chastise yourself over the wrapping. The wrapping is not important."

I didn't believe this in the slightest but as I'd once pointed out to Tony (the recollection could now make me smile in place of want to weep) there had to be room in even the most truthful philosophy for an occasional—*very* occasional—little white lie.

"Here, let me help you."

"Madam, it's all *right*. Thank you."

"No, Mrs. Pond, it is obviously very far from being all right! At least promise me that you will *try* to look for the silver lining, *try* to walk on the sunny side of the street, *try* to banish from your vocabulary, forever, such awful words as 'futile.' Remember that in thirty years' time" (and I studied her most lovingly) "well, let's say in twenty years' time, you will be looking back on all of this and thinking—oh if only I could have those sweet and precious days returned to me! That morning, for instance, when I sold the wedding dress . . . if only I had realized *then* just how happy I was, if only I had struggled *then* to appreciate each dear God-given minute!"

I smiled at her and spread my hands.

"How many minutes *are* there, Mrs. Pond, in the course of twenty years? How many breakfasts, lunches, dinners, teas? How many opportunities for joy?"

She gazed at me and I saw her lips begin to quiver. I wasn't dismayed. A purification in tears. A baptism. A mulching for the young green shoots, the new and tender leaves, the freshly pet-alled flowers. I was ready to take her, warts and all, into my warmly reassuring arms, to soothe her, tell her she was not *inherently* rapacious, that all she needed was to reawaken love (or else to find it for the first time—which I thought in fact was probably more likely).

"You're nobody until somebody loves you," I would say, "and believe me I do know. Love is the answer; someone to love is the answer . . ."

But by then she was shaking—positively shaking—and staring at me in a fashion that really seemed half-crazed. "Happy!" she cried. "Happy! Oh, I'll tell you how to get happy! Care about nothing—care about nothing—that's the only way you're ever going to do it!" And as she spoke she flailed her arms... and in one of her hands was a pair of scissors. I stepped back rather than embraced her.

"Yes," I said, "yes, that's certainly *one* point of view. Indeed I believe it's rather Buddhist. If sorrow is caused by desire then get rid of that desire. For those who are up to it I'm sure it sometimes works. But *I* wouldn't want to waste much of my time or precious energy upon it. Strictly for the unintelligent is what *I*'d say! Oh, gracious—you're not a Buddhist, are you? I do hope I haven't spoken out of turn."

Again no answer. But at any rate she used the scissors just to cut the string. Also her shaking seemed to have lessened. Even to that extent, therefore, I had been able to calm her.

Hallelujah!

"Yes, I can certainly see how it would work." I lied smilingly, wanting to consolidate the good I knew I'd done. "Care about nothing! Perhaps you've found the key! There was recently a ninety-minute programme about some Buddhist monks. Unfortunately I didn't watch it."

Before handing me the box she scrutinized my bank card. She scrutinized the cheque. For the first time it occurred to me that this was going to bounce.

I laughed. "Oh, Lordy Moses," I exclaimed. "Then get thee to a nunnery."

No, I didn't exclaim it; in fact I said it rather gently, not at all in angry Hamlet's tone. (And *she* was no Ophelia.) But it suddenly seemed the one entirely valid response to such a situation—a literally inspired piece of counsel—although admittedly a touch ambiguous... since I wasn't fully sure whether it was directed more towards her or towards myself! All I knew was that if life had been less kind to me I could now have been travelling right behind her on that horrid downhill path.

(*Behind*, I mean, because of the obvious discrepancy in our ages. *Right* behind, perhaps not.)

She still hadn't spoken.

At the door I shrugged. Last time she had opened it for me and on that first occasion too. This morning, clearly, I had given her too much to think about. "Of course," I mentioned, "there is that other all-important thought. Yet here I have to leave you all alone with your god and your conscience and your priorities!" I gave her a moment in which to try to adjust to this. "But is it so much fun-nery...in a nunnery?"

She probably thought I was being flippant. However, if she really thought this, was there any point in my affirming it was just my style?

"By the way, you'll have seen I wrote my address on the cheque. So please come to visit. We'll continue with our merry little chat and by no means neglect—now, what does Billy Graham call it?—that all-important follow-up! I think what he really meant was...tea and sympathy. Or in our case *sherry* and sympathy: because this time we'll do our very best to make it stimulating! Yes?"

———

On my way home I was reminded of something. By Doreen's words, not Mrs. Pond's.

Roger had never thanked me for those two pounds. It was most *odd* when you came to think of it. It wasn't so much that one wanted to be thanked, but—

Yes, it was.

And he had never even mentioned them.

I didn't like it when a person became careless over things; even quite trivial things.

44

HE SAID everything I'd ever wanted to hear. *I* said the things which I had always wanted to say. It was bliss; it was sheer enchantment. I was twenty-five and beautiful and I moved through every day and night in a kind of dream, a dream of heaven which I took to be reality. I was happier than I would ever have supposed to be possible... as if we were living now in Eden long before the Fall. Yes, he was Adam and I was Eve and though we weren't in the least ashamed of our nakedness I at length covered mine with my white dress to signify the purity that had always been his— that had always been awaiting him. And I wafted through my days and through my nights in a dream of heaven which was here on planet earth. And I looked radiant in that white dress: my mirror told me so but more especially did his eyes as he stepped towards me and held me close and together we waltzed across the gleaming ballroom floor, with chandeliers glittering beneath my dainty feet and all the other dancers stepping back to clear an avenue in whispered admiration—"Who is she? Isn't she lovely?" —an avenue that led on to further enchantment amongst shimmering rock pools and coloured lights and down narrow winding paths all tucked away from view. And I *was* radiant. I was a princess—with my lovely black ringlets and my rosebud mouth, with my cheeks bearing the bloom of rouge and happiness, with my feet enwrapped in those scarlet satin slippers which would make me dance forever. (But that was a story which had ended tragically; this one was going to be so very different. I *know*—let me change the red to pink!) And yes it was all a fairy tale: the great four-poster in the magic glade to which we ran laughing in our wedding clothes—he had acquired his somewhere on the way. I shan't describe what happened in that bed any more than I've described what happened in my own; but oh the feel of him, the feel of him, the feel of him. Bursting stars against a backdrop of black velvet.

The bed was like Elijah's chariot (no—on second thoughts maybe not—*poor* Elijah!) or like some mythical Arabian carpet. It bore us smoothly to exotic climes while all the time the orchestra was playing, dreamily romantic, far below: we could just make out—still—the glittering barge on which it played, moored on an ornamental lake strung across with Chinese lanterns.

And I sang to him as we floated.

"Oh, fuck me once and fuck me twice and fuck me once again; it's been a long, long time..."

Then I giggled.

No, *that* couldn't be right! Surely?

Well, why ever not? As he willingly turned over and took me in his arms again and prepared to carry out all my commands (while the moonlight played such naughty tricks: that sexy fleece upon his chest looked spun from purest gold!) he was finally able to demonstrate how much he'd learned from Bing.

"Rachel—you—are—quite—a—girl!"

And I returned the compliment.

We were off on a honeymoon that was going to last through centuries.

45

IT WAS Celia who eventually turned up. She told me that she liked my dress; yet I could see she had her reservations. (I had of course removed the train—and just as obviously I wasn't wearing the veil!) I saw things far more clearly now: I saw them through *his* eyes as much as through my own.

"Celia, why has it taken you so long? I wrote to you eight days ago."

"Yes, we noticed. I'm afraid the letter was delayed."

"Is Roger on his way?"

"No, he can't come. Exams looming. But he sends you all his love."

"Oh, yes—the poor soul! Yet I'm sure that he'll do well. If ever a man was born to carry all before him, that man was Roger Allsop. How's Tommy?"

"Spending the day with my mother. Oh—he too sends lots of kisses."

But she was again speaking absentmindedly. And she kept on glancing at me when she thought I wasn't looking—she would never meet my eye for longer than a second. I had quickly realized why. She felt scared to witness such certainty, such calm... such evidence of attainment. For all that's said about it people still aren't comfortable in the face of liberation. They feel threatened. They affect a cynicism. Only cynicism can conceal, to some extent, the size of their own failure.

"What did you want to tell us?" she said.

I came directly to the point.

"Well, about your all living here, Celia...I've had to change my mind."

I thought she turned a little pale. I went on.

"I can see now that it wouldn't work. Yet I didn't want to put that in a letter. It might have seemed perfunctory."

"But we gave notice to the agent—oh, days ago, straight after your party!—and the new tenants have already signed a contract!"

"Oh dear. What a shame."

"We thought it all so settled."

"Yet if only you had come to see me sooner! I can't apologize enough."

She didn't look appeased. I tried to introduce a calmer, more congenial note.

"But naturally it makes no difference to Thomas's inheriting the house."

"Well, at least that's something!" she said. "Are you sure?"

She was disappointed, clearly; I had to make allowances. "Yes, of course I am."

"Mark said you hadn't yet been in to sign the papers." Her tone was almost lifeless.

"Well, I can't begin to tell you, Celia, how extraordinarily busy I've been!"

She didn't reply to this. When she spoke again there was still that taste of coolness in her voice; before today I simply hadn't encountered it.

"Why don't you think that it would work?"

"Because I'm in love and—well, it was silly of me, I was all mixed up, I'd taken too much wine. I *ought* to have seen. We're going to need our privacy."

She disregarded all the rest. "You're in love?" she said. I might have told her I was Willie Shakespeare in disguise.

She even felt a need to repeat it—"You're in *love*?"

"Yes! Head over heels!"

"Oh."

"Yes *oh* indeed. Oh, oh, oh! Fly me to the moon and let me play among the stars!"

"We didn't even know that you had met anyone."

"Oh, what nonsense! Most certainly you did!"

She simply shook her head.

"You can scarcely have forgotten," I said. "Why, you were even introduced!"

She looked at me as though I might be suffering from delusions; but then mercifully she must have realized it was her own memory which lay at fault not mine. In addition to being disappointed she was plainly very tired. A dangerous combination—as I knew only too well from remembering my own disappointments in London.

"Are you meaning to live with him?" she asked dully. "Is he going to move in?"

"What need? He was here long before I was. Long, long before I was. Except in a way, of course, he wasn't. But up until now he hasn't said too much about that side of it and I haven't liked to push. You see, it's all immensely complicated. I'd rather let him reveal things in his own good time; or perhaps I'd better say—at his own good pace! I mustn't risk giving him a stammer, you understand, or making him feel in any way an oddity."

She still seemed uncertain how to respond. I held up my hand to show her the lovely little band of gold he'd given me. (I noticed, impatiently, that the varnish was chipping off a couple of my nails. There and then I made a vow: on no account must happiness be allowed to turn me slipshod! When had I last washed? Life was so full of incident these days now that I had a man about the house. And not just any ordinary man either; rather one who had most likely had to be celibate for well-nigh two centuries. Oh, he was such a devil! No rest for the wicked! And anyway—let's be honest about this—sometimes for one reason or another a person simply can't be fagged to wash. I think that's true?)

"True?" I asked.

"What?"

I didn't want to start regarding her as unintelligent. Therefore having shown her the ring I stood up and pirouetted for her—as I so often did for my husband. "And this of course was my wedding dress—though plainly doctored now to some degree." I gave her my usual tinkling laugh. "I can hardly bear to take it off."

"So you're...married already?" This also seemed extremely lame.

"Oh my! I would have to blush a great deal if I weren't!"

Dimplingly I covered my face and feigned sweet girlish modesty. She looked towards the door.

I asked: "But aren't you going to congratulate me?"

Though even then she hesitated. "Congratulations, Rachel."

"*Heartiest* congratulations, I hope."

She nodded.

"You may kiss me if you like." Yet I don't know why I said that. I really didn't care whether she kissed me or not.

But she did. And it was a woefully lacklustre performance. Was Roger making typically thoughtless demands on her, stopping her from getting her beauty sleep, forgetting she had a mother's duties to perform as well as a wife's?

"You know, it's suddenly occurred to me, Celia. I don't believe you look at him—not any longer—in quite that same old way. Do you remember? In the garden...when we were sitting on my wrought-iron bench? Well, never mind: with you two it was always just a question of time, wasn't it? I knew that from the start. Now, my dear, which would you prefer: tea or coffee?"

She declined them both however. "I only meant to stay five minutes." But she didn't look as though she'd ever find the wherewithal to get up from her chair. "So, Rachel, this man...why have you never mentioned him?"

"But I *have*! How can you possibly utter such a falsehood?"

Oh, Lord, that sounded harsh; I instantly regretted it. Especially since she looked so completely unsure of herself and of the world around her—it was a little touching, unexpectedly pathetic.

Whatever they might lack materially at least she and her husband had always seemed to possess confidence.

"Celia, you *must* forgive me! I realize it wasn't a falsehood, merely a misunderstanding. And in my simple unworldliness, you know, I'd thought the whole thing would work out so very nicely. It was he who made me see it wouldn't."

"He?"

"Yes, dear. Horatio."

She still looked dazed. It must sometimes be such an awful strain, I thought, having to live up to Roger.

"Perhaps you'd like to say good morning to him? I'm sure he'd appreciate it."

It was almost a whisper. "Is he here now?"

"Good gracious, no. Do you think that we'd ignore him if he were? The wicked man is still just loafing in his bed—*our* bed, I should say. But all the same he can definitely hear you because he *is* here in a manner of speaking; and all you have to say is, 'Good morning, Horatio, isn't it a lovely day!' or something of that sort. He won't mind you calling him Horatio. He's already very used to the free-and-easy manners of our present age!"

She said: "Good morning, Horatio. Isn't it a lovely day?" She didn't sound at all well.

"Poor Celia. It *has* been something of a shock, hasn't it? I can see that. But have no fears about the rest of it: I give you my word that this afternoon I'll go straight round and sign those papers. And listen, dear—surely you don't have to get back immediately? Can't you just say bollocks to your lord and master? There's a little coffee place across the road where I can buy you a cup of hot sweet tea and a bun and we'll continue with our pleasant little talk. Wouldn't you like that? Then spare me half a second; I'll fetch my parasol and hat."

"Your hat?" She must have gathered from my tone that it was something rather special.

"Yes, it's new. Just wait until you see it!"

But obviously she must have felt she couldn't. I was away for literally three minutes—I hadn't even put it on—yet when I got back she had let herself out of the house. I looked up and down the street but she'd already gone.

People were sometimes so peculiar.

It was a pity, I thought. Oh, not for the sake of the tea or the conversation—entirely immaterial!—but she was evidently upset and the sight of my latest acquisition would have cheered her up no end. It was white and floppy and broad-brimmed: a picture hat the like of which—at least until I had stumbled on a most important truth—I'd never had the opportunity to wear...not being a member of the haut monde or a frequenter of Royal Ascot or even of Buckingham Palace garden parties—I mean of course not until *now*! So what was this vitally important truth? Very simple. I had realized merely that you have to find your own opportunities...and that the day is all but spilling over with them. In short the world can be yours if you will only wear the right sort of hat. (Wasn't there a slogan once? "If you want to get ahead get a hat." I could have written it myself!) And pinned to the side of *this* right sort of hat was a soft full-blown red rose, incredibly real-looking, which matched perfectly—picked out quite beautifully—the theme of roses on the dress. And the long red ribbon which I tied under my chin made it a hat so very much like Scarlett's...

Yes, what a pity that Celia hadn't seen it.

Anyway I called up the stairs again, just to tell *my* lord and master that I was still going across the road for a cup of coffee, but that I'd try not to stay too long...home was always the best place for any girl to be; especially—one might add—for any girl as newly married as I was!

But it had occurred to me that Doreen's mother hadn't yet seen my full regalia. And Doreen herself could possibly be there.

Even her boyfriend who went weightlifting? The one with the rippling back?

Well, if he was—and if I behaved myself impeccably—I wondered if he might let me take a peep?

46

But roger—when he came on his own that evening—was more than just upset and disappointed. He was extremely angry.

Not one second of charm wasted on either congratulation or compliment. His anger blazed in the hallway. I hadn't time even to take him into the breakfast room, where in the morning I had entertained his wife.

"Look here, Rachel! What *is* all this? I can't believe what Celia told me."

"About my marriage, you mean?"

"About your marriage—about your extraordinary change of heart—about every single damned thing!"

"There's been no change of heart. Simply a change of mind."

"Do you realize we shall soon have to be out of our flat? Do you realize we shall soon be homeless and probably living on the street because we shan't be able to find anything else we can afford? Do you realize this is all your fault?"

"Please, Roger, there's really no need to shout! And no need to be ridiculous! Can't you simply tell them you're sorry but that you've made a mistake?"

"Oh, don't be stupid! Weren't you listening when Celia told you the flat's already taken? That contracts have been signed?"

"Stupid," I felt, wasn't quite the word for somebody who had bought you caviar and duck and champagne, had had silver christening gifts engraved, had made your son her only legatee. (I had kept my promise and directly after lunch had returned to Thames

& Avery.) This house—together with its contents—was absolutely everything I had.

And possibly on reflection Roger began to feel the same way. He was certainly impulsive but he wasn't unfair. He had a mercurial and passionate nature—and wasn't that at least a part of what I loved him for?—but there was no real meanness in it. He started to cool down.

"Look, Rachel, I'm sorry—I didn't mean all that! I'm worried about my exams, as well as about providing for my family. Couldn't we just talk this through?"

"Of course we could, my darling. First tell me that you like my dress."

"Yes, I . . . I like your dress."

"Now come and sit down and we'll have a glass of sherry and you can say it with a bit more conviction! For after all"—and now I felt confident enough to make a joke—"nobody in his right senses could fail to like the *dress* even if he didn't think so much of the woman who was wearing it!"

He gave a sickly smile but wasn't yet sufficiently recovered to join in with my laughter.

"I bet you lead that poor girl one fucking hell of a life," I said companionably, as we sat down. (I forgot to fetch the glasses and decanter.) "Do you flare up like that *very* often?"

He only shrugged. He still looked rather sullen.

But I met him halfway. "I have to say, though, I can see why she might irritate you. She sometimes does me. I'm not implying she hasn't got character—oh, no, not at all! Yet she *can* be bland, I do admit that. Also just a bit colourless."

"Celia? Bland? You must be dreaming! Oh, I can assure you she has character, all right!"

He actually sounded a mite more bitter than partisan. As though you'd mentioned to Macbeth that you thought his wife was charming—but hadn't anyone told her about those female assertiveness courses she could enroll for?

"Really?" I said. "Well, you should know best—and we're all such a mass of contradictions, aren't we? This morning, for example, she didn't sound half as desperate as you do."

"Then she should have!"

"Yes, I see. Oh dear. But couldn't you go to stay with her parents for the time being? They've a large enough house and possibly Mrs. Tiverton doesn't get chased around it naked any more. (One wonders if she ever did?) And I could come as often as you liked, to take young Tommy out on treats."

There! It sometimes took outsiders to hit on the really obvious solution.

"In fact, come to think of it," I said, "I can already see a certain similarity between Celia and her mother. But please don't get me wrong: I *do* like Celia. How could I not, indeed, as the mother of my first godchild?"

I tried another little joke.

"To tell the absolute truth I occasionally like her a little more than I like you!"

I don't know if he appreciated that. It seemed to me he hadn't quite—not *altogether*—recovered from his sulks.

Of course I had to remind myself that he was still extremely young. Men matured so much slower than women.

But he did have a lovely body.

"It was that which I first admired about you," I said.

"What was?"

"The way you looked without your shirt. All those muscles!"

He didn't even say thank you. I really feel that people should be taught—and at a suitably early age—how to respond to compliments.

"For, in some ways, I *do* prefer you in your jeans. I'm glad you're wearing jeans now. It would even give me something of a thrill, you know, if you were to take off your shirt again tonight. I should really like to sit and gaze—as on some splendid piece of statuary! Or do you think I'm being too forward? But why not say what's on your mind when it's only something nice and almost certain to give pleasure? It's such a pity to be shy!"

He was staring at me but still not speaking. It sometimes appeared to me—particularly of late—that my conversations were getting progressively one-sided.

"However, going back to this business of your raising Cain? Celia, at any rate, can look after herself...whether she's Lady Macbeth or Little Nell. But I won't have you giving my young godson a hard time. I just won't!" As I had done before, I admonished him with a forefinger that was only partially humorous. "Otherwise, my good man, you'll find you have *me* to deal with!"

"Rachel," he said. He appeared now to have relinquished all his anger. A well-timed compliment can often help.

"Yes, my dear?"

"I..."

"Don't be afraid to say it, whatever it is. For all my present fierceness, Roger—not so *enormously* fierce, I think you must agree—I'm still extremely fond of you. Why! You should only have heard me taking up arms on your behalf when...! But no—I shouldn't be saying that. I'm so much hoping that you and Horatio are going to become friends!"

"Mr. Gavin?"

Yet it wasn't truly a question. It was more in the nature of a world-weary comment—as though a vain and incredulous lover were at long last being forced to acknowledge the existence of a rival.

"Yes, sweet, you and Mr. Gavin."

"Your husband?"

"Oh, such jaded resignation!" I smiled. *Dear* Roger. He was just a disappointed little boy who had never been meant to have his nose put out of joint. A little boy who was now discovering that life could occasionally be hard. I so much wanted to reassure him.

Yet how ironic it was. He and I: two pilgrims. Both looking for paradise; for meaning, for fulfilment. The universal quest. But one of us still only at the beginning of *his* journey, whilst the other had almost reached the end of hers.

One...very young in lifetimes. The other...maybe at last about to leave the wheel. But not on her own. That was the blessed wonder of it all: one of God's most infinite of mercies. When the time came I'd be stepping off it hand in hand with the man who had returned to claim me. To love me. To lead me.

And therein, evidently, lay the germ of the great comfort I could bring to him, my disappointed little boy.

"Darling, don't you see, that's how it works! And I wonder if one day (though possibly not for some time: let's say in another century or so?) I shall be the one true love returning to take care of *you*."

Such momentous words. I knew he couldn't grasp them for the present.

I smiled. "My real name so far as I know—my previous name, anyway, *so far as I know*!—in this life it seems you can't be sure of very much; and there could so easily have been others in between...Is it already getting complicated?"

I felt it probably was.

"Well, anyhow, let me get straight to the point. Perhaps it will make things clearer if I explain it to you like this." Now I gave a laugh. "Miss Anne Barnetby—meet Mr. Roger Allsop!"

I held out my hand. He didn't take it. I wasn't offended. I understood precisely what he was going through.

"Indeed," I said, "Miss Anne Barnetby (possibly this will be a little easier; are you beginning to catch on?), Miss Anne Barnetby—meet Miss Rachel Waring! Or should I say—meet the *former* Miss Rachel Waring."

I paused.

"But *now* Mrs. Gavin, Mrs. Horatio Gavin. Proof that I've fulfilled my destiny, my ultimate and oh so lovely destiny! No, forgive me: *our* ultimate and oh so lovely destiny! Dear Anne, we didn't make it *then*—we were still so silly, headstrong and misguided, still such a *painfully* immature young person (not unlike a certain somebody not a million miles away from us right now!) but just look at how it's all turned out! Bingo! You must be every bit as pleased as I am to find that we've finally come home. Relieved and proud and thankful. Oh, yes! I think we've changed a bit during these past two hundred years!"

"Rachel...?" He hadn't spoken for a long time. His voice was almost an intrusion.

"Yes, sweetheart? Your Rachel is still here. So is your Anne. So, perhaps, your Ariadne, your Penelope, your Jane. Who knows... possibly your Christopher, your Julius, your John? I always liked the name Penelope for some reason. Maybe that means something?"

Leaning forward he placed a hand upon my knee.

"Rachel," he said, "I think that you're not well."

His charm may have lost some of its usual dynamism but none of its usual potency.

"Darling," I said, "I never felt better in my life. As if I'd just come home from a long sea voyage."

I giggled.

"Or as if my husband had!"

"I think you need someone to look after you."

"Oh, I do! I do! Don't we all?"

I lifted his hand off my knee and held it lovingly in my own. I kissed the back of it.

"And I can't tell you how colossally blest I feel!" I shook my head in happy disbelief at what had just occurred: the kiss on the back of his hand: a kiss which had said so much and which—*clearly*—he had warmly and sincerely welcomed.

There was a silence. No longer an angry or resentful silence. Just an intensely companionable one. Two kindred spirits, kindred pilgrims, who would valiant be.

"But why are we talking about *me*? It's you and Celia and the baby, you're the ones we should be talking about! Where are you going to find a place to lay your heads?"

"Not here?"

How could I resist a tone so wheedling and seductive? But I knew that I had to.

"It wouldn't work, my darling. Horatio was absolutely right. At least...well, I think he must have been. He's had so much experience. I trust him implicitly."

"We could look after you," he murmured.

"That's very sweet, Roger, but as I've just said..." I fondled his hand some more. "What about *your* parents if not Celia's?"

"They live abroad. In any case we don't get on with them. And Celia's mum and dad—we'd all be at each other's throats before we'd closed the front door."

"But they were all right at the christening...and, surely, just while you're on the lookout for somewhere...?"

"What about here, just while we're on the lookout for somewhere?"

"Oh, Roger, you do make it hard for me! What about a cheap hotel? Couldn't both sets of parents agree to club together?"

"No, I couldn't take it from them!"

"Well, I can certainly understand that. Taking money from anyone at all, it puts you so completely under their thumb, doesn't it? Yet even so...?"

"It would only be for a week or two," he said. "A month at the outside. And we'd make very sure we didn't get in the way."

"Yes but on the other hand...You know what it's like to be on honeymoon? You surely can't have forgotten already...?"

I was aware that I might be sounding coy. It didn't suit me.

"Even though it was only with Celia," I added.

But he must have sensed that I was weakening.

"*Please*, Rachel. Anne. Jane. Penelope. Remember the Co-Optimists? 'All for one and one for all'? Our commune? Our sharing? My singing to you from the bath?"

Oh, Roger the Troubadour. Roger the Fearless. Roger the Bold. How are the mighty fallen! *Troubadours* don't beg!

"Yet what if you saw me skipping through the house in the... in the altogether?" I laughed. "I mean *me* in the altogether, not you! Skipping through the house in my birthday suit? With flowers entwined in the tresses of my maidenhood? Marigolds, scarlet pimpernels, forget-me-nots? Whatever was in season, obviously."

"I should consider myself extraordinarily privileged. I should take a small step backwards and gaze in admiration."

"You wouldn't feel embarrassed?"

"No, not at all. Any more than you would if it had been *me* skipping through the house in my birthday suit. Or even if it had been the two of us doing it together."

Well, I have to confess, this cast a fresh complexion on matters. (And by the bye I wasn't sure that *maidenhood* was any longer one hundred percent correct!) But just as I was in the throes of vacillating still further—even about to cave in altogether—Roger stood up.

"Oh, you're not going?" I exclaimed.

But I felt a measure of relief along with disappointment. He gently pulled away his hand.

"No fear!" he smiled. "I haven't had my sherry."

Now, *this* was certainly Roger the Bold—leaping down from the yardarm with a vengeance, and a cutlass in his mouth!

"It's just that it's quite close in here. May I take my jumper off?"

"Of course you may." I was preoccupied. "I'll fetch the sherry; I *hope* there's still some left! And while I'm gone I'll perhaps have a quick word with Horatio? You see, it could be that up to now he hasn't fully grasped the..."

"Situation" I was going to say but Roger was unbuttoning his shirt.

And when he'd removed it he said, "Rachel. Is that really all you want? Merely the shirt?"

There was a pause. Keeping to the truth isn't *always* quite so easy as one might suppose. "Oh, dear heaven! My goodness! I'm not altogether sure." My mouth and lips felt dry.

"But it *is* warm. Wouldn't you like me to take anything else off?"

I dispensed with words. I nodded. In fact I found this easier. He unzipped his jeans.

I didn't know if I had nodded quite enough.

And soon his jeans had been discarded.

He then pulled off his socks. Finally—and with an air distinctly roguish—he began to push down his underpants.

But he took it completely at his ease: no rush: merely an inch or so at a time; possibly less. Roger the Tantalizer! (I was again reminded of the William books; and simultaneously of Paul—but what unsuitable moments to remember him!) And then he walked towards me. *He* came to *me*.

He held me to him; we could scarcely have got closer and how I could smell the heady mix of his deodorant and cologne! (Oh dear! *Had* I remembered to wash?)

And how I could feel his enormous winky pressed hard against my wedding dress.

47

Rachel Anne,
Rachel Anne,
Who'll never be without a man...!

THAT WAS the chant the other children used to sing in the playground. Not just the girls either; the boys would join in as well, with equal affection, perhaps with even greater affection, since no matter how much the girls liked me there was always, naturally, just the slightest dash of jealousy colouring their admiration. Indeed, as Eunice once put it—Eunice my best friend and eventually, though only very briefly, my successor as Head Girl: "It's a good thing that no one can help loving you, Rachel, because otherwise we'd all be sticking pins in your effigy! We girls would. Do you realize that none of us ever gets a look-in if you're around? It's always *you* whose books the boys want to carry—always *you* they want to kiss and take to the pictures. Life simply isn't fair!"

Possibly because I *did* realize this I was always extra nice to everyone, in an effort—I felt it was almost an obligation—to atone. I always shared out my sweets at school (and my mother's, God bless her) for these of course were the postwar years, when sweets were still on ration. I lent my clothes and I helped people with their homework and I willingly wrote their lines for them; I *would* have sat their detentions if this had somehow been manageable. I tried to have a cheerful word for everyone and never a spiteful thought about a soul. When they made me a prefect I was renowned as the most lenient prefect in the school—yet I never received any cheek or had any problems over discipline. "Oh, what it is to be both beautiful *and* kind! And to excel at sports as well as classwork! No wonder all the younger girls have massive crushes on you!"

It was one of the teachers who said that. Another on some later occasion put it slightly differently. "And to cap it all, Rachel Anne, I do believe you're a saint, on temporary loan to us from heaven! And what's more," she added, "it must be pretty *glum* up there while you're away!"

Yes, more than anything else there were three things I felt especially proud of: first, that everyone automatically thought I must be earmarked for heaven; second, that they all appeared to consider me such *fun*; and third that I was always such a triumph in the school play. (One mildly aggravating note, however: although I repeatedly tried to emphasize in my curtain speech that the production was the result of months of hard work on the part of everyone involved—a team effort of the most inspirational order—no audience would ever quite allow me to get away with that!) I particularly, of course, remember the last play that we did. It was called *The Mask of Virtue* and Laurence Olivier happened to be out front. I say "happened"; but even if I had believed in such things as coincidence or luck I would have known his presence wasn't merely fortuitous. Tipped off on some mysterious grapevine he was there as talent scout, unassuming yet glamorous, silent, courteous, intent.

And, my word, *was* he glamorous! My mother and he came round to my "dressing room" immediately after the show. He congratulated me but not fulsomely—with caution almost—and spoke to me unsmilingly about details of my performance. "Darling," said my mother, for a moment laying her hand lovingly upon my shoulder, "we're going to leave you to get changed. Make yourself look even more beautiful than ever. Mr. Olivier is taking us out to supper!"

"Larry," corrected the young man. "Larry to my friends."

He took us to the Savoy Grill. I hardly knew what I ate. He

was the most attractive man in the room—in the whole of the West End—in the whole of the known world. As my mother declared later, "The eyes of everyone in that Grill never looked anywhere else; I don't suppose they'd ever seen another couple like yourselves!" He was in his middle-to-late twenties; about eight years older than I was.

In the taxi to the High Street he wrote down our number. "May I ring you in the morning?"

But then he laughed. "No—dash it—I can't wait until the morning! My mind's made up! In a few weeks we're taking a production of *Hamlet* to Denmark. To Elsinore itself! Rachel? Will you play Ophelia?"

We sat up, my mother and I, till nearly three, chatting in the kitchen in our nightgowns, over our cups of hot chocolate.

"Darling, I'm so very proud of you! *What* an evening! *What* a triumph! If only Daddy could have been there!"

"Oh, Mummy, he *was*—in spirit!" Indeed, he nearly had been—in person! He nearly hadn't died whilst saving another soldier's life.

But his earthly presence would have caused complications. And besides... it was good to think of him waiting for me up in heaven—and being able in the meantime to lean out over the side and keep a fatherly eye on my progress.

"I feel I want to cry," said my mother. "I don't mean just because of Daddy but because I can now see this is going to be the last night of your childhood; you'll be leaving me before either of us knows it. It's only right and proper that you should—you have your own exciting life to lead—but, even so, I can't pretend..."

She smiled satirically at her own silliness and took a sip of chocolate.

"Mummy, I shall never leave you. You know that. I mean, not in the furthest reaches of my heart and soul."

"Yes, I do know that, my dearest." She patted my hand. "And it makes me feel quite guilty and ashamed."

"What!"

"Yes. Frequently I feel I haven't been as good to you as I'd have liked."

I protested, loudly and indignantly. "You've been a perfect mother!"

"Shhh! Shhh! You'll wake the neighbours!"

"Then you mustn't talk such nonsense!"

"Bless you for saying that, my love."

"I mean it!"

"Yet all the same—bear with me—I still want to beg your forgiveness for any little ways in which I *may* have failed you. No, please—this is important—don't say there's nothing to—"

"Then I forgive you *everything* with all my heart," I interrupted, with a laugh. "And you must do the same for me! Extend to me your forgiveness for every little way in which *I* may have failed *you*—and for every little way in which I ever shall."

"Oh, there's—"

"Come on. Fair's fair!"

"Very well. My forgiveness is absolute!"

"And mine, too. What a ridiculous conversation! Especially as I now believe that, even when we think we have something to forgive others for, we're really only blaming them for the faults which lie in ourselves."

I took a thoughtful sip.

"For instance . . . just about the last thing in this world I can imagine! But supposing you ever became possessive? Domineering? Would I afterwards be justified in claiming you had ruined my life? ("O misery me, she stole from me my birthright, my inheritance, my due!") No, certainly not! For I could always have *broken away*, couldn't I? And if I wasn't up to doing that, then the fault was in me—yes?—not in you."

"Oh, in that case you might say next that even if I dropped a little arsenic in your bedtime drink the fault would lie entirely in yourself!"

"Yes!"

"And the other way about. *Much* more likely, if I'm to turn into this creature you describe!"

"Yes!"

We roared with laughter. "Oh, poor Mrs. Fowler," I gasped. "Poor Mr. Richards! Poor Neville and Joan!"

"And what's more," she said, "the fault *would* be in me! And I forgive you unconditionally!"

We grew more serious for a moment. "Besides," I said, "there's always a pattern. There would always be a purpose. God would be leading us forever on. To eventual sunlight and eternal growth. No matter what; through whatever form of hell. I firmly believe that."

We stood up and put the saucepan and the cups in water, and the biscuit tin away. We hugged each other. "I know what *I* believe," said my mother. "That you, darling, deserve to win through to success and happiness and glory as nobody else I know!"

"Correction: as *everybody* else you know. Life is a vale of tears, life is a battleground and who are we to judge the merits or demerits of a single travelling soul?" I had my two hands to my breast as I declaimed this and we both declared I wore the mantle of my Aunt Alicia!

———

In bed, despite the lateness of the hour and the silence of the pub across the way, I lay awake for a long time—though strangely not thinking so much about the future as about the past. This was indeed the last night of my childhood and it isn't everyone who can point to it so accurately—yes, even as it's passing! I loved my little room. I regretted to think of it now slipping away from me. My bed was at the very heart of it: my craft, my sanctuary, my dreamland: the place where I'd been tickled, pampered, healed—most comforted, most demonstrably loved—the place where I'd hung up my Christmas stocking. Home.

Home was the spot it was always so good to get back to, even from the best of holidays. (Even from the holiday I'd spent in Paris that year when I'd turned seventeen!) I loved our fortnights by the sea—especially, perhaps, when my father had been there to bury me in sand, build me castles, make me kites; give me piggybacks, teach me how to swim. Yet even after he was gone we still managed to have lots of fun, my mum and I. We would stroll out to fetch the papers before breakfast, filling our lungs with fresh sea air, and have an early cup of tea at a café on the front, watching the seagulls wheel gracefully above the prom. We would listen to the band and sometimes request particular pieces of music. (One year—this was all postwar of course—my mother rather fancied the bandleader; we laughed a lot about that. I requested *The Dream of Olwyn*.) We would go to the fol-de-rolles at the end of the pier. We would have a late-night mug of Ovaltine at Fortes and we would sit up companionably in our twin beds, reading our novels and each eating a Crunchie bar—like Eunice and *her* mother sometimes used to do on holiday. (Arabella's, too, had once had a thing for a bandleader; but *he*, it appeared, had never responded in the smallest way!) Oh, it was all such fun. Yet just the same it always felt so good to return. "Back to our little grey home in the west," I remember saying on one occasion, "or anyway to our little grey home in Paradise Street." Not that it was really grey, just a bit smoke-begrimed, and it wasn't really in Paradise Street either: only *my* room and the bathroom overlooked that. But the very fact I had said it (or *sung* it!)—didn't that show how this mean little thoroughfare somehow meant more to me than the far more respectable High Street? After all, Paradise Street was the road in which Paul had lived, along with his rabbit; it was the road which led to the recreation garden, where my friend the street orderly resided—and where I had once read *John Halifax Gentleman* in the space of a single day. It was the road which led to the Classic cinema in Baker Street.

Home…I thought of how we used to sit together listening to the wireless, my mother possibly doing some darning, myself—since it was generally only show tunes or the like—getting on with my homework. (But naturally, if we were listening to *Much-Binding-in-the-Marsh* or *Educating Archie* or a play, then homework would take second place.) On Sunday nights we used to eat hot toast with dripping and switch on *Grand Hotel*. Most often this was after we'd just got back from the first performance at the pictures.

Home... Saturday afternoons in summer by the lake in Regent's Park, our having walked up a lazily drowsing High Street, carrying our books and our deckchairs and our frozen lollies... Visits to my Great-Aunt Alicia (the rift between my father and his aunt seeming so unimportant now that my father was dead... "and especially," whispered my mother, wickedly irrepressible, as we stood waiting for the bus in Baker Street—our being for the first time en route to Neville Court—"now that *we* are poor!"): always a Lyons cake avowedly baked that very morning by Bridget, despite its coronet of bright yellow or orange icing, unarguably professional and a good inch thick; despite also the sponge or scones or rock cakes , undeniably authentic. Always a plateful of delicious biscuits—these, it was conceded, *could* have come from the grocer's—and a scolding for my mother if she drew attention to the number I was eating. Always a song from *Bitter Sweet*. Luxury. Insulation. Permanence.

Songs around the piano at the pub. (The first time we went in, my mother was prepared to lie about my age but this had proved unnecessary.) She once, after a great deal of persuasion, sang a solo: "Other People's Babies." She scored such a hit with it. I felt so proud. It seemed she had an unexpected gift for blending comedy with pathos: you almost thought as you listened that here was a real nanny, old now, unwanted and living mainly on memories but still rich and happy with the warmth of them. That song became my mother's speciality. (It sometimes saddened me to think about the wealth of untapped talent in the world.) I too had a speciality, although it never achieved quite the same level of success—which I was glad of. (I must admit that I deliberately held back.) Something by Cole Porter.

Experiment—
Make that your motto day and night;
Experiment—
And you will someday reach the light...

We used to spend at least one evening there a week..."our local," as we used to call it. At first we had meant to sip only sparingly at our sherries but we soon discovered everyone was just so anxious to buy us drinks it would have seemed ungracious to refuse. People were so very *pleased* to welcome us there! "Oh, don't leave us yet! Don't leave us yet!" Before they'd finally consent to our departure we always had to offer a finale: "Be it ever so humble there's no place like home."

So altogether—I realized it even then, lying in bed with a silly, small-hours lump in my throat—home would always be a part of me. And I was glad.

I knew that I would always miss it.

Despite the excitement of Elsinore—and Larry—and my career; and of all that lay ahead.

48

SOMETIMES, even towards the end of November, I went to sit in the park. Luckily the weather had continued mild, so I was still able to wear my picture hat and just a cardigan over my beautifully embroidered dress. I went to the park because I needed the exercise and fresh air. I went there because I could no longer afford to go into cafés or look for down-and-outs, and because when I searched for ordinary housewives or widows waiting by their garden gates for somebody—almost *anyone* would have done, poor souls—to tell about their latest operation or the shameful way in which their daughter-in-law was treating them . . . well, maybe it was the approach of winter that sent them scurrying indoors. I don't know. But the ducks on the lake were made of sterner stuff and I could always talk to *them* for as long as we all wanted.

But, yes, poor souls. Those women had so little; I had so much —so unreasonably much. I had Larry and Horatio. I had Roger and Celia and Thomas (and *that* situation, despite my lover's misgivings—Larry's?—Horatio's?—really did seem to be working out; we were all so happy with it; even the lawyerly Mr. Wymark was now considering moving in: a real little commune) and I was healthy, beautiful and very much admired. Not simply was I in my prime; I was one of those rare and fortunate creatures able to appreciate her prime while she still had it, not pine for it as soon as it was gone.

And something else. The best of all—obviously. The *very* best of all!

Yes!

Dear Lord.

At last!

I was *blooming*!

Which was naturally the reason why I needed exercise. And fresh air. Every day, it seemed, my bulge grew bigger. I was so glad that I didn't have to wear a coat.

I felt extra proud I looked so well: all rude and glowing despite my marathons of throwing up: for I'd observed that people couldn't help but stare; simply couldn't help it. Young men gave whistles. Yet it wasn't embarrassing—not in the slightest. I accepted it rather as a film star must, not as her due (good heavens, no, that sounds so *horribly* presumptuous), but with grateful recognition and a lot of secret pleasure. I thought of Rudolf—and kept on inclining my head in humble yet gracious acknowledgement.

I had also written a letter to a famous women's magazine, in which I had said it was so important not to take your husband (or husbands) for granted; not to grow careless over your appearance or personal hygiene habits simply because you were married and therefore your man (or men) was hooked and landed. A woman's appearance, I said, was such a lovely, precious and God-given thing and of course she had a sacred duty towards it *even after marriage*—oh, how I stressed that point! Wives, I said, should always be lovers too and I wrote out for them the whole wise lyric of that probing song, only putting in dots where I couldn't quite recall the words. I offered, indeed, to write them a series on marriage and beauty and its attendant responsibilities; on how to hold your man (or men); my life with Larry; my brief idylls with Rock Hudson and Robert Taylor and James Dean; and—above all— on some truly marvellous fucks I'd had and on how to prepare yourself for motherhood.

It was kind of them. They seemed so pleased with the idea that they sent two of their most important editors to discuss it—a man and a woman. They joined me one morning in the park. (Obviously I wasn't difficult to find. My renown was spreading far and wide; they could have asked practically anybody.)

"Hello," they said, and sat down on the bench, one on either side of me. I had expected to meet them in London but had forgotten that the journalistic nose, once it had scented a scoop, wouldn't wait to let the hair grow from its nostrils.

"So good of you to come," I said. We shook hands. They seemed touchingly surprised by my politeness, a sad indictment of the rest of their contributors. This made me more resolved than ever not to let them guess my disappointment: I'd been imagining, you see, how it would feel to be welcomed into their Fleet Street offices, introduced to a number of their colleagues, taken out to lunch: a personality, someone of just a little consequence.

But never mind all that. I cried gaily: "You should have given me some warning, though! If I'd known you were coming I'd have baked a cake!"

"No need for cakes," said the lady. I wasn't certain that she understood the joke. "Isn't it peaceful here?"

"Yes, it's a lovely park. I like to feed the ducks." And really it didn't matter much: it had only been a very silly little joke.

"We hear you sit here often."

"Oh dear," I said. "What it is to be famous! I feel I should apologize!"

We all smiled at one another…"The three of us," I assured them, "already the very best of pals. Luckily, you know, I could always get on with anybody—absolutely anybody!"

"Would you like to accompany us now?" suggested the woman. "We've got a car just over there."

"I'd prefer to stay in the sunshine for a while if that's all right with you?"

"Very well then—though I can't say I've noticed a great deal of sunshine!" That was clearly *her* idea of a joke; so I laughed politely. She glanced at her wristwatch. This had a broad leather strap—must have been meant for a man. (I'd have thought editors would automatically imbibe the ethos of their own magazines: the style-setting bits, in any case. No, apparently not.) "Five minutes more," she said.

"Oh, yes!" I finished it for her. "'Five minutes more, give me five minutes more, only five minutes more in your arms...'"

Suddenly worried, however, that she might see some sort of message in this I added hastily: "Your watch reminds me of Sylvia's."

"Does it?" She nodded, then evinced mild interest. "And who is Sylvia?"

I had to laugh again—well, naturally I did—although I soon supplied her with a serious enough answer. "Holy, fair and wise is she! That's right—the best woman friend I ever had, apart from my mother. And as a matter of fact shortly before my mother died I had joined ENSA and happened to be out in the Middle East servicing our brave young fighting men. And do you know what they'd say to me? 'Ma'am, you have given us back our reason for living; you alone—single-handed!' Indeed it was sometimes difficult to know how to answer them, revealing all the gratitude I felt in my heart, yet with prettily becoming modesty. I'd say, 'Oh, fiddle-dee-fuck, my dears; oh, fiddle-dee-fuck!' I think I got that more or less right, don't you?"

I smiled, reminiscently.

"Well, anyway, Sylvia stood proxy for me at my mother's deathbed. She told me it was the sweetest thing she'd ever seen. My mother said just before she went—I mean before Mummy went, not Sylvia—that she saw friends coming along the road to greet her and she heard wonderful music; Sylvia told me that she passed with a beam of joy upon her face. And I hope that when the time comes just such a thing can happen to all of us. The big adventure! Well, Sylvia herself was so affected that she's now contemplating taking the veil. She really has earned that soubriquet, *holy*. She watches *The Sound of Music* at least once every six or seven days."

There was perhaps a slight discrepancy here but it didn't matter. Few people worried too much about chronology. Detail should always be subservient to spirit.

"Shall we go now?" asked the woman.

"Oh, just a little longer. Please! It is so pleasant here."

She complied. I wanted to reward her. What further little titbits could I find?

"Well," I said, "he was always kissing me and holding my hand. He didn't mind in the least who saw.

"He would say, 'How's my pussycat?'

"'I'm fine, puss. How are you?'

"'What kind of a day did you have? Well, sit down and tell me all about it.'

"And he would say, 'Happy Christmas, puss, my puss!'

"We were the most popular couple in Hollywood, the most envied, the most glamorous. He told the press: 'I don't suppose there ever was a couple so very much in love.' I said at the same time, 'Our love affair has been simply the most divine fairy tale, hasn't it?' And they printed it, you know, in *Life* magazine. Glorious."

I looked to the woman for comment. She said, "Very nice." I hoped she hadn't thought I was belittling *Feminist* by mentioning *Life*. The man just grinned. He was my strong and silent type, not particularly good-looking, yet he evidently possessed some of the skills which Fleet Street must demand. I moved a little closer and pressed my own thigh up to his. Actually *I* didn't get much of a thrill out of it; but was pleased to suppose that he had.

I smiled at him. "Hey, genius. I'd like you to meet your Scarlett O'Hara."

But those were neither my own words nor certainly my normal voice. It was my west-coast American drawl, my gently comic take-off of dear Myron. Before our very eyes Atlanta had risen from the water, a roaring furnace of flame and smoke and showering sparks; and I stood there in my broad-brimmed black hat, with the fire's reflection leaping in my eyes and my complexion prettily aglow in the rosy flickering light; and I heard him say, "The end to years of searching! Nearly fifteen hundred interviews, over ninety actual tests, the most publicized hunt in screen history! Now here she stands before us: the perfect choice, the perfect girl... Hosanna in the highest!"

"Well, fiddle-dee-fuck," I cried. "And thank 'ee kindly, sir."

The flames died down into the water. Old Lord Fauntleroy's drawing room, temples from *The Garden of Allah*, forests from *The Last of the Mohicans*, skyscrapers from *King Kong*—all of them had sunk beneath the burning lake. The ducks returned. I was stricken with anxiety; jumped up at once to get a clearer view. Oh, thank God! Thank God! In that most awesome conflagration not a single feather singed.

The editors had stood up too. Fleet Street might well be a jungle but—clearly—any contact with courtesy could still produce benefits.

I sat. They did the same. Three merry jack-in-the-boxes—well, two of them maybe less merry, like thick Russian novels on either side of a Wodehouse. I might have enjoyed a short period of gloriously undiluted fun. I remembered the Marx Brothers.

"One blessing," I exclaimed. "At least *this* Christmas we shan't be eating roast duck!" None too surprisingly my joke was wasted on the woman.

Perhaps that made it even funnier?

But then I frowned. No more *Happy Christmas*, either. "Happy Christmas, puss, my puss!"

For he had aged so rapidly. Had become an old man while I was still a lovely girl. Had it been wrong of me to take him? Should I have left him there in Shangri-La?

The answer was—oh yes! oh yes! But could I have done it? We rode a streetcar named Desire and so few of us ever had the strength to ring the bell. The stops were all request.

Now, therefore, as I remembered this, the sky grew dark. No

warning, absolutely none. A whole canopy of cloud: massive, menacing, undeniable.

Not undeniable. Undefiable! *Was* there such a word? Well, if there wasn't there ought to be—and, oh, what a difference just one letter could make!

For no one had ever triumphed through taking the path of least resistance. *Defy*, not deny—that was the name of the game. I thought I had been learning this.

But, no, what I had been learning was only the following: it grew so very difficult to be valiant 'gainst all disaster. Resilience and gaiety and awareness . . . they all became so *wearing*. Required such quantities of superhuman strength.

And suddenly I felt frail. I couldn't go on in this fashion—rise and shine, rise and shine—unerringly, day after day after day. Waiting for that red, red robin to come bob, bob, bobbin' along. (Along.) Because *I* hadn't got superhuman strength. Sometimes I prayed for just the ordinary kind; yet occasionally had to wonder whether God could even be listening.

Life *was* a vale of tears. So why had I thought that I could somehow skirt around it, keep my magic pink dancing shoes clear of the water?

They were good and damp right now.

No more "What kind of day did you have, my puss, sweet puss? Sit down and tell me all about it!"

And even dear little Doreen had never come to tea. Nor—a scrap less disappointingly—had Mrs. Pond.

And he had thrown my Oscar out into the garden because he had said that I was growing highhanded.

But I truly couldn't help it. Hadn't he seen that? Not any more than he could.

Oh, Larry.

And why, God, why—why little Alfredo Rampi?

Did *anybody* have the right to live in a fool's paradise so long as just one person shrieked?

And was that *all* that it could ever amount to? Purely a fool's paradise?

I stood up. (They both jumped up beside me.) "Shall we go?" the woman repeated.

I think I even smiled; I tried to smile; I had my baby to consider.

We made our way along the tarmac path. Each had given me an arm; I couldn't be insensible to that. "Who claims," I said—and now I certainly put on a smile—"who claims the age of chivalry is dead?" Admittedly, I addressed this more to the man than to the woman, but it didn't prevent my feeling that at any moment we might all start skipping along in unison—

"We're off to see the wizard,
The wonderful wizard of Oz!

"—and do you think," I asked, "that if the wizard had four sons, and one of them suffered unbearably, he wouldn't still want to see the others happy?"

This I addressed equally to the pair of them; but neither seemed to have any deep thoughts upon the subject. In the end I felt obliged to answer my own question.

"It would definitely even things out somewhat and I do believe things need to be evened out, don't you? Possibly that's one of the main purposes of heaven?"

But, no, I couldn't get them going. I just couldn't get them going.

That was such a shame. I myself had found it helpful.

I mean—amazingly helpful. For I saw now that, after all, the path we might have been skipping along (but you have to make allowances for people) didn't show so much as a blister, not so much as a blob, of tar or asphalt or macadam. Oh, I should have realized! I felt so guilty; so ungrateful. How could you not notice a thing like that? How could you not notice the sheer lightness and pleasantness of shiny yellow brick?

"Oh," I cried, "will he have a heart on hand to give me? Or a brain? Or the noive?"

I accompanied this with my usual ripple of gay laughter.

"And which do you think I am going to need the most?"

Yes, *ungrateful*! The sky was certainly a little cloudy but at least it showed sufficient blue to make a suit for a sailor; or, at any rate, to cover any coffee stains. All right, so people shrieked in the darkness—probably thousands of small children there amongst them—but though I must never forget any of those poor suffering souls, though I must never stop trying to reach out to them in prayer, this was no reason for *me* not to attempt to sing in the sunlight. What kind of series was I going to write for them anyway? *All is doom, doom, doom; we must hang up our handbags and howl*!

No, they didn't want anything lugubrious. They wanted to hear about cheerful things; well, naturally they did; everybody did.

"Shall we sing as we go?"

"You sing," said the woman. (He merely grinned. My word, he *was* the strong and silent type!)

"What shall it be, then? Oh, I know what it *ought* to be. 'We're busy doing nothing, working the whole day through, trying to find lots of things not to do...' Me as Bing Crosby, you two as William Bendix and Sir Cedric Hardwicke. Oh, I wonder how *that* name originated, don't you?" No response. "I mean, one can understand, quite easily, how something like 'Armstrong' would have first got going." To illustrate, squeezed my escort's bicep—"Oh, my!" I exclaimed. "But...'Hardwicke'? I suppose that's why they added an 'e' to it? What cowards!" But it was a happy little conundrum.

In the car, my companions sat warmly pressed on either side of me—for, as I had foreseen, they had a chauffeur. I felt so cosseted. The journey took about ten minutes. We drove to a large grey house hidden behind high grey walls. It was an imposing place in which to have a branch office—imposing if not pretty.

"Have you driven all the way from London? I *am* grateful. How early you must have started! Long day's journey into night, indeed!"

I amended this, still doing my best to entertain.

"No, long day's journey into sparkling morn! The grass all dewy beneath the apple trees. A real success story!" I let them think about the loveliness of it all: the mushrooms ready to be picked, the windfalls lying in the orchard, the housewives running to the market. "In fact, my dears, I'll let you both into a very tiny secret. If I should ever write my memoir, that's exactly what I'm going to call it. *Success Story.*"

Unfortunately, though, I was being a spot *too* entertaining. I missed what was written on the board by the gates. I hadn't wanted to miss anything.

We went inside. It was by no means as luxurious as the London office would have been.

There was a long bare corridor and people in white overalls. You'd have supposed that even in the provinces there would be *some* attempt at fashion. As for myself, I think I'd have felt quite out of place in all my finery if I hadn't remembered that this was just my ordinary humble workaday wear—not donned specifically to impress.

My two friends now left me in charge of another woman, a woman who had thick, unfortunate ankles. I was taken into a reception room with unpleasant brown lino. Somebody brought me a cup of tea. It was strong and sweet (I don't take sugar), served in a thick white cup with a generally grubby appearance. I took no more than just a sip—having carefully wiped the tiny portion I was brave enough to set against my lips—though, in the process, bequeathing it a vividly scarlet smear: perhaps more of a dynamic symbol, however, than merely an irritating waste of Max Factor. Yes! I felt like Virginia Mayo! I was painting the clouds with sunshine!

But anyway.

"Please," I said, "I think I should now like to be driven home."

I stood up and adjusted my hat and gloves; even in retreat a lady had to look her best. Exits were every bit as important as entrances.

Naturally it was to my new companion that I had turned; there was no one else in the room. She sat stolidly beside the closed door.

Then I picked up my parasol and reticule—I always refer to one particular handbag as my reticule, although it's made of leather and is really quite capacious. I smiled as brightly as I could...and just as if I hadn't been affected by the depressing chill of institutional walls (for that is what in all honesty they now felt like: *institutional!*) or as if I hadn't been made sick, almost literally so, by that cup of tea-infused molasses. I told her that it wasn't her fault; no, not at all; but that—how could I put this?—the *ambience* wasn't right: not exactly one the Queen or Mrs. Thatcher might feel thoroughly at home in. I pointed out that for anyone to benefit from our discussions we should have to be sitting in far softer and more conducive surroundings; and I mentioned that my instincts about such things were simply never wrong.

But attitudes seemed to have changed a little.

Perhaps, I thought, it hadn't been tactful of me to display my own neat ankles. I could so easily have kept them covered by my dress.

"Yes, I'd like to go now," I reiterated.

"Only a little more patience, dear. Doctor will be here at any moment. While we wait, why not just finish the rest of your nice tea?"

"Doctor?" I asked.

She nodded.

"You mean, about the baby?"

"I mean about anything you'd like to discuss with him."

"That's very thoughtful—very thoughtful indeed; an attention which I really hadn't expected; I can see that *Feminist* looks after its employees. Yet between ourselves I should so much rather talk to my own physician. I was planning to, anyhow, within the next few days; but I didn't want to rush off and bother everyone the *instant* I found out. I refuse to be a fusspot."

"Doctor will be here at any moment," she said. She was probably well-intentioned but it was as though she hadn't listened to a word. My goodness, maybe I ought to apply for the position of Personnel Chief: how I should insist on proper training, on stamping out ineptitude! But that was for the future. In the meantime I began to grow impatient.

I said: "I know I shall be writing a series of articles on motherhood and marriage and what to do if one breast hangs lower than the other, which I appreciate is quite a problem for the vast majority of women. But I'm afraid I don't altogether see why *I* should need a checkup on account of it. My own tits are enviably symmetrical."

I avoided glancing at hers.

"Besides, they should have given me some warning. They probably have no idea how difficult it is to perform your ablutions in a wedding dress!"

What's more, I had no intention of letting them find out. But I didn't tell her that.

"May I get past you, please?"

"Sorry, dear. You've got to stay here until the doctor comes. Then they'll take you up to bed."

"*Bed?*"

And suddenly I understood.

"I've come to the wrong place, haven't I? This isn't a publishing office!"

"No, dear."

"You make it sound like a hospital. Now, why in the name of holy shit have I been brought to a hospital?"

"Well, it's far better that—"

I hit her with my reticule. I swung it with every ounce of energy I had; and caught her squarely on the chin.

My tome on King David was probably what did it. I'd been

saving it up, yet luckily, only the day before, I had decided to make a start on it—normally the only book I carried was *Pride and Prejudice*. But it seemed right for King David rather than Mr. Darcy to keep himself in trim by flooring latter-day Goliaths. (And had he been looking at her ankles he would scarcely have noticed the difference.) She only swayed for a second or two; but this appeared to be enough. In no time I was out through that door and running down the corridor.

And God *was* listening. There was nobody in sight.

As I ran, the truth occurred to me. There had simply been a most appalling error. A case of mistaken identity. Totally horrific.

This was a lunatic asylum.

It flashed upon me in all its dreadful clarity. Some poor soul had been certified; and her physical description couldn't have been a lot dissimilar to mine.

Which meant she must be fairly young. Oh, sweet child, I felt so sorry. How unimaginably terrible to know that, somewhere out there, there could be people—your own family perhaps; your own good friends (as you had thought!)—people ready to put their names to any deed so unspeakably shameful and wicked and self-serving. So utterly lacking in compassion or empathy. How you must feel! Oh, dear Lord. Yes, how you must feel!

But I would discover who she was and I would visit her regularly. I would strive to restore her confidence, her self-respect, her capacity for trust.

I knew that if at present she was feeling frightened she'd think she would *always* be feeling frightened. I should try—oh, how I'd try—to soothe away those fears.

Had I said that it was unimaginable? I now found out it wasn't, not in the slightest. I found I could imagine it only too easily.

Yet in the meantime I still had my own predicament to consider—no one could deny that, for the moment, I had got myself into a bit of a pickle. (No, not I; circumstance!)

Fortunately it wasn't any more than just a bit of a pickle, but even that could be degrading—not instantly lending itself to interpretation as a merry jape. "*Oh, guess what happened to me this morning? I do hope you're not going to believe it! I was carried off to the loony bin!*"

No, of course I could pass it off as a joke. Almost anything could be appropriated to make an entertaining story.

Besides, this one was really very funny.

But, even so, that didn't stop me running. I don't know why I ran. I ran instinctively.

Out through the entrance hall, out through the open gates, out onto the main road.

There was a bus approaching and there were people standing at a reasonably nearby stop. It must have helped that I had King David as an intermediary. A man after God's own heart!

I heard impassioned shouts. With both hands lifting my dress, despite the parasol I held in one and the reticule I still clutched in the other, I ran after that bus in my flying pink satin slippers—and thanked heaven it was all downhill! "Hold on, little one." I had no option but to pray that telepathy would work. "Mama doesn't mean to harm you. It's a bumpy ride but it'll very soon be over."

I could imagine him standing there, red-faced, thumping his little fists against the walls of my stomach, desperate only to get out and climb into my arms for loving reassurance.

Naturally the three or four who had been standing at the stop were the first to board the bus. I awaited my turn in anxious suspense, not daring to ascertain the progress of my pursuers. The conductor helped me on: a coloured man and such a gentleman.

But most of the passengers at once moved further down inside, as though even in so short a time something of those bare stone-floored corridors had managed to rub off on me.

Three schoolboys from the upper deck came jostling and gawping on the bottom stairs.

And the bus would not set off.

"Please ring the bell," I said to the conductor. "There's no one left to come."

But still I was so breathless that I wondered if he'd understood.

Apparently he had. "We're a few minutes early, madam." He glanced uncertainly towards the front and then I saw that the driver was getting down from his cab.

Oh, God, I thought. Dear God. Please help.

I watched the driver and conductor conversing on the pavement. I saw the passengers—both those who'd backed away and those who had stayed put—looking curious or impatient or embarrassed. A few were sniggering. I saw men in white coats running down the hill. One of them carried something which I thought might be a straitjacket.

But a straitjacket would harm my baby; no way I'd let them use it. I'd explain the awfulness of the mistake—although at present I couldn't set great store by the intellect of anyone who came from that place.

I thought again, Oh, God, please help. If I go down on my knees, unashamedly bearing witness in front of all these people—will you help me then?

So that is what I did. Although there must have been the germs and the dirt off a thousand pairs of shoes, shoes that might have stepped in any kind of nastiness, and there were also torn-off strips of ticket and a couple of screwed-up tissues and even a scattering of squashed raisins, that is what I did. I went down on my knees in my rose-embroidered silk.

And I said: "It isn't me I'm asking you to care about. It's my baby, my son, my small Horatio. Your son, as much as mine. And it's my duty to protect him. Somehow I've just got to get him home!"

I attempted, on the backs of my once-white gloves, to wipe away my tears.

"You see, that's where I know that we'll be safe. That's where I know that we'll be happy. There are people there—good people —who will always do their best to look after us. At home."

I tried to curry favour. I reminded God of how, even from childhood, I had hoped one day to find my place in heaven.

But then I corrected this.

"I mean, *our* places. I no longer care what happens just to me."

Yet now those men in the white coats had boarded the bus and the passengers were again starting to inch forward.

The men were pulling me up off my knees.

But they did it quite gently; and their gentleness released a miracle.

Furthermore, something else did. For one of them held out to me my picture hat—which, during my crazy downhill flight, I hadn't even realized I had lost. Not a straitjacket at all...my lovely white picture hat! I now saw why some of the passengers had been laughing. Clearly, my hair must have looked *such* a mess! Apart from its not having been brushed recently, let alone washed, I knew that it required its long-overdue dose of *Love that Blonde!* All its dark roots had to be practically waving for attention.

So with trembling hands I shoved the hat back on and tried to tie the ribbon underneath my chin. But I couldn't do it—oh, how I'd got the shakes! When he saw this, another of the men did it for me...although really the sides of the bus were far too constricting to accommodate such a gorgeously broad-brimmed hat. And how everybody laughed—myself included! Indeed, the nature of everybody's laughter had now altogether changed; even the schoolboys'. All those dear hearts, they were laughing *with* me, not against.

Therefore there had been a splendid reason for the whole terrifying episode. Hadn't there? Everyone had learned his lesson. The world had become a nicer place.

I truly shouldn't have forgotten, yet *again*, that this was how it all worked: that this was a new beginning—the kind of new beginning to end every other new beginning I had ever known.

I was crying once more but now my tears were tears of joy. A joy so intense I felt my heart must break—could any mortal bear to be so happy? I brushed from my knees a few of the squashed raisins and I smiled at the men who stood about me: the hat-retriever and the ribbon-fixer in particular, although they had all, all of them, been so exemplary. "I have always," I said, "depended upon the kindness of strangers." Didn't that seem the best, the very aptest way to put it?

And then, just a second or two before my legs finally gave out and I sagged between the strong protective arms that held me, I looked around at my fellow passengers and at the driver and conductor, both as black as your hat, and I flashed them all a rapturous and heartfelt beam.

All movement stilled and they appeared to freeze into a tableau: a tableau brilliantly coloured yet at the same time restful. I saw this busload of passengers now standing in a garden. (Perhaps the bus had broken down.) It was not unlike the recreation garden of my childhood only far more beautiful. And the passengers were far more beautiful—patently I didn't know them but I would have vouched for great individual transformation—and there came unutterably lovely music from a new and ornamental bandstand. I bestowed on everyone my blessing. Or at least I had intended to. I had wanted to let them know that everything was fine—fabulous—fantastic!

I had meant to say:

"Oh, fiddle-dee-fuck, my dears! Just fiddle-dee-fuck!"

ACKNOWLEDGEMENTS

Every effort has been made to trace the owners of copyright material but in some cases this has not been possible.

"If Love Were All" from *Bitter Sweet*. Words and music by Noël Coward © 1929 Chappell & Co. Ltd.

"I'll See You Again" from *Bitter Sweet*. Words and music by Noël Coward © 1929 Chappell & Co. Ltd.

"The Boyfriend" from *The Boyfriend*. Words and music by Sandy Wilson © 1954 Chappell & Co. Ltd.

"It's Only a Paper Moon" from *Take a Chance*. Music by Harold Arlen. Words by Billy Rose and E.Y. Harburg © 1933 Harms Inc. (Warner Bros.) British publisher, Chappell Music Ltd.

"Ten Cents a Dance" from *Simple Simon*. Music by Richard Rodgers. Words by Lorenz Hart © 1933 Harms Inc. (Warner Bros.) British publisher, Chappell Music Ltd.

"September Song" from *Knickerbocker Holiday*. Music by Kurt Weill. Words by Maxwell Anderson © 1938 de Sylva, Brown & Henderson Inc. British publisher, Chappell Music Ltd.

"I Wonder Who's Kissing Her Now" © 1909 Chas. K. Harris Music Publishing Co. (USA). Reproduced by permission of EMI Music Publishing Ltd., 138–140 Charing Cross Road, London WC2H oLD.

"Baby, It's Cold Outside" by Frank Loesser from *Neptune's Daughter* © 1948 Frank Music Corporation. © Renewed 1976 Frank Music Corporation. International copyright secured. All rights reserved. Used by permission.

"Dancing in the Dark" from *The Band Wagon*. Music by Arthur Schwartz. Words by Howard Dietz © 1931 Harms Inc. (Warner Bros.) British publisher, Chappell Music Ltd.

"Belle of the Ball." Music by Leroy Anderson. Words by Mitchell Parish © 1951/53, Mills Music Inc., New York. Reproduced by kind permission of Belwin-Mills Music Ltd., 250 Purley Way, Croydon, Surrey, England.

A Streetcar Named Desire © 1947 by Tennessee Williams. *Theatre of Tennessee Williams Volume 1*. Reprinted by kind permission of New Directions Publishing Corporation.

Love Scene: Laurence Olivier and Vivien Leigh. Published in Great Britain by Angus & Robertson, 1978. My grateful acknowledgements to Jesse Lasky and Pat Silver, who wrote this entertaining book.

OTHER NEW YORK REVIEW CLASSICS*

For a complete list of titles, visit www.nyrb.com or write to:
Catalog Requests, NYRB, 435 Hudson Street, New York, NY 10014